# PROM MOM

# PROM MOM

## A NOVEL

## LAURA LIPPMAN

*wm*

WILLIAM MORROW

*An Imprint of HarperCollinsPublishers*

PROM MOM. Copyright © 2023 by Laura Lippman. All rights reserved. Printed in the United States of America. No part of this book may be used or reproduced in any manner whatsoever without written permission except in the case of brief quotations embodied in critical articles and reviews. For information, address HarperCollins Publishers, 195 Broadway, New York, NY 10007.

HarperCollins books may be purchased for educational, business, or sales promotional use. For information, please email the Special Markets Department at SPsales@harpercollins.com.

FIRST EDITION

Library of Congress Cataloging-in-Publication Data has been applied for.

ISBN 978-0-06-299806-4

23 24 25 26 27  LBC  5 4 3 2 1

*This book is for everyone, 2021–2022, who texted,
emailed, or DM'ed me: "How are you doing?"*

# PART I

# BEFORE

*What was she thinking?*

# THE GIRL

THE LIGHTS WERE off in the bathroom, but the door was ajar and sunlight had begun seeping into the room. The day came at Amber in a series of unpleasant sensations. Hard—she was lying on the floor. Cold—she had on only her strapless bra, the floor was tile, the air conditioning had been set low.

*Sticky.* That was the blood. So much blood. She didn't know a body could lose this amount of blood without going into shock. Maybe she *was* in shock? She had taken a first aid course at the Y and remembered what to do for someone else in shock—get them to lie down, elevate the legs—but no one ever told you how to know if you yourself were in shock. Besides, she was already lying down.

"Joe? Joe?"

No answer. He wasn't here, of course. Why hadn't he tried to check on her? Was he so busy mooning over his ex-girlfriend that he couldn't be bothered to see if Amber was going to rally and make it to the after-party? He must have gone without her— fair enough, given how she had demanded the only room key and bolted from the prom, never to return, but couldn't he at least have pretended concern?

*He doesn't really like you,* her mother had said when Amber had told her about the invitation. *Not in that way.* That's okay, Amber had replied, and it had been okay, because she believed it was only a matter of time before he realized he did like her. She had thought it would happen last night.

Instead, she had rushed up to the room alone, assuming she was sick from the crab ravioli at dinner. The ravioli and the swigs of whatever had been in Zach's flask, although she had tried to take only the tiniest swallows, what her stepfather called "nips." No one could get drunk from those little sips, those nips, could they?

Her head was pounding with a cartoon frenzy and it was impossible to separate what had really happened last night from what she wanted to believe had happened. Her stomach had started cramping badly about twenty minutes into the dance, but she had ignored it until Joe danced with Kaitlyn "for old times' sake." Amber felt as if she was about to throw up, and that had to be done in privacy, always. "Give me the room key," she had demanded, her fear and shyness making her sound rude, imperious, as if she was mad at Joe.

She *was* mad at Joe.

Back in the room, she had taken off her dress and laid it across the bed, fearful it would be stained. She then crouched by the toilet in her bra and underwear, waiting to vomit.

She was still by the toilet, but she had not vomited.

She struggled to a sitting position. There was so much she couldn't remember, so much she couldn't forget, and those opposing camps warred with each other until her thoughts were more jumbled than ever. Her situation would make more sense if this were a dream, because, as in a dream, nothing made sense. She should be waking up in the bed, next to Joe, not on this sticky bathroom floor. She shouldn't be waking up at all, because the plan had been to stay up all night. When she had never come back downstairs, the others had probably gone on without her to the after-party. But why hadn't Joe come back to change into the more casual clothes he had brought for the trip to the reservoir? How could he not have checked on her, even once?

She pressed her palms against her temples, then into her eyes, not wanting to see what the creeping daylight would reveal. She would have to take care of things, take care of herself. It wasn't Joe's fault Amber had gotten sick, even if it was watching him dancing with his ex, Kaitlyn, that had prompted her to keep bringing the flask back to her mouth. And it wasn't Joe's fault that the sudden pain had made her desperate to be alone. She didn't want to throw up in the public ladies' room adjacent to the ballroom. She could imagine nothing worse than other girls listening to her retch.

Now she could.

There was nothing left to do but drag herself to her feet and turn on the bathroom light.

*Oh god, oh god, oh god.*

*You can do this.*

The voice kicked in, the voice that had been with her all her life, telling her what to do when no one else had any advice for her. It was the voice that had told five-year-old Amber to wait quietly in the bookstore where her mother left her while she shopped. The voice that said, *Say nothing*, when she was accused of cheating on a test because her grade was so high. To pretend ignorance when a teacher asked who might have defaced her locker.

*Clean first, then shower.*

She worked quickly, using all but one of the bath towels, then took a shower. She changed into the clothes she had packed for the activities that had been planned for the morning. If the evening had gone as anticipated, she'd be at the Towson Diner right now, having eggs and hash browns and maybe a Diet Coke. Twenty-four hours earlier, her gravest worry had been that the others would tease her for not liking coffee.

Joe's overnight bag was on the luggage rack, zippered. Why hadn't he come back to the room? *Kaitlyn*, she thought miserably. *Kaitlyn*. He obviously still yearned for her, despite everything that had happened between Amber and him over the past year.

She left the prom dress behind, draped across the bed. She hated abandoning it, but it would be ruined if she tried to put it in her bag—crushed, maybe even stained—and she had too far to walk to carry it over her shoulder. Besides, it would look odd, walking down York Road on a Saturday morning, a party dress slung over her shoulder. *Don't draw attention to yourself*, the voice told her. *Just try to get through the day. Maybe it will be all right. You don't really remember doing anything, so maybe you didn't.*

She wore rayon pants with a small floral print, elasticized at the waist, a loose-knit yellow T-shirt, and lace-up espadrilles, which were flat, but not particularly good for walking, and she already had blisters from the shoes she had worn the night before. How thoughtfully, how pridefully, she had assembled this outfit, stalking bargains at stores she seldom could afford. She had chosen the espadrilles because their pale green color uncannily matched the tiny pistils of the flowers on the pants and the laces made her feel dainty, like a ballerina. She had not expected to be walking far in them. What had she expected? The after-party downtown, then back to the hotel to change into this very outfit, sunrise at Loch Raven, breakfast at the Towson Diner. They had pledged not to sleep a single minute until they were home, reunited with their own beds.

Of course, that was before Joe had danced with his ex-girlfriend and Amber had started feeling those weird stomach pains and gone up to the room. She honestly couldn't remember what had happened after that. There was no denying what she had seen in the room, but she had no memory of it. She was in shock. She should see a doctor. No, she should *not* see a doctor.

When she reached Regester Avenue, she lingered for a moment on the sidewalk, regarding her house as a stranger might see it. The small, treeless front yard was decorated for spring—the five plaster geese that marched in formation year-round, from biggest to smallest, wore gingham-checked sunbonnets; the second largest, presumably the mother, had a matching apron. A month ago, there had been Easter baskets and giant eggs, but those had since been replaced by flowers, real and fake. In early June, right before

Flag Day, the yard would be transformed into a bower of patriotism, all red, white, and blue, which stayed up past the Fourth. August brought a back-to-school theme. Halloween, Thanksgiving, Christmas, Winter Wonderland, Valentine's Day, Spring. Amber knew that most people found her stepfather's house tacky, even creepy, but she had always taken comfort in the way the calendar marched through their front yard, the constancy of the geese. Every season, every month, the geese were always there.

Her stepfather was in the kitchen, reading the paper. Rod asked if she had a good time at the prom. "It was fine," she said. He had been her stepfather for ten years, but she never stopped feeling a little shy around him, a perpetual guest in his home. Her mother was always emphasizing how *lucky* Amber was that Rod treated her like his own daughter, and the consequence was that Amber didn't feel she was worthy of his kindness and attention at all, much less his love.

She went straight to bed, which was to be expected, as her mother and Rod assumed she had been up all night. The hotel rooms were changing stations, really, or so the parents had been told. They also were told that the girls would be staying in one room, the boys in another. Had they believed it? Amber had almost believed it, until she saw the flat glare in the eyes of Susannah, Zach's date. "Of course we're not staying in the same room," she said. She was smiling, there was no edge to her voice, but the look in her blue eyes unsettled Amber.

Amber put her bag in the room reserved and paid for by Joe's parents, while Zach stowed his bag in the one that Susannah's parents had provided. It was the nicest hotel Amber had ever been in, but then, the only hotel Amber had ever visited was a motel in Ocean City, where she, her mother, and Rod crowded into a one-room studio the last week of every June, when the Atlantic was still cold and the rates were low. She wouldn't have minded if she and Joe had a little time in this room, just the two of them. They'd been alone only once since January, in late April, the day they had agreed to go to the prom together.

Who had Joe danced the last dance with? Kaitlyn? But Kaitlyn had a date, the college boy she had been seeing since last summer. *Just a dance?* she had asked Joe when she came up to their table. *For old times' sake?* Amber's heart had lurched at how Joe's face lit up. In that moment, she realized how Joe looked when he loved someone. He had never looked at her like that. But he liked Amber; she knew he liked her. He had told her things he had never told other people, not even Zach. They had something special, even if they had never defined it.

In her own bed, with the Laura Ashley comforter her mother had found 90 percent off at C-Mart, she fell into a dreamless sleep in spite of herself.

It was past noon when she came downstairs for a lunch of tomato soup and grilled cheese sandwiches in pj shorts and a baggy T-shirt, hair tousled, traces of makeup still smeared on her face despite the vigorous shower she had taken at the hotel. She was glad, for once, that her mother was not the type to pepper her with questions. Rona asked only: "Well, was it everything you thought it would be?"

"No," Amber admitted, tipping a bag of pizza-flavored Goldfish into the soup. This was how she had eaten her soup since she was a child. The goldfish got soggy quickly, so you had to eat very fast, scooping them up with a spoon like some game at the Ocean City boardwalk.

"I tried to tell you. Boys like that Joe Simpson—"

"Mom, I have a headache."

"Were you drinking?"

She decided to tell the truth. *Tell the truth whenever you can,* her inner counsel advised her. "Only a little. And only because everyone else was."

"That's not like you, Amber."

It wasn't. Her mother had inadvertently hit on what had been bothering Amber since she had awakened on the bathroom floor. Amber was not the same person she had been twenty-four hours ago. She would never be that person again.

The police arrived while Amber and her mother were clearing the lunch dishes from the table. "Don't say anything, baby," her mother said, and Amber almost jumped out of her skin. But she already knew not to say too much. Anyone who watched television knew that.

The detectives, two men, said they needed to take her to see a doctor, which made Amber feel hopeful for a moment, that maybe the doctor could figure out what had happened, which still made no sense to her. Maybe she had some weird, unusual sickness and that would explain everything. But then she realized that would not be the point of the visit.

"Why does she need to see a doctor?" her mother asked.

"We believe your daughter delivered a baby last night, Mrs. Deluca."

Impossible, her mother said. She'd know if her daughter was pregnant, she said. Amber felt the same way. It was impossible.

A maid had found a newborn wrapped in a towel on the floor of the bathroom in room 717. The room was registered to Joe Simpson, but he told police he had stayed out all night with his friends after his date got sick and locked herself in their room, taking the only key. He had tried to go to the room to change at about four a.m., but Amber wouldn't open the door. He had breakfast with his friends at the diner and drove home from there.

"I woke up and the baby was dead," Amber said, even as her mother and Rod shushed her.

*Did Amber want to tell them anything more about last night?* Amber shook her head no over and over again. She had nothing more to tell. She had said the only thing she knew to be true. She remembered nothing except pain, searing pain. Pain and blood and darkness, and then suddenly it was sunrise.

Still, she could ask a question, right? Asking them a question wasn't the same thing as talking.

"My dress?"

"What about it?" asked one of detectives, a Mr. Lenhardt, who had the kindest face she had ever seen, but maybe it was simply that Amber realized in that moment his would be the last kind face she would see for a long time. No one was ever going to be kind to her again.

"I left it behind in the hotel room. Do you think I could have it back, when everything is over?"

*September 19, 2019*

AMBER LET THE real estate agent lock the door of Rod's home, which was the only way she could ever think of the house on Re-gester Avenue. It was Rod's house, even if she and her mother had shared it with him for ten years. And now she would never have to enter the house again, not even for the closing, whenever that happened.

She had flown up from New Orleans two days ago, met with the lawyers, found a real estate agent, endured the walk-through, taken copious notes on her phone. When the agent was not actively disparaging the house, she crowed about how executing the punch list would cost less than $5,000 and yield more than $30,000 at sale. Less her commission, of course.

Amber had almost cried out, "I don't have $5,000."

Then she remembered: She did. Or would, when Rod's estate was settled, almost a million dollars, an unfathomable amount of money in some ways, yet also *too* fathomable. Amber wasn't stupid. She was only thirty-eight, so a million dollars, amortized—was that even the right word?—over a lifetime was, at best, maybe $20,000 a year. Or, if she invested the $1 million and it yielded 3 percent every year, that would be $30,000. Nothing to sneeze at, but it wouldn't keep you in unlimited Kleenex either.

It was enraging, now that she thought about it, how little a million dollars meant. People on reality shows, the competitive ones, were forever saying the prize money would change their lives, but now Amber had won the prize without even trying and she couldn't see how her life would be different. She grossed almost $25,000 a year from her Etsy shop, augmenting those earnings with her gallery job and shifts at the Upperline. Maybe she could quit Upperline now, but she wasn't sure she wanted to. The goose had laid the golden egg, yet she was more dissatisfied than she had been before she knew such eggs existed. Would she finally go to Paris, that long-ago dream? No, she had come to terms years ago with the fact that Paris was never meant to be.

Still—*a million dollars*. How had Rod saved a million dollars, above and beyond the equity in his house, which also would be Amber's? Her mother would be furious if she knew her second husband had been able to put away that much money, given how modestly they had lived. But Veronica "Rona" Deluca had died ten years ago, bequeathing her daughter nothing but a vague suggestion that Amber was responsible for the cancer that ravaged her, if only because it was connected to her reproductive system. "This is what I get for having a kid," was one of the last things Rona ever said to Amber, in one of their monthly phone calls.

If it hadn't been for Rod, Amber wouldn't have even bothered to come home for Rona's funeral. That had been her last trip to Baltimore, in and out as quickly as possible.

"Do we really need to replace the venetian blinds?" Amber asked the agent as they sped away from the house in her cherry-red Lexus. Regester was one of the few east-west streets in this part of Towson that had no speed bumps, no traffic-calming curves. That was all you needed to know about Regester Avenue: Feel free to run over its kids.

"Honey"—she was almost a decade younger than Amber, yet treated her with a breezily patronizing air as infuriating as it was comic—"those blinds are the *worst*. They have to be at least twenty years old."

*Older. They were there when I was in junior high school.* But she didn't bother to say that. She typed into her Notes app: **Blinds must be changed.**

"And the garden figurines, the geese—what should I do with them?"

"Take them straight to the dump. No one wants that stuff."

Amber knew the real estate agent was right, but she almost winced on Rod's behalf. Even as a child, she had understood that Rod had too much stuff in his front yard, that people who talked about THAT house on Regester were not complimenting it. But the yard had made Rod happy, and young children loved it. In some ways, Rod's front yard was the first gallery of Amber's life. She had yet to meet anyone, whether in a gallery or a museum, who doted on their installations the way Rod had fussed over his yard.

Maybe she could sell the geese on Etsy. If only there were a Depop for yard art. Depop loved a good narrative.

The real estate agent turned right on York Road, heading north. "Are you from here?" Amber asked.

"Moved down after college," she said.

*That would be a no.* Amber disliked people who didn't answer yes-or-no questions with a yes or a no. "It's just that, to get to the airport, I would have taken York south—oh my god, stop, please stop."

"What?"

"Pull into this little strip center. I need to see something."

"Sure." Said with an eye roll of a tone, two drawn-out syllables ending on a sigh.

This particular strip center, built in a faux Tudor style that Amber thought of as fairy-tale quaint, had been the nexus of Amber's teenage years, bookended by a hardware store and a duckpin bowling alley. In between had been a toy store and a copying store. (Because people in the '90s had needed places to make copies. Funny to remember what a big deal it used to be, making copies.) And a Baskin-Robbins, where Amber had worked during high school.

Today, only the hardware store remained. The duckpin bowling alley was a restaurant. The Baskin-Robbins, where she had leaned into so many cartons of ice cream, feeling the cold on her cheeks and the burn of boys' gazes on her exposed cleavage, was a florist. The copying store was all poke bowls and acai smoothies, and the toy store was—*vacant.*

Vacant. Available. A blank canvas for someone with an imagination.

She got out of the agent's car and peered into the toy store, which, for all she knew, had led many lives over the past two decades. Think of how many lives Amber had managed in the same time span. Tinker, Tailor, Soldier, Spy. Felon, Student, Saleswoman, Gallerina, Waitress. The toy store's most recent incarnation appeared to have been some kind of clothing outlet. There were racks and hangers, nothing more. A plain white rectangle of a space, it could be virtually anything.

"How much would a property like this rent for?" Amber asked. "By the square foot?"

"I wouldn't know," the agent said. "I don't do commercial."

Amber took note of the number on the FOR LEASE sign, capturing it on her phone. Her flight was in three hours, and she had checked out of the hotel. But Rod's house was hers; the furniture was still in place. ("Arrange to sell furniture and stage house" was also in her Notes app.) She could sleep there tonight if necessary and, according to Southwest.com, switch her flight to the next day for only an additional $30.

"You know what," she told the agent, "I realize there's one more thing I need to do before I leave town. I'll grab my bag from your trunk, if you don't mind, and then Uber to the airport later. I'll be in touch about getting the house ready for market."

"No rush," the agent said. "By the time we get through the punch list, it will be November, practically the worst time of the year to put a house on the market."

"Yes, well, I'm sorry my stepfather didn't think about that when he was dying."

The woman was immune to insults. It was downright admirable, this impenetrable ego that did not allow for the possibility that she could ever be the butt of a joke. How Amber longed for a skin that thick. She had always been self-conscious, even before she had anything to be self-conscious about.

"Okay, I'll be in touch. I know a handyman who can do most of the things we discussed. I'll get the estimates and forward them to you."

There was a Starbucks on the west side of York Road. Amber crossed over, rolling her suitcase behind her, and called the leasing agent listed on the sign. He was enthusiastic about her interest, but couldn't meet her for at least another two hours. That was fine by Amber. She got out her laptop and researched what she could about galleries in Baltimore, folk art in particular. She called Miss Margaret back in New Orleans, wanting a sounding board, although her mind was already made up.

"You'd really stay up there?" Miss Margaret asked. "After all this time? And all that happened? I thought you wanted nothing to do with that town. You were all over sighing and complaining about going back for even two days."

"I think I can improve the house, get more money for it, if I'm willing to be a DIY'er."

"While you're losing money every month trying to run a *gallery*."

It was funny to Amber how Miss Margaret made *gallery* sound like an epithet, given that she had owned a successful one for twenty years.

"You know it's something I've always wanted to try, and it makes more sense to do it here. Too much competition down there."

"So should I be rooting for you to have a big success and never come home, or should I be counting on you going broke, like every other hobbyist who ever tried her hand at this, and coming back with your tail between your legs?"

"I'm *not* a hobbyist," Amber said. "Don't be cruel, Miss Margaret. You know what I have in storage, my contacts, my instincts, my eye, my *talent*. I could run an amazing gallery."

"Look, I'm going to miss you, that's all. I don't like many people.

I can't afford to lose one of the few I actually enjoy talking to, especially when she's my best employee."

"I'll miss you, too. And New Orleans. I'll miss New Orleans something fierce. But it's, well, a sign, this space being available in *that* shopping center. I need to know if I could be just, well, me again. Me and nothing more than me."

Who would she be if she moved back here? How would she be known? She had to find out.

"It's a sign the way the sirens calling to Ulysses were a sign. You can't go home again, Amber. You, of all people—I'm surprised you want to."

"I am, too."

She stared out the window at York Road, changed and yet not as changed as she would have expected. Twenty years was nothing; twenty years was an eternity. She pressed a button on her phone and whispered to it, almost conspiratorially, "Siri, please google Joe Simpson Baltimore Towson High School."

Siri boomed back, always so proud of herself: "I found this on the web!" Alumni news, a profile from the *Baltimore Business Journal*, but nothing in the first page of results from 1997. Why should there be? Joe Simpson might have been a jerk, ditching what he believed to be a merely queasy Amber on prom night to pursue his ex-girlfriend, but that wasn't something people remembered twenty years later, was it?

Instead of talking to Siri, who would shout her words back to her, Amber typed her next query into Google: *Amber Glass, Joe Simpson, Prom Mom, Cad Dad*. Ah, here they were, the headlines and images she had fought so hard to erase from her memory and her life. But also: There was Joe in his tux, undeniably handsome. And, Amber had to admit to herself, undeniably miserable. Even before he knew how the evening would end, he wasn't happy to be going to prom with her.

She sipped her coffee, which wasn't as milky as she liked. If she took the space across the street, she'd become a regular, and she'd playfully cajole the baristas into making her latte more of a café au lait. She imagined herself picking up a venti here in the mornings, then going into that restaurant after work, the one in the old duckpin alley. But she would not live in Rod's house, not for long. That was still going on the market. She'd rent a place, as she did in New Orleans. She could never see herself as a home-owner, if only because it made it difficult to leave somewhere fast. She had to be prepared to *go*, always.

Still, maybe this was Rod's true bequest to her; maybe he knew she needed just a touch of serendipity to return to Balti-more. Quiet, stoic Rod. He had married her mother when Amber was only six. Amber's father was long gone and out of touch, but her mother had forbidden Rod to be a father to Amber in any way—no adoption, no financial help of any kind, no surname, although Rona had happily become Veronica Deluca on all *her* official papers. What if she became Amber Deluca now? But no, she had to know what it would be like to be Amber Glass here, in the old neighborhood. Did people remember her, or did they just remember an event?

At least one person had to remember her.

*Joe*, Amber thought. Joe Simpson. For a few months in her ju-nior year of high school, Amber had moved through the world as if she were living in a movie, an extremely specific kind of movie, where the most desirable boy in school realized that he was in love with his mousy little tutor. It had been a silly fantasy, but it had been powerful enough to block out reality—her thickening waist and expanding breasts, the disappearance of her period. *He loves me, he loves me, he loves me,* she had told herself in the weeks leading up to the prom. Yet he had never said those words, not even close. *I love him, I love him, I love him.* She had never said those words out loud, but she had expected that love to transform her, change her life.

Maybe it still could.

JOE TOSSED THE ball for his serve, marveling as he often did at how much depended on the toss. The score was 40–0, and Joe was up 5–3, having broken Zach's serve in the last game. He could wrap this up with one good serve. He sent the ball scorching on an angle that kissed the corner of the box. Not an ace, but Zach barely got his racket on it, whiffing the ball into the net. Zach's backhand had fallen apart over the summer, and he now had legitimate yips. Joe hit to Zach's backhand whenever possible. It was a game. You were supposed to try to win.

Zach slumped on a bench and toweled his face, trying to be a good sport about dropping two sets. "You're on fire lately."

Joe shrugged, took the compliment.

"I wonder how many more weeks we have outdoors," Zach continued. "I hate being in the bubble over the winter, having to drive over to Pikesville."

"I hate it, too," Joe said. "I don't like that pressurized air. But, thanks to climate change, we can probably play outside for another six to eight weeks. Almost to Thanksgiving."

"Are you here this year or going to see Meredith's parents?"

"We do her folks in the even years, my mom's in the odds, so thank god we're here."

"I thought your in-laws were okay, as in-laws go."

"They are. Even when they're irritating the hell out of me, I remind myself they raised Meredith, so they deserve some credit, if only for that. But I don't think any man ever stops feeling like a guest in his in-laws' home."

"When you have kids," Zach said, "you don't have to do that stupid do-si-do between households. Grandparents come to *you*."

"Yeah, I think I can handle visiting my in-laws on an every-other-year schedule, thank you very much." Joe and Meredith had agreed even before they got engaged: no kids, ever. Everyone said they would change their minds, that they were too young to know what they wanted, but they had never wavered. Yet people with kids continued to lobby them, even as they began aging out of the possibility. Misery loved company.

"You want to grab a bite?"

"Sure. Meredith has her book club tonight. Where do you want to go?"

"I'm yearning for souvlaki or a gyro. You up for the Towson Diner?"

The question was probably innocent, but it felt like Joe's serve, Zach aiming for a weak spot, payback for Joe winning. It wasn't that he consciously avoided the Towson Diner, but it wasn't his favorite place. The Towson Diner was a boy in a tux, living his last carefree hour.

"Sure," he said. "Why not?"

And once he said them, the words became true. *Why not?* The diner never did a thing to him. The hotel, either, come to think of it. Five years ago, he had arrived at a symposium at the Sheraton and been unable to get out of his car. But, as Meredith kept telling him, Joe had a legitimate form of PTSD, and he needed to con-front it, one memory at a time. "No one remembers 'Cad Dad' but you," she had said. "So let's bury him once and for all."

At the diner, Joe defaulted to his regular order as a bottomless pit of a high school boy: chocolate shake, Reuben, french fries, but with mayo on the side instead of ketchup, a preference he had acquired from Meredith.

It was fucking great. "This is fucking great," he said to Zach.

"If you can't eat like this after two sets of tennis, then what's the point of the tennis," Zach said, attacking his gyro. It looked good and Joe wanted to share, but that didn't feel like something two men did. Spouses, yes. Women, sure. But not men.

They ate in happy silence, friends for more than thirty years. They kept their questions to generalities. *How's work. Amazing,* they assured each other, and Joe knew he was speaking the truth and assumed Zach probably was, too. A personal injury lawyer never had to worry about drumming up business. Joe, meanwhile, had bought a Class C shopping center up in Cecil—try to say that three times fast—that he was planning to flip on his own in order to impress his boss, who also happened to be his uncle. *How's Meredith, How's Amanda. Great,* Joe said. *Busy,* Zach said. They talked a little bit about politics, speculating on next year's presidential race, careful not to reveal which candidates they liked, not because they were inclined to disagree on politics, but because they understood some things were better left unspoken. They were men who voted their wallets, and it was not clear, more than a year out from Election Day, who would best benefit their bottom lines. They ordered beers, but only one apiece. "School night," Zach said, and Joe replied: "Oh, we drank so much more on school nights."

*Was that even true?* Joe had been a good kid, beneath his popular jock veneer. A little drinking, a little weed, but overall a good kid. Excellent grades, except for that one blip in fall of senior year, when everything fell apart and he had to work with a peer tutor, who happened to be Amber Glass. God, the randomness of life. Your high school girlfriend, who you think is the actual fucking love of your life, breaks up with you on the eve of the first day of senior year. You crater—cut classes, cut practice, walk around like you're Kurt Cobain. The school recommends you use the peer tutoring program, and fate—was it fate?—assigns you to Amber Glass. Joe had never bought into his mother's belief that Amber was an out-and-out schemer, but she'd definitely had an agenda.

But here he was at the Towson Diner, and it was fine. The high school reunion, two years ago, had been fine. No one cared, no one remembered. A boy had sat here once in a tux, tie untied, boutonniere long gone. Now that boy was a man, a man who had reclaimed and rebuilt his life. A bad boy could become a good man, as Meredith had told him many times.

"The girl I went to prom with—" he began.

Zach looked wary. They talked about high school. They talked about life after high school. They never spoke about prom night.

"Yeah?"

"What was her name?"

"Don't you remember?"

"Yeah, I'm just curious if you do."

Zach looked into his beer glass as if it were a magic mirror in some fantasy film. "Something . . . weird. Her name was weird." A pause. "*She* was weird." Said tentatively, as if he was worried Joe might disagree, or even take offense. Zach had *hated* Amber, and that was before everything went down.

"Ya think?"

The two old friends laughed and toasted. They had turned forty this year, which was supposed to be a dangerous age, but Joe didn't feel like he was at midlife, so how could he have a midlife crisis? He tried to be grateful, consciously grateful, every day. He wasn't perfect; he still made mistakes. He could do better and he would, he promised himself. *He would*. The main thing is, he always tried to do his best.

And Meredith deserved the lion's share of the credit. God, the miracle of Meredith—if it hadn't been for that nightmarish prom night, which had led to his decision to defer college for a year, then his abrupt change of heart to choose a small private school instead of a Big Ten university, he might never have met her. Twenty-one years in and he still felt a little anxious when he was away from her. She kept him steady; she was his rock. She would be buzzed tonight from all the book club wine, irritated by the women who had failed to read the book. She would be *frisky*.

"We're lucky men, Zach," he said, knowing it was true of him and hoping it was true for his friend, yippy backhand aside.

MEREDITH SURVEYED THE dining room table. Platters of cheese and meats, homemade pimento cheese (her mother's recipe), crudités, fruit. Inevitably, there would be women on keto or Whole30, but they could eat the vegetables and the meats, maybe the hummus? She was unclear on all the rules of the various diets. Meredith had never dieted in her life. Oh, she watched what she ate and exercised rigorously, but she had been spared the body obsession that plagued almost every other woman she knew, perhaps because her body had failed her so fundamentally when she was young. A near-fatal illness at age eleven has a way of changing one's perspective.

She refused to "theme" her refreshments to the book, a practice she found frivolous and, in the case of tonight's book, *Beloved*, potentially offensive. Meredith had resisted book clubs for a long time, and she had joined this one only because she had been assured by her best friend, Wendy, of its seriousness: Discussions were substantive, and no one ever failed to do the reading.

Wendy Asher was a sweetheart, but if she thought these halting discussions that boiled down to thumbs-up, thumbs-down were substantive, well, in the parlance of Meredith's hometown: *Bless her heart.* There were always at least two members who tried to fake their way through it, relying on Wikipedia or film versions, while others seemed intent on talking about anything except the book. The one promise that the club had kept was selecting books that had won major awards. The choice of *Beloved* had been prompted by Toni Morrison's death at summer's end. The selection had been Meredith's, but she did not have high hopes for an elevated conversation.

*Why do you continue to go,* Joe had asked once, *if you dislike it so much?* Meredith wished she knew. She had been like this all her life. Dutiful to a fault. Kind, prone to caring for others, but seldom without this inner caustic voice salting her compassion. Only Joe was spared her harsh judgments, which was how she had known Joe was the one for her, her actual soulmate. From almost the moment they had met, she had recognized that he brought out her best nature. Not only the need to care for him—that was instinctive, she cared for everyone, beginning with her parents—but also a profound and singular passion. *This is my person,* she told herself, lying in Joe's dorm bed the first time they had sex, *and I am his*. They were only nineteen, she had no right to be right—and yet she was.

Meredith was seldom wrong. Which came in handy on tests, but it was more burdensome in life than others might suspect. She saw how the evening would unfold. Sweet Wendy, mindful of her assurances that this was a serious book club, would try to keep the more frivolous members on topic. Darla would drink too much, topping off her glass after every three sips. (As the daughter of high-functioning alcoholics, Meredith could never stop keeping tabs on those who drank too much.)

Anne would worry about reverse racism, which she saw everywhere, and which she refused to acknowledge wasn't really a thing. "Why can she say this, when I can't say—" Brynn wouldn't have read the book. She almost never did, and she didn't even try to fake it. How strange, Meredith thought, to join a club and fail to do the one thing the club was about. She supposed some women simply needed a reason to get out of the house. The club had been formed when the members' children were young; perhaps the women had been too sheepish to call it what it really was: the Drink-and-Complain-About-Your-Husbands Club.

Within two hours, all her prophecies had come true. Meredith sat, nursing her glass of wine. *Beloved*, for all its technical virtuosity, had left Meredith cold. She just didn't have much to say about motherhood. She had learned not to reveal that childlessness was her choice. When the topic came up, she said: "It just wasn't in the cards," which was true, yet allowed people to assume there had been fertility issues, especially if they knew about her childhood cancer. Some people were pushy enough to pursue the topic. "What about adoption, or surrogacy, or—" and Meredith would repeat: "It just wasn't in the cards." Once, at a party, Zach's wife, Amanda, got sloppy drunk and said, "You were smart, not ruining that body of yours for kids, but then, given that you're a plastic surgeon, I guess it wouldn't have been a big deal to get everything fixed. Hey, does your practice do vaginal rejuvenation?"

Meredith almost wanted to congratulate Amanda for managing to misunderstand her on every possible level. She had even been tempted, for once in her life, to tell the truth to someone other than Joe: *I decided never to have kids because I ruined my parents' marriage. There's a reason that two of the best liver specialists in New Orleans ended up having drinking problems, and it was me, their daughter.*

Hostages to fortune, it is said of children. Meredith would add: Hostages to happiness. She could afford to love only one person completely. That person was Joe.

Wendy offered to stay to clean up, which was really an offer to gossip, but Meredith hugged her and gently pushed her toward the door. She could clean up faster on her own. Within thirty minutes, both dishwashers were humming, and she headed upstairs. Joe, who had come in through the garage entrance while the women were gathered in the living room, was upstairs in their bed, freshly showered. He was better-looking at forty than he had been at nineteen, but then—so was Meredith. Heads turned when they walked into rooms. Maybe it was because they had devoted their lives to their devotion, never taking each other for granted. Their love kept them shiny.

She undressed in front of him. He watched attentively, as if he had never seen her disrobe before. She let her hair out of its upsweep, unbuttoned her blouse, slid out of her jeans. She took her time, putting things where they belonged—clothes in the hamper, earrings in the velvet-lined jewelry drawer in the ridiculously over-sized closet, really a dressing room, large enough for a small sofa, not that anyone ever lounged in it. The previous owners had stinted on nothing in the house's renovation, then had the bad luck to divorce right before the free fall of 2008 and been forced to unload it at a bargain price.

Meredith's movements were not overtly sexy, but she could tell Joe wanted her. The only bum note came when she took off her socks; one could actually hear, even over the buzz of CNBC, the way the fabric peeled away from her rough, battered feet, almost as if her soles were covered in Velcro. Meredith's feet were hideous, rough and dragon-like from her treadmill runs. After she and Joe made love, she would get up and vaseline them, put on sweat socks. After.

"Who are you tonight?" Joe asked, rubbing her shoulders.

"Who do you want me to be? What do you want me to do?"

He whispered a favorite scenario in her ear and she took charge, which they both enjoyed, and by the time they were finished, she fell asleep promptly, too tired to get up and put on her socks. Her rough feet scratched against the sheets, and she angled them in such a way as to ensure that they would not brush against Joe in the night.

*October 25, 2019*


JOE GRABBED HIS keys from the peg by the front door. Although the house had a three-car garage, he preferred to park under the porte cochere. Wasn't that the point of a porte cochere? Besides, the gate to their driveway was achingly slow; once he got to the top of the hill, he didn't want to wait for the garage door to open as well.

"I'm heading out," he said into the intercom next to the door, which allowed one to speak to the front gate and various rooms throughout the vast house. He felt like the school principal, making the daily announcements. "I'll order from the car. What was it you wanted—garlic soup and—"

"Soupe à l'ail, with a poached egg," Meredith croaked, blowing her nose. "And a baguette if they have it."

"Feed a fever, starve a cold, stuff a Meredith," he said, an old joke between them. Meredith became ravenous when ill. Ravenous and picky. She was always demanding and discerning about food, a trait that Joe found distressingly common in New Orleanians. He liked food, too, but he didn't need to *talk* about it all the time.

And when Meredith got sick—and she was prone to colds and flus, much to her disgust—only restaurant meals would do. She had heard about the garlic soup at this newish French restaurant on York Road, and when she came down with her usual fall head cold, nothing else would do.

"Carryout?" echoed the person who answered the phone. "We do not normally do *carryout.*" Joe felt as if a *monsieur*—and an insult—were implicit.

"Do you have a bar?" Joe asked. Assured they did, he said: "I'll come in, I'll have a drink, order my food, and then ask for take-home containers. Is that cool?"

A beat. "Certainly," the supercilious voice on the phone said. "Whatever pleases you."

*What would please me is not being lorded over by some dude who's answering the phone at a "French" restaurant on York Road.* But Joe always tried to focus on solutions. Too many people got distracted by one-upmanship, the urge to be the alpha in any encounter, social or business. Joe wanted only to get out with what he wanted. Most of the time, that meant being nice, and, luckily, nice came naturally to him.

He hadn't realized that the bistro, which Meredith had heard about from one of her friends, was in the quaint faux Tudor shopping center that had been central to his childhood. How funny to think he had once played duckpins where he now sat nursing a Peroni. He had ordered the garlic soup and bread, then added a pot de crème on impulse. He would poach the egg for the soup himself, rather than gamble on it surviving the ten-minute trip back to Ruxton. He made a good poached egg.

He wished he had time to walk the streets of his old neighborhood while the food was prepared. Joe considered Stoneleigh the platonic ideal of a place to grow up. Big but not gross houses, lawns large enough for badminton and croquet, basketball hoops in driveways. He had tried to persuade Meredith to move there when they were ready to buy their first house, but it was too suburban for her tastes. "I like a little more grit," she said, pushing for Fells Point, convenient to Hopkins, where she was a resident at the time.

"But Stoneleigh has such a great school district," Joe had argued.

"Why do we have to worry about schools when we're not having kids?" Meredith countered.

"Resale value, baby. Resale."

They had compromised on a North Baltimore neighborhood known as Keswick. Like a lot of compromises, in Joe's opinion, it succeeded only in making them both vaguely dissatisfied. Then the housing market collapsed and he had been able to buy the Ruxton place crazy cheap, just south of $2 million, although they ended up losing a little money on the Keswick house. By then, Meredith had joined a practice at Greenspring Station, which made her commute a breeze. She wasn't sure why they needed a 15,000-square-foot house and, frankly, neither was Joe, but it was such a steal—and convenient to L'Hirondelle Club, where they now were members.

Meredith had been skeptical of joining a country club, too, but

Joe really did network there, and she had been placated by the fact that it didn't have a golf course, only tennis. Meredith frequently joked that golf was her only dealbreaker—except Joe knew she wasn't joking. Meredith really *hated* golf. When they traveled and stayed in nice hotels, she was upset if the golf channel was included in the cable package. She believed golf courses destroyed marriages and the planet.

His beer finished, his food ready, he decided he could at least walk the length of the little shopping center, a mini trip down memory lane. The place also interested him professionally, since he had invested in his first shopping center up in Cecil County. Of course, what worked on York Road in Towson wasn't going to fly on Pulaski Highway in North East.

Copy place gone, ice cream store gone, hardware store the same at least. He couldn't even remember what the place in the middle had been, and now it was clearly in the middle of a transformation. Drop cloths on the floor, a woman on a ladder rolling paint on the ceiling. Oh, this was the old toy store. What was it going to be now? A name had been stenciled on the door, but not yet painted in. The font was bold, unfussy.

**AMBER GLASS GALLERY.**

A sign. A literal fucking *sign*.

He couldn't believe she had come back. Joe had been reluctant to return in his twenties, but Meredith had gotten into Johns Hopkins, so he'd had no choice. And while being "Cad Dad" wasn't great, it was nothing compared to "Prom Mom," the honor student who hid her pregnancy from everyone, then killed her baby. His mother had always maintained that Amber Glass was crazy *and* crazy like a fox, that she had set Joe up to be the fall guy for some other man's mistake. Others, too, had been happy to speculate on

the identity of the father of the not-quite baby, a child so premature that it was a toss-up if it would have survived.

As if sensing his presence, the woman on the ladder turned her
head toward the door. Given the October dusk, she wouldn't be
able to make out more than his form. Whereas he could see her in
sharp detail, down to the eyes that matched her name. Not that
he really could see her eye color from here, but it seemed to him
that they glowed gold in the dark. Like an animal's.

He turned briskly and walked toward his car. Ten minutes
later, he was home, although he couldn't have told you a single
detail about the drive, or the poached egg he managed to make,
sliding its silky perfection into Meredith's garlic soup and then
bringing the well-staged meal to her on a Lucite bed tray.

"You okay?" Meredith asked, eating with a zest that few people
with a head cold could muster. "You look pale."

"Oh, I'm fine. Market had a hiccup today. I'm a little spooked."

"I thought it closed up?"

Ah, Meredith, loyal listener of NPR. "It did, but Amazon fell 1
percent." Thank god he had *Marketplace* on in the car.

"Do we have Amazon stock?"

"A little."

He could tell her. He should tell her. Meredith knew all about
Amber. He had told Meredith everything years ago, the month
that they met. She had never judged him; quite the opposite.
That's why he loved her.

Yet, somehow, he could not bring himself to mention that
he had seen Amber Glass for the first time in more than
twenty years. Had she seen him? He didn't think so. Would she
even recognize him? He wasn't sure he would have known her
without the name stenciled on the storefront.

Her name. What was she thinking? *Shameless*, his mother had said of her. *That one is shameless. Made her mess and tried to drag you into it.* His mother had wanted to hire a private detective, force a paternity test. The lawyer his dad hired had explained there was no gain in proving someone else had fathered the baby. "Amber has a legal issue; Joe has a PR issue," the lawyer had said. "He ditched his date on prom night, left her alone while she was clearly ill. But he didn't know she was about to have a baby, much less that she would kill it. Making a stink about the baby's paternity—that's only going to make the story juicier."

He wanted to lie on the bed, bury his head in his wife's lap, have her tell him, as she had told him many times, that he had no reason to feel guilty. But there was a tray full of food in front of her, and her forehead was warm to the touch. It was not fair to ask her to take care of him, not tonight. He needed to be solicitous of her for once.

"Do you want me to sleep in the guest room?" he asked.

"Absolutely not."

He cleared his wife's dishes, took his time tidying up, allowed himself some idle googling in the little office alcove off the kitchen. Should he reach out to Amber? *No.* It was one thing to embrace his own redemption, another to open that Pandora's box. He wished her well and he hoped, not just for his own sake, that she would be allowed to resume her life without the past rising up to haunt her. Staying away from her would be the greatest kindness Joe could confer.

Thank god a gallery in that location was destined to tank.

MEREDITH FELT BETTER after she ate. She almost always felt better after she ate. If you could eat, you were healthy. Those who could not eat were . . . something else. The cold, or maybe the decongestant, had left her with a bit of brain fog.

But now insomnia, her old and troublesome friend, had come for her. Three thirty a.m., the worst time to be awake. Even if she managed to fall back to sleep, she would get maybe two hours of true rest. But it was too early to rise and *do* anything. She resisted reaching for her phone on the nightstand. Turning on a screen was the worst thing one could do. Besides, the light might wake Joe.

Meredith used to take pride in how little sleep she required, especially during med school and her residency. She remembered a time when it was common for people to brag about being able to function on four to six hours sleep. Now everyone spoke about "sleep hygiene" and developing good "sleep habits." Well, she had good sleep habits, for the most part, except for the huge television in the bedroom. But try to tell Joe that he couldn't fall asleep while watching television, just try. Once asleep, he slept soundly, like a beautiful machine in slumber mode, although he was prone to bursts of nonsensical speech.

She eased out of bed, careful not to disturb Joe, put on her robe, slipped her phone in the robe's pocket. Might as well get credit for the steps she was about to take.

They had lived in the house for a decade now, but it still felt new to Meredith, or maybe simply a little unfinished, under-furnished. It was so big. Why did two people without children require such a large house? The ruder people in their lives had asked them this question straight out, and others probably wondered. Yes, the purchase price of the house had been a bargain; they had picked it up in a short sale in 2009, from a desperate owner. (An oxymoron, the short sale had taken forever.)

But the cost of maintaining the house was not similarly affected by the global housing market crash. Joe paid the bills out of their joint checking account, and Meredith's stomach always lurched a little when she saw the cost of heating it, cooling it, tending its lush, verdant grounds. Repairing it. Her own parents owned a charming wreck of a house that had burned through all their discretionary money and forced them to keep working at an age at which they might otherwise have retired. Having a needy house was almost as dangerous as having a needy child. But Meredith, although incensed that Joe had made an offer on the house without consulting her, had come to love it.

She lapped the second floor, then went downstairs, where the layout made it possible to walk infinite loops, for everything was arrayed around a central staircase. In warmer weather, she sometimes went outside on what Joe called her midnight patrols, but it spooked her, walking in the dark. As a child, she had briefly been a sleepwalker, and her parents had told her frightening stories of finding her blocks away, barefoot on Nashville Avenue. Just another way in which she had tortured them.

She was eleven when she was diagnosed, in remission at thirteen, officially cured at sixteen. A "survivor." If only her parents had survived as well. Oh, they had lived, of course. But Meredith's needs had drained her mother and father, bankrupted the reservoirs of affection in her parents' marriage. She was pretty sure that the drinking had not been a problem until then, nor had the tit-for-tat indiscretions. But they stayed together. For her, she assumed.

Sometimes she wished they hadn't.

She checked her phone: 850 steps already, almost a half mile. Imagine having a house where it was possible to walk that many steps without going in tiny circles. It was obscene. Joe continued to justify it on so many levels, but Meredith didn't bother. *We can entertain in a grand fashion!* They did start having a large holiday party, another wretched expense. *The grounds afforded them privacy! They could put in a pool if they wished.*

They did not wish. But sometimes they did have sex outside, on one of the chaises, which was enjoyable if the bugs weren't too bad.

She also had a huge, lovely office in the basement, which she didn't even need. But she had been touched by Joe giving her the space and taking the cozy, shelf-lined alcove off the kitchen, the space that Realtors had finally learned to stop calling "mother's office."

She decided to make herself some warm milk, although she knew from experience it wouldn't put her to sleep. But it was something to do. The kitchen, renovated the year before they bought the house, seemed dated to Meredith based on the bits and pieces of HGTV she caught. (It was by far the preferred station in the waiting room at her practice.) The wood was too dark, the granite counters ordinary in a world where people now used poured concrete or even glass. They should probably update it soon. Paradoxically, her parents' kitchen, which had not changed for thirty years, had aged better. When she had been at her sickest, they put an antique chaise in place of the dining set, and once she was well, they kept it there. People loved that chaise. During parties, holidays, it was considered the prime location—close enough to the action to be in on all the conversations, yet far enough from the work areas so that one was rarely asked to pitch in.

But Meredith never sat there again, under any circumstance. The chaise stank of illness to her. Maybe it made no sense, but she was ashamed she had been so sick so young. It seemed a moral failing and had left her prone to every kind of virus.

*I destroyed my parents' marriage*, she whispered to Joe in bed after they had been dating about a month. They were nineteen. She was a sophomore, he was a freshman. The words *I love you* had not been said yet, but it was only a matter of time. First came the confidences, the sharing of secrets. *They fight all the time. They drink too much. They cheat on each other. I don't ever want to be a parent.*

*Me, neither*, Joe said. *Although, I guess in a way, I sort of was? Only I didn't know it. I had no idea. Honestly, I had no idea.*

The story he told her was shocking. Or should have been, she supposed. But Meredith was not shocked. She felt only empathy for this young man, caught up in something terrible through no fault of his own. She absolutely understood what *that* was like.

*I can't ever forgive myself*, he said.

*I forgive you. And maybe one day, that will help you see that you should forgive yourself.*

And with those words, she had bound Joe to her for life. Oh, they had their ups and downs—they were young, it was overwhelming to find the love of one's life at nineteen, everyone and everything told them that they could not be sure. But Meredith was sure enough for the both of them.

Ugh, she had let her thoughts wander and the milk had scalded. She poured it down the sink, leaving the pan to soak. She checked the clock on the stove—four fifteen. Was it worth trying to go back to bed? She would inevitably be rewarded with a perversely wonderful sliver of sleep, only to have the alarm go off at five thirty. Oh, wait, it was Saturday. She could sleep in.

Theoretically. But she was sick of bed after spending yesterday there.

She slid back into the sheets. Joe sat straight up. "What's going on?" he demanded. "What are you doing here?" It took her a second to realize that he was talking in his sleep. She placed a hand on his left shoulder and he relaxed, settling back under the covers.

AMBER WORKED LATE, almost incapable of stopping, even after nightfall. She wasn't sure painting after dark was the best decision, but she was going to have to apply at least two coats, so she could chase imperfections on the next go-round. She was a skilled painter by now, having done most of the rooms at Rod's house, which, despite the real estate agent's pessimism, was already under contract. She could have paid someone, but it was hard to unlearn the habit of thrift, essential to her life for so long. Now Rod's estate was almost settled, and the projected numbers in her various accounts—checking, savings, brokerages—were staggeringly unreal, numbers she had never seen before.

Yet this gallery could swallow it all, and quickly. It was a tough business. She had seen it up close. And this was a counterintuitive location for any gallery, but especially one that would seem avant-garde by Baltimore's standards. She had already started introducing herself to concierges at the best Baltimore hotels—Four Seasons, the Ivy, Sagamore Pendry—and telling them that any guests who visited the American Visionary Art Museum would be interested in her shop. Maybe she should prepare a brochure or a one-sheet once she had the first exhibit up?

She had thought a lot about the best show with which to kick off the space. Her specialty, most of it warehoused back in New Orleans, was art by the incarcerated. *Not* the works of notorious prisoners, which did not interest her, although she went back and forth in her mind about the paintings of John Wayne Gacy. His work was powerful, but his crimes were too horrible; the paintings weren't good enough to transcend his evil.

She cared about the art, not the rap sheets of the artists. And while there were fewer and fewer prison art programs, she had built up a network of artists and collectors over the years, bargaining shrewdly for pieces from some of the best-known prison artists of the 1970s and '80s. These were her standout pieces and always fetched good prices.

But she knew her stodgy hometown and had decided to start with something accessible—flowers. Bright blossoms, a burst of color as the world moved toward its darkest season—it would all be very safe and pretty. Amber could show her truer colors later.

She put the lids back on her paint cans, folded up the ladder, made sure the lights were out in the back. No alarm system, not yet, as there was nothing to steal. Only an old velvet sofa and a mini fridge in the back room. Going on midnight, her car was the last one in the lot, but she felt safe.

Or, at least, as safe as she ever felt. Twenty-two years was a long time to move through one's days with the expectation that someone was going to call you out, reveal who you were. And although she had been released into the world at age eighteen, absolutely free and her record sealed, she never lost the fear that she would be locked up again. It was terrifying to have done something so awful that you couldn't remember it. Who's to say it wouldn't happen again?

Her duplex, a rental, was a few miles south of the gallery, in a hidden enclave known as Stone Hill. Amber hadn't even known the place existed when she was growing up in Baltimore, but she had chanced on an Airbnb and persuaded the owner to let her have a month-by-month lease. The tiny neighborhood, once home to mill workers, could have been a film set. For Amber, its real charm was the privacy it afforded. She wanted to live on a street where no one ever happened by. Puritan Street led nowhere; no one ever drove down Puritan Street unless they had a reason.

*Puritan Street.* The name amused her, as did the retro kitchen. She spent most of her time in here, at a marble-topped bistro table, starting the day with a homemade café au lait, ending with wine, her laptop open and trained on the social media pages of Joe Simpson and his wife, Meredith Duval Simpson.

She had taken his name. *Interesting.*

Joe was on Facebook, but barely. Meredith, however, had a large presence there, and even more so on Instagram, which she used to promote her plastic surgery practice. She was beautiful, Amber had to concede that. And accomplished. She not only had her practice, but she made annual missions to Central America, where she worked on children with cleft palates and other facial deformities. So, beautiful, accomplished, *and* virtuous. Joe had chosen well. Definitely a cut above Kaitlyn. (Amber had found her, too, but she was boring, a mother of three in Howard County, and she had really let herself go.)

As for Joe, he seemed successful as well, but the only impression he left on social media was that he played a lot of tennis. His wife's account had a few photos of parties at their house, which seemed large and lavish. If one searched for Joe only by his name, this was all one found.

Add "Amber Glass" and "prom," and things turned out differently. There were articles, photographs, a Wikipedia entry. Remove those terms and it all disappeared, like a magic trick. Even

"Amber Glass," on its own, turned up little, thanks to a name that yielded a thousand Etsy offerings. Joe Simpson, denuded of words that linked him to Amber Glass, was simply a successful commercial real estate salesman. All Amber wanted for herself was what had been granted to Joe. Was that so much to ask?

Probably. Apparently. But if that's what she wanted, the smart thing to do would be to stay away from Joe, avoid him at all costs.

Amber was tired of doing the smart thing. She had usually done the smart thing, most of her life, and where had that gotten her?

She would not *try* to meet Joe or cross his path. But this was Smalltimore, after all, and it was probably only a matter of time before they encountered each other. She couldn't help being curious about that moment, fantasizing about it, even. She loved that she had no idea how he would respond to her, or how he felt about her. For the first time in a long time, maybe twenty years, her life held the promise of an exciting story.

*There's simply not a lot of suspense in most people's lives*, she thought, staring through the kitchen door's glass at her small backyard. If you think about it, we usually know how things are going to go, what's likely to happen next, whether it's a movie or your life. Amber had made a new life for herself, first in Florida, then in New Orleans, but she couldn't help wondering how the old life might have gone if it had not jumped the track. Was that weird? It didn't feel weird to her. She had a right to know what she had lost, even if it meant putting herself at risk for losing it all again.

*Weird* would be sending Joe a Facebook friend request. *Weird* would be following Meredith on Instagram. Yet she did the latter this evening, telling herself that there was no way Joe's wife knew anything about her, or would even notice a new follow from

AGlassGallerina. Heck, people who had money to fix their faces and bodies were in the income bracket that bought art.

The little Oriole stove looked beautiful in the moonlight. She took a photo and posted it, including multiple hashtags. #Baltimore Oriole #NotThatKindOfBaltimoreOriole #vintage #LifeIsGood.

*May 1997*

# THE DRESS

**"AND YOU'RE PAYING** for the dress?"

The question caught Lynn off guard, but then, everything Rona Deluca said was couched in the sly tone of a woman with an agenda. A strong stage mother vibe—no, that wasn't it. Rona Deluca appeared to be someone who had been waiting her entire life for the world to take notice of her. If the long-desired attention had arrived in the form of a reporter who wanted to document her daughter's search for a prom dress, so be it.

Over lunch in the Nordstrom cafe, Rona had barely let her daughter get a word in edgewise. True, the daughter, Amber

Glass, was shy. But Mrs. Deluca was actively interfering in Lynn's attempts to draw her out without being too interrogative. Lynn wanted to be a fly on the wall, and she was grateful that Trish was the photographer assigned to this piece, because Trish had the ability to work unobtrusively, even in a tight space such as this dressing room. True to the maxim, the experience was already being shaped by being observed—they had needed Nordstrom's permission, and the store, inevitably, had gone overboard, setting aside one of its grandest dressing rooms. They weren't even in the area closest to the teen department, but across the floor, where the store's most expensive dresses were sold. Lynn and Mrs. Deluca had been offered tea and champagne as they sat on the love seat near the three-way mirror. Lynn had said no, of course. Mrs. Deluca had asked if there were any cookies to go with the tea.

Maybe this VIP treatment was the reason she believed the *Beacon-Light* would pay for the dress itself. And Lynn had picked up the check at lunch. Yes, all of this would be confusing to someone unaccustomed to reporters—trying to gauge what they would pay for, what hospitality they could accept, what they must refuse.

"Uh, no, we can't buy Amber's dress, Mrs. Deluca. That would almost be like a form of checkbook journalism."

"Oh, sure, I get that," she said.

Amber, standing on a round platform in a much-too-fancy and grown-up red dress, appeared to blush, although it was hard to tell, given her olive-gold skin. *Amber* was such a good name for her. Skin, eyes, hair—she was all over amber. Not beautiful, not yet, but she was going to be one day, when she shed the baby fat.

Not that Lynn had been looking for a beauty when she began

calling schools, asking for teachers and guidance counselors to recommend a girl who might be right for this story, her editor's brainchild. She had needed someone who didn't take going to prom for granted, a girl who wouldn't be jaded about the experience. True love not required.

Amber, a junior at Towson High School, fit the bill. Honor student, had represented the county in a statewide forensic competition, placing second in extemporaneous speech, so she must be able to talk under some circumstances.

She also was altruistic, volunteering in her school's peer tutoring program, which was how she had met the boy who was taking her to senior prom, a lacrosse player named Joe. Lynn had inferred that the date was a bargain struck for convenience. He was a senior who had broken up with his girlfriend, or she had broken up with him. God knows, with Mrs. Deluca forever chattering, it was hard to piece the details together.

Not that Lynn cared about the boy. She was here for the *ritual*, the totem, the dress. Lynn barely remembered her own prom date, but the dress lived in her memory to this day. She and her mother had gone to every department store in Baltimore—and there had been a lot, in 1977. Hutzler's, Hochschild's, Stewart's. All gone now; there wasn't a single local one left. In the end, they had found what she wanted at the Bloomingdale's outside D.C. It was simple—Grecian inspired, a pale coral. Not the kind of dress that boys liked, but Lynn, like Amber, had gone to her prom with a friend.

Styles were all over the place this year. Super sleek, but also a kind of prairie froufrou. The dress Amber was modeling now was the most expensive she had tried on yet, $300, which might be why Mrs. Deluca had brought up the subject of who was paying.

"I really think I need an Empire waist," Amber said. Lynn noted that she pronounced it correctly—but then, according to her guidance counselor, she was a wiz at French, too. That was the subject in which she had tutored her prom date.

"What's that?" Mrs. Deluca asked.

"High-waisted, right under the—" The girl didn't even want to say the word *breasts*. Lynn couldn't tell if her modesty was characteristic or if it was extra shyness brought on by having a writer and photographer present.

"I had such a cute figure when I was Amber's age," Mrs. DeLuca said. "Same boobs, but skinny all over."

*Not exactly a quote I can use.* Lynn wrote it down anyway.

Lynn had hoped for some conflict between mother and daughter; that was part of the ritual, too, right? For the daughter to push to look older, while the mother tried to temper her with a restraining hand. She had expected Mrs. Deluca to urge Amber to try on the high-necked Gunne Sax dresses that were so popular this year while Amber lobbied for something low-cut and shiny. This article was supposed to be, well, heartwarming, but Mrs. Deluca had a way of flattening every promising moment.

The saleswoman, clearly quite good at her job, came in with another armful of clothes from the juniors department, known as the "Brass Plum." Ugh, what a name, probably some remnant of the '60s, when people were forever coining nonsensical combinations of adjectives and nouns. "Try this one," she said.

"Oh, no," Mrs. Deluca objected. "That's all white. It looks like a wedding dress."

"It's not white. It has really subtle gold tones. She's going to glow in it."

She did. It had the Empire waist Amber wanted, but the skirt was floaty, with an underskirt providing the gold effect. She twirled in it, saying: "This is it, this is it, this is it." Well, at least Lynn had her kicker. Now she just needed 700–800 words to go in front of it.

Mrs. Deluca turned to Trish. "I have so few photos of Amber. Do you think you could give me copies of the ones you're taking?"

Lynn and Trish exchanged a look. It was not an uncommon request, but it was an awkward one. The paper *sold* prints to people, its corporate owner having figured out this was a reliable if small source of revenue. They were forbidden to give prints away.

"I'll tell you what," Trish said. "I just finished the roll I was shooting. I'm going to put another roll in, fire off some shots, and I'll give you that. You'll have to get it developed, but the prints will be yours."

Lynn watched Amber twirl again, her happiness infectious. She almost wished she were a teenager again. Almost.

Later, when Amber Glass became known as Prom Mom, those were the shots that appeared in tabloids. Mrs. Deluca didn't even give Trish the credit, claiming to have taken them herself, probably to avoid copyright issues. Which, in the end, kept Trish and Lynn from getting in trouble with their bosses, so maybe it was for the best. The shot of Amber that ran in the features section, one in which she was caught in mid-twirl, also showed up in a lot of newspapers, properly credited to the *Beacon-Light*. But the photo that made Mrs. Deluca the most money was the only known photo of Amber with her date, and, in fairness, that *had* been taken by her mom, in that ridiculous front yard. A smiling girl, a frowning boy, and a bevy of geese in hats and aprons looking like the most ridiculous shotgun wedding ever.

*November 14, 2019*

MEREDITH FELT SHEEPISH when the other doctors on her mission trip filed past her business-class seat on the flight out of Guatemala City. "Living high," Steve Epstein said, and she simply smiled, trying to find an expression that combined contrition and bemusement.

"Joe upgraded me with his miles," she said to Anne Langtry, whom she had known since med school.

"He's a good guy," Anne said sincerely as she headed to the rear of the plane, without even a trace of envy.

Normally, Meredith would have refused Joe's offer; it seemed antithetical to the spirit of a healing mission to travel in business class. But the connection time in Miami was tight and seat 2B was an advantage she could not refuse. Thank goodness she was traveling with only a carry-on. And that she had Global Entry, which would speed her through immigration. She should be okay.

Except—the plane did not move. Five, ten, fifteen minutes passed. The pilot came on the speaker and explained that there was a light on the dash and although this very aircraft had flown from Miami to Guatemala City problem-free only hours earlier, a mechanic must check it out. "Shouldn't take too long, folks." Meredith looked around, disturbed by the other business-class passengers' obvious relief at the pilot's accentless English. So many people had told her to stop participating in this mission, that it was too dangerous. Even Joe had begun to question the wisdom of these trips, hectoring her to stop, even sulking a bit. "Do you really need to keep doing this? Haven't you paid it forward by now?"

She couldn't begin to convey to people who had never visited what Guatemala was really like, especially around Lake Atitlán. She'd move there if she could. If only she could lure Joe down for one of the mission trips, she knew he would be charmed by life around the lake, especially San Pedro La Laguna, where the weather was wonderfully mild in November.

She checked her watch. Thirty minutes past departure. She emailed Joe's young assistant, Bobbie, and asked her to be ready to book a hotel room in Miami. "Something near the airport, and check the flights, so I can be on the first flight out of there to-morrow."

Forty-five minutes, an hour. While the business-class seats had their own entertainment systems, the plane also had ceiling-mounted video screens, where a sitcom was playing. The show looked oddly dated to Meredith, but then she figured out—it was supposed to be taking place in the 1980s. She had almost no memory of that era, the decade of her birth.

No, she had no nostalgia for the '80s, and even less for the '90s, other than meeting Joe at the end of that decade.

She scrolled through the photos in her phone, before-and-after shots from the last week, although the afters were not true *afters*, only post-surgery. The patients had long healing times ahead of them, sometimes more surgeries. Joe had once glanced over her shoulder, saying after a long pause: "I don't know how you do it, honey." She could not find the words to explain to him that these unfinished faces disturbed her not at all. That was her preferred word—*unfinished*. Not disfigured, merely incomplete.

In the field, she spoke slowly and carefully to her patients, making eye contact, wishing she understood how her words were being translated by the helpers using the local dialect. She was pretty sure she heard "Dios," which could be a reference to God; it was one of the few words that was the same in Mayan and Spanish. She wasn't crazy about having God credited for her work. God, even if one was a believer, had failed the child; Meredith was picking up the slack. Did that make her superior to God? She smiled at the idea. Meredith didn't believe in God, hadn't for a long time. Nor did she believe in perfection, and she was strict that this word never be used in her practice. Instead, she liked to say that her patients, even the rich ones in Baltimore who probably did believe in perfection, were seeking *improvements* or *changes that would enhance their confidence.* She was wary of anyone who used the word *perfect*, and she hated how often people applied it to her. To call someone perfect, although it seemed complimentary, was a dig, a way of denying them their humanity. A robot was perfect. Meredith was a person, albeit a highly competent one.

"The captain's going to turn off the seat belt sign," a flight attendant announced. "Feel free to use the bathrooms and stretch your legs. And we will be coming around with water."

A woman from economy class beelined up the aisle, and the flight attendant blocked her: "This bathroom is for business class only." Her tone was polite, if steely.

"I don't need to use the bathroom," the woman said. "I need to explain that it's very important that I get to Miami tonight. I am attending a wedding tomorrow."

Meredith hid her smile behind the in-flight magazine. The woman sounded as if she truly believed her urgency would be enough to get the plane aloft.

Another thirty minutes. The show about the 1980s family was now on its third episode. Meredith was warming to it in spite of herself. Was this how Stockholm syndrome worked? She was resigned now to spending the night in Miami. The woman who had to attend a wedding made her way up to the front of the plane again, announced how vital her trip was. At that moment, the intercom crackled, and Meredith sensed immediately that this plane was going nowhere tonight. Before the captain spoke, she had packed up her purse and started strategizing.

"We're sorry, folks, but we're not going to be allowed to take off tonight. We're going to let you off and you'll need to go to the gate agent to get your voucher for a hotel and rebook your flights for tomorrow—"

Meredith was third in line at the gate, a huge advantage, and her rebooked flight was an improvement in some ways—first thing in the morning, via Dallas, with a more generous connection window. She shared a cab to the hotel with another business-class customer, a woman uninterested in idle conversation, thank god. Meredith had no small talk in her tonight.

Riding through the streets of Guatemala City, Meredith saw the dangerous place that Joe and others imagined—the razor wire, the armed guards. Although she was an adventurous traveler and fearless in the countryside, she would not leave the hotel in search of dinner tonight.

She was at the end of a long, leisurely meal in the restaurant when Anne and Steve showed up in the lobby. Meredith flushed with guilt. They must have been sitting very far back in the plane. She lowered her eyes to the book in her lap, hoping they would not notice her.

They didn't. She was sure of this because, as they waited for the elevator, Steve absentmindedly put his hand on the small of Anne's back. This was not something a man would do casually to a female colleague, and it was notable to Meredith because Anne was married. Happily, Meredith had thought. And maybe she was. People were complicated. Happily married people had affairs all the time.

Meredith didn't approve, of course, but she also didn't judge. What really bothered her was that she hadn't suspected. When had this started? Were they that good at deception or was she that obtuse?

Back in the room, she called Joe on his cell, then the landline, leaving messages on both. "I miss you," she said, the simple truth. If he had picked up, would she have shared the gossip about Anne and Steve? She thought not, although she couldn't say why. They were not particularly gossipy people, Meredith and Joe. Were they incurious? Or was it because they were both so private about themselves? Meredith did have a disproportionate fear of being talked about, which dated to her childhood. She remembered being in Langenstein's when she was recovering, hearing one woman whisper—no, not even whisper—*That's the Duval girl, she's been terribly sick, poor thing.* She had never felt so ashamed in her life.

She understood then that if people said such things within earshot, they said far worse things still behind one's back.

She fell asleep, only to be awakened by sounds through the wall. Whoever was in the next room was making love, the headboard bumping the wall, a woman's moans steady and even. It sounded gentle and sweet. Anne and Steve? No, this was a couple with a history; there was something familiar about the act to them, yet they were still clearly enjoying each other. Like Meredith and Joe.

She fell back asleep easily.

JOE HAD NEVER realized how much he used the stretch of York Road below Stevenson Lane until he started trying to avoid it. Wells Liquors, occasional takeout from Café Zen—it was a rare week that went by without him needing to drive past the Amber Glass Gallery.

Meanwhile, Meredith kept agitating to visit that French bistro in person. He told her someone from the office had gotten food poisoning there from bad oysters. "Was it before Labor Day?" Meredith had asked, and Joe had almost been offended on behalf of his nonexistent friend and his nonexistent food poisoning. "No," he had told Meredith, "it was in September."

"Well, anyone can get a bad oyster," Meredith said, then let it go. Meredith was that rare woman who, when dropping a contentious point, really dropped it, instead of slipping it into her purse or back pocket for a future argument. It was another reason Joe loved her so much. He should have told her about the gallery right away, after he discovered it. But she had been sick, and he hadn't wanted to upset her, and if he told her now, it would seem like a big deal. When it wasn't.

Still, he was going to have to take Meredith to the French bistro eventually. Was it possible, he wondered, to park so that one didn't pass the gallery? He should check out the parking situation, do a little reconnaissance mission.

"Opening Show," a sign in the window of the now freshly painted Amber Glass Gallery promised. "November 15 through December 15." The lights were on, but no one was inside. He crept from his car as if he were eight years old, playing the wide-ranging game of hide-and-seek in which the children of his block had virtually no boundaries as long as they stayed east of York Road. There was a glare on the windows from the streetlights, so he cupped his hands over his eyes to peer inside. Lots of paintings of flowers, crude and amateurish.

"Would you like to go in?"

He turned and found himself face-to-face with Amber Glass for the first time since May 25, 1997. She had a cup of Starbucks in her hand and only mild curiosity in her eyes. There was no spark of recognition, although Joe knew he still looked remarkably like the boy he had been. (A boy, he reminded himself fiercely, only a *boy*.)

Amber, on the other hand—her poise, fusty and prim on a teenager, finally suited her. She was extremely—what was the term—*put together*, everything just so. Outfit, shoes, makeup, hair. This was a woman who probably took hours to get ready to leave the house. Meredith could be ready in fifteen minutes and was still a knockout.

"Sure," he said. "I'm in commercial real estate. I'm always curious about new businesses."

It *was* Amber, wasn't it? Height was right, hair was the same color, only worn up now, in the kind of bun that allowed a lot of tendrils to escape. The body was different, but maybe it was only that this Amber dressed to accentuate it, especially below the waist. Her skirt was leather, knee-length, but snug. The Amber he had known had been shy. He had sometimes thought that if she had the option to be nothing but a brain in a jar, that would be fine with her. She seemed to consider everything below her neck mysterious and shameful in equal parts.

She unlocked the door and ushered him in, gestured at the walls. "This is my first gallery, although I've worked in others and sold online for years."

Still had those strange golden eyes, like a cat.

(*An animal, his mother had said of her. Ignorant, without maternal instinct. She's barely human, that girl. She could have destroyed your life. It wasn't for lack of trying that she failed.*)

"I'm looking for a gift," he said. "For my, uh, wife." Did she really not recognize him? His hair had darkened with age and he wasn't as lanky, but he thought he looked pretty good. He had been pleased, at his high school reunion, how well-preserved he was relative to most of the guys. Interestingly, the women, for the most part, had aged well, far better than the men. And yet not a single one was as attractive as Meredith, who had reverted to her shyest, most Southern self among Joe's boisterous high school friends.

"Does she like visionary art?"

"Like, art that predicts the future?"

Amber laughed, and she was clearly laughing at him. "The show that opens tomorrow features still lifes of flowers and other things in nature, but all the artists lack traditional training."

"I like the colors on that one," he said, pointing to a messy bouquet of what appeared to be peonies, in a range of pink and peach hues.

"Ah, Marian Baker. She's one of my favorites. That goes for $450."

His mind could not help making the calculations—*square footage, rent, overhead*—she would have to sell a lot of $450 paintings to make a profit in this space, even if she had a website. He doubted she would last a year. This store was one of those cursed locations that no one could make a go of. Joe had lost track of all its incarnations over the years.

She continued: "If you like it, I'll mark it as sold, but I'd want to keep it on exhibit through the end of the show, if possible. Obviously, if you're shopping for a birthday or something urgent, we could work something out."

*Oh, she's good at this*, part of Joe's mind registered. *She's a salesperson—she can close a deal.* He had come in here with nothing more than prurient curiosity about the gallery's owner and now he was going to walk out with a commitment to buy a painting that looked like the work of an eight-year-old.

"Yeah, sure. I'll take this one."

"Great, how would you like to pay?"

Shit, how would he pay. A credit card, even a check, would expose his name, which would be awkward at this point. He longed to reach out to Amber Glass, offer her the kind of redemption he had enjoyed, but how could he do that now? Was her redemption even up to him? He opened his wallet. "Could I give you $200 in cash and pay the balance when I pick it up? It's a Christmas gift, and my wife will see the charge or the check. We do everything jointly."

"How nice," Amber said, although something in her voice suggested that she found it more amusing than nice. "A deposit is fine. It's actually a plus for me to open the show with one work already sold. People at the opening will be convinced there's high demand. Of course, most of them will want *this* painting because it's no longer available. People are funny that way. They see that red sticker, denoting sold, and suddenly, it's the only painting they desire."

"Yeah," Joe agreed. In his mind, he was already saying goodbye to the $200. He wasn't coming back. Two hundred dollars was a small price to pay for satisfying his curiosity. This was Amber Glass, but it was a coincidence that she was here, the kind of coincidence Baltimore threw at people every day. It made sense for her to open a gallery in this neighborhood; she had lived here, too, although on Regester, which was Stoneleigh, but not really *Stoneleigh*. She had worked in the 31 Flavors that was now a florist. He wouldn't have thought she harbored any nostalgia for the old neighborhood, given her past, but who can predict what people will yearn for?

The main thing was—she seemed okay. She looked good, she had a business, she probably had a life, a boyfriend or at least friends, a pet. He watched her affix a small red circle to the painting and smiled.

"It's yours to take home after December fifteenth," she said.

"I hope you'll be able to smuggle it into the house without being caught."

Again there was a sense of mirth percolating beneath her words, as if she found him comical. Did she think he was whipped for sharing accounts with his wife? He and Meredith had gone to premarital counseling and learned it was a good thing for a couple to pool their money. They both had discretion up to a certain amount, but they talked over big purchases. Except the house, Joe remembered. That had been one of the biggest fights in their marriage, the only big fight in their marriage, his decision to put in an offer on the house without consulting Meredith first. But it was an auction, there wasn't time, and it was such a steal. She had grown to love it, so all's well, etc. etc.

"Right, December fifteenth," he echoed. He felt a little guilty, but she was going to come out $200 ahead on the deal, assuming she could sell the painting after he failed to pick it up. She wrote $200/*Bal Forward* $250 on a carbon-backed receipt—charmingly old-fashioned, but awfully impractical. And she didn't even ask for his name. Not that he wanted to give it, but still.

"It seems so far away, but it's really only four weeks. The holidays are rushing toward us."

Joe felt a weird déjà vu. Had Amber said something to him like that, all those years ago? Something about the future rushing toward them?

"Anyway, see you then."

"Feel free to come back sooner if you like, or even to tomorrow night's opening. Maybe your wife will fall in love with the painting and then be doubly gratified when she receives it as a gift."

"Maybe," he said, moving swiftly toward the door. Meredith had outstanding taste—she would never go for this crap, and would never have any desire to visit this gallery. She probably didn't even remember Amber's name. What had happened to Amber Glass? The Amber he had known wanted to go to Paris, study the greats, and here she was in Baltimore selling paint-by-numbers art by nonentities. Oh, well, he had had grand plans for himself as well, and those had been sidelined for a while. Now he was striking out on his own, ready to build his own empire. Everyone went at their own pace.

The door had almost swung closed behind him when she called out after him: "Anyway, it was good to see you again, Joe."

THAT WASN'T HOW *I expected it would go*, Amber thought as she locked up for the night.

*It was better.*

Of course she had recognized him. She had studied his recent photos on Facebook and his wife's Instagram account. But she would have recognized him even if she had never seen his adult likeness. He was still the boy she had known.

*The boy she had known.* That was their real secret. Not the sex, delicious as that had been, but the things they had confided in each other. They had told each other their dreams, things they had never told anyone else, which was far more terrifying and intimate than sharing their bodies.

Once in her car, she impulsively chose to drive the streets that she had walked as a teen, always hoping to bump into Joe. In the summers, in particular, she had devised the most roundabout route possible so she could pass the swim club on her way to her shift at Baskin-Robbins. His family had a membership. Hers, of course, did not. Impossible to tell from the street if he was there, but sometimes she thought she recognized his laugh, sweeter than the other boys'.

She never ran into Joe on those rambling walks—not that it mattered. Stoneleigh seemed magical to her. She often walked home through its winding streets after dark, marveling at the lives glimpsed through the windows, the fireflies that seemed more abundant here, the delighted laughter of younger children. She could never work out where the teenagers were, but she supposed they all had cars and used them to flee the streets she found so delightful. Chumleigh, Avondale, Pemberton. Bristol, Oxford, and Sheffield. Tred Avon, which sounded the most British of all to young Amber, but turned out to be named for a river on Maryland's Eastern Shore. Then again, many of the place names in Maryland were from England, so who knew?

Amber was no Anglophile. She cared only for France. She took honors French and was the rare ninth grader to be admitted to La Société Honoraire de Français. France was her future; she believed herself a French foundling, dropped on Rona's doorstep like a baby in a fairy tale.

She was shrewd enough not to attempt to look French, something that couldn't be done when a girl did most of her shopping at Caldor. Besides, she hated to think what her classmates would say if she had put on even a perfectly knotted scarf, much less a beret. But Amber had a plan. She was going to attend UMBC, taking out loans if necessary. (It would have been necessary: Her mother had made clear that Rod wasn't to contribute a penny toward Amber's college, not even a loan.) She was going to go abroad her junior year—and she was never coming back. She belonged in France.

Ah well, Amber always had a lot of plans back then, and not a single one had panned out. Wait—one had. She had wormed her way into Joe Simpson's life and persuaded him to take her to prom. Of course, it's not like she could have willed him to start flunking French in his senior year of high school. But he did, and there she was, the star French student who had signed up for the school's peer tutoring program because she thought it would look good on her college applications—not that she was too worried about getting into UMBC, but it might be an advantage for certain scholarships.

So in the fall of 1996, Amber walked to Joe Simpson's house on Chumleigh, where they would sit at the highly polished dining room table and conjugate and translate, trying to save his tanking GPA.

He was miserable, clearly. Suspended from the lacrosse team, failing and flailing. But he didn't care about the team or his grades. He cared only that his high school girlfriend had dumped him the night before the first day of school. He talked about it endlessly, which fascinated Amber. She hadn't known that boys did that, spoke about heartbreak. She realized it wasn't really flattering, that it meant Joe did not take her seriously—not as a romantic prospect, or as a girl, or even a person. Did he think she had no friends to whom she might spill his secrets? She didn't, but he couldn't *know* that, and it was her choice to avoid close friendships. Amber survived high school by pretending she was an alien who needed to pass unnoticed in this human world until she was called back to the mothership. France was the mothership. She belonged in France.

She helped pull Joe's grade up to a C, then a B. "Still might not be good enough to go to Michigan, but I was only applying to Michigan because my mom went there and it's Kaitlyn's first choice. I might switch up, go opposite."

"What's the opposite of Michigan?" Amber had asked, fascinated by the array of Joe's options.

"There's this school in St. Petersburg, Eckerd, that has a good marine biology program. Maybe that's where I'll go. Who wants to be in Michigan in the winter when you can be in Florida?" Amber had never heard of Eckerd and was confused why a college was named after a drugstore, but she looked into it and learned it had a strong language program, with ample opportunities to study abroad.

The days got shorter, fast; it was dark by the time she finished working with Joe. They always ended with ten minutes of conversation, or sometimes Amber would simply point to items in the house and Joe would (or would not) reel off the names.

One day in early November, when the dusk brought a chill and the air seemed full of woodsmoke, although no one burned leaves in Stoneleigh, not anymore, Joe said in perfect French: *Would you like to go to my room?* And Amber had answered automatically, *Of course, I would like to see your room.*

*I'm serious*, Joe said in English.

*Oh*, Amber said. Then: *Moi aussi*.

His room was surprisingly tidy, neater than hers, if she was honest. It looked polished and yet sterile. The nightstand and the bed were clearly a set. There were framed reproductions of vintage travel posters. Egypt, Greece, Morocco.

"Voulez-vous voyager à ces endroits?" she asked.

"My mom decorated it," he said.

"En français," she said teasingly, getting close enough to wag a finger in his face and then blushing at the lameness of her gesture.

"Oh, I'll do it in French," he said and before she knew it, he was kissing her. She was amazed at how swiftly things progressed from there, but not unhappy. She had no recollection of how they ended up on his bed, or how her clothing seemed to fall away, then his. She was enjoying it, she was ecstatic. It was simply too fast. She pulled back and tried to convey this to Joe—she wanted him, she wanted this, but maybe not so fast?

"Please don't be a tease, Amber. Kaitlyn was a tease."

"You mean you never—"

"No." Then quickly. "I mean, never with Kaitlyn. Of course I've—"

"Of course."

But she was sure that he was a virgin, like her. Neither one of them spoke of birth control; Amber felt it would dull the romance of the moment. And she did want it, god she wanted it, wanted him, just—not so fast.

"We better get back to the dining room," Joe said when they were done not even five minutes later. "My mother will be home from work soon."

She followed him down the stairs, dazed and happy and terrified. Was she—? Were they—? At school the next day, he smiled and nodded at her in the hall, as he always did, always had. Joe was nice to everyone.

But when she showed up at his next tutoring session he said, in English, "Maybe we could start in my room and then study?" She was all for it, especially when Joe showed her that he had procured condoms. They were very careful, all that fall and into January.

Then Joe aced his French midterm and submitted his college applications and there was no reason for Amber to go to his house. She walked the sidewalks of Stoneleigh, through the winter and into the spring, and one day she actually did run into Joe and they ended up back in his room and when they were done, she said: "I want you to take me to prom, Joe. Just as a friend. Lots of people do it."

"O-kay," he said, drawing the syllables out. "My mom's been on my back to go. Hey, I got into Michigan."

"I thought you wanted the opposite of Michigan?"

"Oh, I was just being reactionary. It's a big school. I'll probably never see Kaitlyn there."

He had no comment on her body, how it had changed since they had last been together. Maybe it hadn't changed. Maybe it was all in her head, the bloated belly, the tender breasts, the morning queasiness. She went home and told her mom she had been invited to the prom and she would need something to wear and her mother said, "Well, don't think I'm going to pay for a dress you'll wear only once." Amber said she would use some of the money she was saving toward college.

She never did see that dress again. Did it live on, in some police evidence locker? Did they throw it away?

Stoneleigh still seemed charming to Amber and it still smelled of woodsmoke, but maybe that fragrance was just what decaying leaves threw off when they fell. She cruised past Joe's house, as she always thought of it. His mother, now widowed, still lived there. Amber had found her on Facebook. She had not tried to friend Caryn Simpson. She knew Joe's mother would not want her as her friend.

Amber also knew how she was supposed to tell her story. She was a victim, used by a careless boy who wanted only sex, then left to deal with the consequences on her own, her life destroyed, his barely disrupted. There was a world of difference between Prom Mom and Cad Dad. Joe enjoyed not only forgiveness, but something better still—forgetfulness. He had been afforded the chance to move through the world unmarked. Amber could never assume that would be true of her; she was always at risk for exposure.

Yet when she saw a light on in the window of the room that was once Joe's, all she felt was a rush of desire, the memory of their bodies colliding.

She didn't care what anyone said: Joe Simpson was the best thing that had ever happened to her, and that fall had been the best time of her life so far.

*Christmas Eve, 2019*

MEREDITH MADE IT to the gym a few minutes before one, an hour before its early closing, grateful that she needed only forty-five minutes for cardio. She didn't have to work today—there was no reason for a plastic surgery practice to be open on December 24 and she'd be plenty busy after the New Year—but she had spent a terrible morning at the mall, trying to figure out a gift for Joe. What an unfamiliar humiliation, being part of the last-minute shoppers, fighting for parking and then trotting through the "luxury" wing of Towson Town Center, a salmon moving upstream no matter which direction she headed.

Louis Vuitton, the Apple Store, Tiffany, Burberry—Meredith didn't have a clue what to give Joe this year, an unusual problem for her. She could buy him a good suitcase at Tumi, with a card inside promising a trip. But, no, that was too similar to last year's present.

Meredith took gift-giving seriously, almost competitively, especially when it came to Joe. This would be their twenty-second Christmas together. Last year, she had surprised him with a December 26 trip to Anguilla. With his assistant Bobbie as her collaborator, she had cleared both of their schedules, rented a villa, packed his bag. Then she wrapped a Tommy Bahama shirt and placed it under their tree. He tried to be a good sport when he opened the box, but she could see how deflated he was. A shirt, and not even an expensive one at that. Joe had become increasingly fussy about his clothes—bespoke suits from Christopher Schafer, Mack Weldon underwear, shirts from Ledbury in Richmond, going so far as to drive three hours for fittings. Dan Brothers shoes because he had heard that the pro athletes who visited Baltimore favored the Federal Hill store. If he was going to wear a "tropical" shirt, it would probably be a Paul Smith.

"You always forget to read the card first," Meredith teased him. The card not only detailed their itinerary but included coupons—daily sex, Joe's right to stipulate all activities and dining choices. She had promised herself not to worry about the sun, unkind as it was to her fair skin, and not to check the news on her phone. The latter probably meant more to Joe than the daily sex. He liked to be, if not Meredith's *sole* focus, at the center of her life, and he usually had been. He basked in her attention, which she had to admit was in short supply these days. Lately, he had floated the idea that she could stop working, or at least cut back on her hours, if he started earning the "big money."

*How does one top a gift like Anguilla?* she thought, mounting an elliptical and beginning the interval program she had designed for herself—thirty seconds at top speed, thirty seconds of recovery, on and off for forty-five minutes, her machine's television screen tuned to MSNBC. The news was terrible. Meredith could no longer remember a time when the news had not been terrible. She wondered if some of her former patients were among those detained along the border. The children whose mouths and faces she had operated on—some would be old enough to try to make the journey north on their own now. And if the younger ones had ended up accompanying older siblings or parents—

She was moving too fast, neglecting the recovery intervals, which were as important as the thirty seconds of acceleration. *Slow down*, she told herself. *Focus.* Maybe if she lost herself to an endorphin high, her subconscious mind would present her with a gift for Joe. Another trip? She would love to go to Mardi Gras; they hadn't done that since 2015. But it was too late to book one of the good hotels, which meant staying with her parents. And no one wants to stay with one's in-laws on a romantic getaway, not even if they have a big house in New Orleans with a little guest cottage in the backyard.

"Guest cottage," Joe had said the first time he visited. "You mean former slave quarters, right?"

"This house was built in the late 1890s, Joe. No slaves were kept on this property. And you know my parents didn't arrive in New Orleans until the late 1960s."

Meredith was not disingenuous about race in general or New Orleans's problematic history in particular. She knew that her parents' house, in its early life, had availed itself of the labor of people of color, and that those workers had not been paid a fair wage for their services, much less treated well. That inequity lived in the bones of the house, in its soil, but then—it lived in the soil of the United States. She knew the story of how New Orleans schools were desegregated only a few years before her parents enrolled at Tulane. She understood how whiteness had benefitted her during every step of her mostly charmed life.

But she also saw how it benefitted Joe and others from the so-called North. Meredith was the one who told Joe that the Emancipation Proclamation had not freed Maryland's slaves, because the state fought alongside the Union, prompting violent protests and riots. She had reminded Joe that the "tyrant" in the state song, the one whose heel was on the shore, was none other than Abraham Lincoln. Racism came in so many varieties. Meredith preferred the brand she had known in her native New Orleans, where the people with bigoted views admitted to them, practically brayed them, while moving through a largely integrated world. Whereas people like Joe and his family, whose milieu was overwhelmingly white, spoke in a code that they honestly didn't recognize as racist, starting always from the premise that they "didn't see color" or "didn't have a bigoted bone in their body," but—

*That man was lazy, he just was.*

*It was so advantageous to be non-white these days.*

*All I'm asking for is a meritocracy.*

No, as much as she loved Mardi Gras, she could not pretend that Joe would consider it a suitable gift.

She ran through tomorrow's schedule in her head. Joe's mother had an annual open house—chafing dishes, the football game on in the background, neighbors and family coming and going. It was a lovely, durable custom, and Meredith hated every minute of it. Thank god she had a reason to leave early. A few years ago, her friend Joyce had started organizing a caroling party for adults who found themselves admitted to Hopkins unexpectedly over the holidays. Joe had accompanied them once, but it clearly made him anxious. Joe was nervous around sick people. Poor people, too—basically anyone who had known misfortune. He was not unkind, nor lacking in compassion. Joe simply did not like to contemplate the royal flush of luck he had been granted in his life, with that one huge exception, the averted disaster that made him appreciate his life all the more.

The news went to break. There was a commercial for a treadmill, which reminded Meredith of the furor earlier that month after the ads for an in-home cycling program were deemed sexist and strange, almost as if the "wife" had been forced by her "husband" into servitude to the bike. People became so agitated about the commercial that they almost seemed to forget that the people were actors, the story fabricated.

And yet no one seemed to mind last year's ad for the same bike, a spin—ha, Meredith congratulated herself on her own unconscious pun—on "The Gift of the Magi," in which the husband bought his wife a Peloton bike, hid it in their picture-perfect garage, and then began to use it secretly every day. The joke was on him, because the wife had found it, too, and used it while he slept, then slid back into the marital bed, presumably still somewhat sweaty and smelly, unless their perfect little freestanding bonus building had a shower as well. And by the way, wouldn't their spouse's workouts have shown up when they signed on? That couple, carrying on with their twin deceit, irritated Meredith far more than the Peloton POW bride.

*A Peloton!* She was so excited by her brainstorm that her foot slipped and she almost fell from the elliptical. A Peloton would be perfect for Joe, who had been complaining that the short days of winter made it difficult for him to get in the long runs he liked.

Obviously, she couldn't get one delivered in time for Christmas, but she could order one today and then find a toy bicycle or a bicycle Christmas tree ornament to put in a ridiculous oversized box.

A toy bike was harder to procure than Meredith had anticipated, but she found a bicycle bell in the odd little hardware store near where Joe grew up. Rushing back to her car, she noticed the gallery had vintage robots in the window, including a duck riding a bicycle. Oh, that would be better still. But the place was dark, the door locked.

The next morning, Joe opened a box that had once held a crockpot and dug through mounds of tissue paper. "A bike?" he asked, looking at the bell. "I have a bike."

"You never read the card," she said, handing him the envelope that he had ripped from the top of the box before undoing the ribbons and tearing the paper.

"Cool," he said. "Is it really a full-body workout?"

"It comes with hand weights, so I guess they at least do some upper body work. But you already have a full rack of weights in the basement. The thing is, now you can do your cardio at home, no matter the time of day or weather."

Joe then handed her a present about the size of a shoebox. It *was* a shoebox, and the shoes inside were very much what Joe liked—red, high-heeled, peep-toed. Slutty, to use a word that Meredith knew she should not use, and yet—just looking at the shoes made her feet hurt. Meredith could not wear high heels. She tried, every now and then, for Joe's sake, but her feet were flat and she couldn't handle anything more than a modest stacked or kitten heel. These were bedroom-only shoes. Which was . . . fine. They were Fendis, after all.

"What do you think?" Joe asked with a grin.

"Very pretty," she said, determined to mask her disappointment. Not everyone could be like Meredith, a champion gift-giver. Obviously, she could not say what she was thinking, which was that she had given him a $2,000 bike and he had given her $1,000 shoes that would cause her genuine pain if she tried to walk in them.

"*You* never unwrap things all the way," he said. "Check the toes."

"There's tissue paper in them," she said.

"And?"

The tissue paper in the left shoe was empty, but in the right, she found two diamond studs, exactly her style, and far more costly than any piece of workout equipment by many, many multipliers.

"Joe, you shouldn't—"

"I had a great year," he said.

AMBER SWIPED THROUGH the weather app on her phone. She kept tabs on four cities—Baltimore, New Orleans, St. Pete, the three places where she had actually lived, and Paris. New Orleans was going to have the same high temperature as Baltimore today, about 55 degrees. But a Baltimore 55 in December was different from a New Orleans one, where the houses were built to let warm air escape. Amber would rather face a subfreezing Baltimore than a 50-something day in New Orleans.

On such a day in New Orleans, Amber would have spent much of the day in bed, under layers of kantha quilts. Miss Margaret had been early to import the colorful cotton bedspreads, but once they started showing up on websites and Etsy and even the store at Belladonna Day Spa, she let Amber choose what she wanted, at cost, from her inventory. She had ended up with a half dozen, which she draped over her bed, her sofa, her armchair. Amber had put most of them in storage when she moved to Baltimore, intent on traveling light, but she had allowed herself one quilt, and while it didn't provide much in the way of warmth, its riotous pattern of orange poppies and red stripes provided an eccentric bright spot in her duplex, where everything was dark wood and white plaster walls. Amber was used to living in a world of color and craziness. In her shotgun rental house back in New Orleans, she had painted the front room coral, her bedroom navy blue, and the kitchen butter yellow. She had filled the open shelves with brightly colored crockery and Russel Wright plates.

Almost all of those things were in storage now. *Hedging your bets*, Miss Margaret had said. *You know you're coming back.* Amber wasn't so sure, but she had been careful not to bring things with her that might cause homesickness. She had, in a sense, put the New Orleans version of Amber in storage, too, but she wasn't sure she had found the Baltimore version of herself just yet. And if she did find that identity, would it be connected to the girl whose life had been so abruptly bisected, or would it be something new entirely? Could she reclaim herself without claiming all she had done?

She looked around the gallery, where she had recently mounted an exhibit of found-object robot art. The American Visionary Art Museum had sponsored a DIY craft class for kids last weekend, and Amber had piggybacked on that event, a successful cross-promotion. Etsy was awash with such robots, but most of them were too *cute* for Amber's taste. She preferred her robots on the melancholy side, a little banged up, and she had curated this show carefully. (So annoying, the way the word *curated* was thrown around now, when her job involved actual curating. What did it

mean to collect/select in a world where *everyone* claimed to cu-
rate?)

Inevitably, given the season, casual customers had wandered
in, people who assumed the robots were toys and professed disappointment when they learned these were more like sculptures
that did not walk or talk or light up. But Amber had anticipated
that kind of shopper and stocked, for this month only, knockoffs
of vintage robots. She marked them up ruthlessly, but that was
the thing about a gallery. The kind of person who visited a gallery
didn't blink at paying $25 for something that cost $12 elsewhere.
In fact, Amber's prices convinced her shoppers that the toys
were vintage. She told the truth when asked—"No, they're new,
made in China"—and yet, they didn't seem to believe her, or the
labeling on the box. Or they just didn't care.

Miss Margaret had often said, quoting a beloved movie, "A
person is smart. People are dumb." But she always added, "Actually, a person is pretty stupid, too. People see what they want to
see. Always."

Amber's gallery still wasn't breaking even, of course, but that
was not the plan, and she had all of Rod's money now, so no worries. What was the plan, exactly? Amber wasn't sure, but she had
decided that represented progress for her. She had been such a
planner once upon a time. *I will take these AP courses, I will do
these extracurricular activities, I will go to a school with a strong art
history department—and all of those plans were for naught.* She had
a GED earned in a juvenile facility, a four-year degree in French
from Eckerd College, and here she was, no plan at all.

The door buzzed. The gallery wasn't normally open on Tues-
days, but Amber had decided she might pick up some last-minute
shoppers in the morning hours. Her toy robots made excellent

stocking stuffers, and people became desperate in the final hours of Christmas Eve.

She released the door and there was Joe, literally hat in hand, shoulders broad and impressive in a camel hair coat. She wasn't surprised. The only surprise was that he had waited so long. Oh, she understood, when he thrust that $200 at her back in September and avoided giving her his name, that he had *thought* he would never return.

She knew differently.

"I'm sorry I didn't come sooner. To pick up the painting."

"That's okay, I wouldn't have started charging you for storage until next month."

He looked startled, almost hurt by her joke. Amber had forgotten how little experience Joe had in being teased, how his good looks and utter normalcy hadn't prepared him for much beyond praise and respect. She had envied him for that, once. Now it explained so much.

"Anyway, it's in the back. I'll bring it out."

When she returned with the painting, he was standing in front of a "robot" by Kansas artist Anthony Pack, someone whose work Amber had discovered during her days in a St. Petersburg boutique. Pack didn't call his creations robots, but this one, a girl fashioned from a coffeepot, worked for Amber's show. Was it a girl? Amber had assumed so because of the eyelashes and the red mouth fashioned from a metal ring. Miss Margaret was forever reminding Amber that she was too quick to make assumptions based on surfaces, the appearance of things. "Also, you are woefully heteronormative."

"Do you like her?" she asked. *Her*—there she went again.

"It's interesting," Joe said, polite as ever. He had always been polite, kind even. That was why she had been drawn to him, long before they had ever spoken

He looked at the painting in her hands. "Oh, I thought—I don't know why—I thought it would be wrapped? Not like a gift, but maybe in brown paper and string, like you would use for shipping?"

"I don't have brown paper and string. When I ship things, it requires quite a bit more packaging than that."

"If I ducked into the hardware store and got some paper and string, could you help me?"

*Help him.* That was familiar. That was the basis of everything between them. He had needed help and she could provide it. *The irregular verbs are killing me. So are the regular ones, truth be told.* Yes, she had always been ready to help Joe.

"Sure," Amber said.

He was back within ten minutes. "They actually had Christmas paper and real ribbon. I had forgotten how cool that place was."

But the sheets of paper weren't broad enough to cover the painting. Amber had to tape two pieces together and then wrap the painting loosely, so the corners wouldn't poke out. It didn't look great, but it was the best she could do with the materials provided. *Doing the best she could with the materials provided*—Amber's life in a nutshell.

"Now all you have to do is sneak it in the house." Again, that startled, jumpy look. "I mean, I hope you weren't planning to leave it in the car, even if it's overnight. Art needs a climate-controlled environment."

"No, no—it shouldn't be a problem."

"Great."

"How are you enjoying being back in Baltimore?"

"It's fine. Good to be close to family." She had no family here.

"Is that why you came back?"

"No, not really."

"So you decided to come back because—?"

She kept her gaze level, her voice casual. "Unfinished business, I guess you'd call it. Or maybe I just needed to know if . . ." Her voice trailed off.

"What did you need to know?"

"If I could be allowed just to be, after all these years. Be me, me as I am now. Not who I used to be. Not the me people remember. Or think they remember."

"I get it, believe me."

"If you didn't understand," Amber said, "then who would?"

He tucked the painting under his arm and turned to go.

"Joe?"

"Yes?" God, he seemed so jittery. Why?

"You owe a balance of $250. Plus tax."

He paid her in cash and left. She noticed he drove a Range Rover, hulking and dark green, with a vanity plate that read LANTERN. It took her a second—*Green Lantern*, who, Joe had lectured her in his boyhood bedroom, was the noblest of the superheroes. *You can have Superman, Batman, whoever. The Green Lantern is the best superhero.*

Joe the superhero in his own movie. Joe the adventurer, who was going to see the world. When Amber told him of her dreams of Paris, he had said he wanted to see Africa, China, South America, all the places on the posters in his room, posters he hadn't even chosen. He mentioned the Peace Corps as a possibility. Beyond college, had he even left the state? That Range Rover had probably never tackled anything more daunting than his sloped driveway in Ruxton. (She had found photos of the house on a real estate agent's website, posted when the house had gone to auction in 2009.)

He had come by to pick up his wife's Christmas gift. Nothing personal. Yet Amber felt strangely giddy as she locked up at noon. She stopped at Eddie's on her way home and bought a chicken to roast, along with the ingredients for homemade eggnog. She would have a proper feast on Christmas Day, and she would have champagne, real champagne, from France, on New Year's. She felt as if life was finally beginning, and it wasn't because the calendar was flipping to a new year.

*Joe had come to see her.*

JOE SLID THE painting into his rear seat, hoping that Amber's wrapping job would hold together for the long ride out to Freeland Acres. The builder tried to be coy about the development's location, describing it as "the Hunt Valley area," but the bottom line was that it was only a few miles shy of the Maryland-Pennsylvania state line and the commute to the city was a bitch. Practical for those who worked in the northern suburbs, however, and you got a lot of house for $750,000.

Then again, once you were home, you had to drive ten miles to buy a carton of milk.

Anyway, residential real estate bored Joe. To his way of thinking, anyone could sell a house, because most people, at least those over thirty, assumed it was a rite of adult life, like marriage or kids. It was something you did. Take any halfway decent house, paint everything white, stage it with neutral furniture, and someone would buy it. Commercial real estate took vision and a high tolerance for risk. A commercial Realtor had to be able to see the potential in raw land. Eventually, if Freeland Acres did boom, there would be an opportunity for some small shopping centers, dine-in chain restaurants. But it wasn't there yet.

He remembered the first time he had visited the model, only eight months ago. The drive seemed longer now. In fact, he was actively dreading it. Holiday traffic was already building on I-83 in both directions. He wanted to get home and start a fire, enjoy Christmas Eve with Meredith. Christmas Eve was their time, while Christmas Day belonged to his family.

He really hadn't planned to go back for the painting. But then he realized he shouldn't show up here empty-handed. Two birds, one stone. By paying for the painting at Amber's gallery, he had ended the need to ever see *her* again. And now he had a gift for this meeting, a gift that would feel personal, but not too personal.

There was only one car in the driveway, of course. Who looks at a new home model on Christmas Eve? He pulled in alongside the silver BMW and walked in through the unlocked front door.

"Hello?" he called. The house was staged, but it was still a little on the empty side and his voice echoed.

"Back in the kitchen," Jordan called out.

It felt like a trek, the journey from the foyer to the kitchen, but then—if you were the owner, you'd come in through the garage, which led into a mudroom, with the kitchen just beyond it. His heart sank when he saw the spread on the marble-topped island— cheese, crackers, holiday cookies. Everything still in the plastic Wegmans wrappers. Jordan was good at many things, but cooking was not one of them.

A bottle of prosecco was open and resting in an ice bucket.

"Merry Christmas," he said, thrusting the barely wrapped

painting at her. Her surprise was evident and, although he sensed she didn't really dig it—who could blame her?—she was clearly touched that he had given her something unique. "I love it," she swore, and there was no avoiding it then. He had to kiss her.

*I have to kiss you.* He had said those words to her last spring. Funny, how similar the two sentiments were, how much his feelings had changed in the interim. He had met Jordan at an industry party, and she began pitching him hard on Freeland Acres. Of course, he had no interest in buying a new house, especially not all the way out here, but he admired the hustle, saw immediately that she was good at her job. Out of professional courtesy, truly nothing more, he agreed to meet her here one April afternoon, at sunset.

"The view is spectacular," she said, showing him how the house was situated so that the setting sun was captured in the family room and kitchen windows. Those rooms were enormous, while the formal living room and dining room were relatively small. Everything was about the hang now.

He agreed the view was spectacular, but he was looking at her figure. She had a high, tight rump—a word Joe preferred, slangy but not crude—and gorgeous calves, which she displayed to full advantage in a knit skirt and spiky high heels, the kind Meredith would never wear. To be fair, she *couldn't*, they killed her feet, but you couldn't blame a man for liking the look of a woman's legs in shoes like that.

"Do you want to see upstairs?" Jordan had asked. He did. That was why he had come here, right? To see the house. He followed her up, eyes level with that sweet curve.

They first inspected the three "smaller" bedrooms, across the front of the house. She then led him to the master, which took up the entire rear half of the house and would have enjoyed those same sunset views if they had climbed the stairs just five minutes earlier.

"So this is the master," he said. "I guess it's okay."

"Please," Jordan said laughing. "We say owner's bedroom now, or primary. In this case, owner's *suite*."

"Well, aren't you politically correct?"

"Gosh, the terms changed years ago, when I was just getting into the business. When you think about it, you can see why it would be offensive. Although"—she smiled flirtatiously—"I like the idea of someone being the master in the bedroom."

"You strike me as a woman who doesn't have a problem in that department."

"Oh, I don't."

"I mean—" Jesus, what did he mean? "I assume you don't lack for company."

"I don't, but I'm very picky."

"You should be. Hold out for what you want."

"I do." Holding his gaze, challenging him.

"I have to kiss you," he said. "I'm sorry—that was totally inappropriate, forget I said anything, you're just so beautiful. I can't help myself."

Then she kissed him, and what could he do but kiss her back? They ended up with Jordan propped on the sink in the master bath. Sorry, *owner's*. It seemed slightly less of a betrayal somehow, not using the bed. He had assumed it would be a one-off because that's all he had ever done before, one-offs, and not terribly often. He never *wanted* to cheat on Meredith, but when he did, it felt restorative to him, and he kept it safely contained—out of town, at a conference. Made him better with Meredith, in his opinion, replenished something vital. He and Meredith had married young; Joe had missed out on a lot.

But Jordan, who had seemed so knowing and sophisticated, had proven sticky. She assumed they would keep seeing each other, and when he tried to be evasive, she began making noises about what she might do, whom she might tell. Not Meredith; Jordan wasn't some bunny boiler. She just wanted to confide in her friends, maybe her parents. Joe, used to absolute discretion, decided it was easier to meet up every three to six weeks or so and let Jordan's passion dissipate on its own. A controlled burn, as it were.

Then, last month, he had gone to Las Vegas for a conference, and she had shown up to "surprise" him, materializing in the hotel bar as if she were David fucking Copperfield. *Oh, what a coincidence.* He resolved then that he would have to break up with her. He had planned to do it today, in fact. But he couldn't, not on Christmas Eve. The present, those stupid badly painted flowers—look how happy it had made her. He didn't love her, not even close. He wasn't even sure he *liked* her that much. But she was sweet, she meant no harm, and it turned out that when they were alone upstairs in the model home, it was absolutely the master's suite. There was nothing she wouldn't do for Joe, absolutely nothing. He probably could invite another woman into the mix, but that idea was more terrifying than titillating because, as they say, three can keep a secret only if two are dead.

They showered together in the owner's bathroom. He was almost out the door when she called after him—"You didn't let me give you your present."

"Oh, you did fine by me, baby."

"No, seriously." She pulled a small box from the otherwise

empty drawer of the nightstand. A watch, a nice one, Baume & Mercier. "You shouldn't have," he said, and he meant it. How could he wear a watch like this, how would he explain it to Meredith, who had given him the Bulova that he always wore.

"I noticed how old your other watch is."

"Well, yes, it's vintage." It had, in fact, belonged to Meredith's maternal grandfather, who had been the hardest person in Meredith's family to win over. The old man had died without ever warming up to his son-in-law, yet he liked Joe.

"I know you can't wear it—yet." She turned it over; the watch was engraved. *Our time will come.* A line from a movie echoed in his head, something about a stage-one—or was it a stage-five—clinger. This was bad. He had never told Jordan he loved her, never suggested he would leave Meredith. He had thought he was involved with a libertine, someone who understood the implicit contract of their arrangement. How had he gotten in so over his head?

"Well, see you in 2020," he said.

"To 2020," she said, drawing him in for one more lingering kiss.

He put the watch in his glove compartment. Maybe someone would break into his car and steal it. His old friend karma, sneaking up on him. Joe wanted to be good, he did, but he just kept racking up debts. He'd straighten everything out in the New Year, he promised himself. Flip the shopping center, flip the script.

*May 1997*

# THE CORSAGE

**CARYN SELDOM HAD** any regrets about being the mother of three boys, but she felt a pang of wistfulness when Joe's prom approached. She knew she should be glad he was going at all—what a terrible year it had been for him. She understood that little Amber Glass was not exactly his dream date. Which, for Caryn, was a plus. Joe's intense relationship with Kaitlyn had scared Caryn. The depression after the breakup—the spiraling grades, the long, lost fall where he retreated to his room—had been even worse. But Joe had rallied. He had pulled up his failing grades. He had been accepted by University of Michigan, her alma mater. He was going to be fine.

Still, he was her *baby*. Was it wrong to wish she had a front-row seat to the key rituals that the girls' parents took as their due? All she was going to get was a view of Joe in his tux, a boxed-up wrist corsage in his hand. She had suggested that maybe she could follow him to his date's house—

"Jesus, Mom, no. The limo will pick me up at home, then we'll go to her house, then we'll pick up Zach and Susannah. Don't you dare follow us."

"Over on Regester, right?"

"How do you know where Amber lives?"

She had thought quickly: "I had to sign paperwork affirming her participation in the peer tutoring program and mail it to her. She doesn't get credit if she doesn't have that document."

Joe let it drop. And he let his mother pick out the wrist corsage, although he had scant information about the dress itself. White, he thought. Long. No, he didn't know what the neckline was like. If he had still been with Kaitlyn, he probably would have been given explicit instructions on what kind of flower, what color, wrist or pinned. Kaitlyn had been an extremely bossy girl, in Caryn's opinion. Thank god for the breakup, despite the havoc it had wreaked. He would go off to school a free man.

Caryn hadn't planned to take a walk past Amber's home after learning the girl was to be Joe's date. She had long had the habit of weekend walks, and she felt like she was acting on impulse when she said to herself, "I think little Amber lives on Regester."

Caryn didn't have a street number, only a vague sense that Amber lived west of Sherwood, but east of Petworth. Not that there was anything wrong with that. It just wasn't Stoneleigh, not really, but the small houses and yards were well-kept. Besides, it wasn't fair to compare other neighborhoods to Stoneleigh. How she and Dale had extended themselves to buy the house on Chumleigh, back when he was still saddled with law school debt, and they had two boys in diapers. But it had been worth the lean years, and by the time Joe came along, five years later, the family was long past worrying about money.

She recognized Amber's car, not by model or make, but by its color, a distinctive bright green. "Oh, I see the Green Hornet is here, Kato," Joe had joked last fall when Amber's stepfather picked her up after dark, although it was a short, safe walk. Some parents were so overprotective.

The house, well, *irked* Caryn, although it was almost identical to the other houses along this block, except for the tacky geese and lawn ornaments. Why did she care? This was not Joe's girl- friend, after all. He was going to prom because Caryn had told him it was better to go and have a blah evening than to wonder the rest of his life if he had missed something special. "That's for girls, Mom," he had said. "You're talking about yourself, how *you* feel because you didn't go to your prom." He wasn't wrong. Joe was perceptive, even as a small child, highly attuned to the feel- ings of others. That's why he was her favorite, although she never said as much, of course. Her youngest, her baby, her brightest, handsomest boy.

Three days after that conversation, he came home and said, "I'm going to take Amber Glass to the prom." Caryn had needed a second to remember that was the name of the girl who had tu- tored him in French last fall. Caryn had assumed Joe would find another solo senior, a friend also at risk of sitting out the dance. But so be it. The important thing was that he would be with Zach, who was like Caryn's fourth son. He would make nice memories and he would be happy, one day, that he had not allowed Kaitlyn to deprive him of this milestone moment.

Caryn had never cared for Kaitlyn, never. *What a beautiful couple*, people had said during the two years she and Joe had gone together. But Caryn had not trusted that girl with her precious boy's heart and she hated being right about that, truly. Kaitlyn should have had the courtesy, at least, to break up with Joe at the beginning of the summer between junior and senior year, which might have given Joe a chance to bounce back before school started. Instead, she came over the night before the first day and announced she was in love with some Towson University boy she had met in Rehoboth and she planned to keep seeing him.

What did it matter, then, if Joe's date for prom lived in *that* house on Regester, the one with the abundance of lawn "art"—a perpetual parade of geese, a half-dozen yard gnomes, a shining green globe on a white pedestal, an odd Baltimore artifact that Caryn had never understood, despite being Baltimore bred and buttered, as the old saying went. Or that the front door had a tiny corrugated arch, an aluminum eyebrow that couldn't possibly offer any significant coverage from the weather.

Yet that house lingered in her memory when she went to pick out the corsage (at Radebaugh's, of course). She had been inclined to select an orchid wristlet, but she feared it would be too fancy. Amber had probably chosen one of those prairie-like dresses. White roses would be safe—too safe. Caryn opted for a white ranunculus, which ended up going beautifully with the surprisingly elegant dress that Amber had chosen.

By the time Caryn saw the dress, in the photos that Amber's mother clearly sold to the tabloids—thank god, she thought then, that there were almost no photos of Joe—all she could see was the unlikely demon who had tried to derail her son's life. Little Amber had been the real threat, not Kaitlyn. The remains of the white ranunculus wrist corsage were found on the floor of the hotel room at the Towson Sheraton, never to be pressed between the pages of a book, because it was a night no one wanted to remember.

*January 20, 2020*

AMBER WOKE UP early, but not early enough—her underwear and sheets were already bloodied by her always unpredictable period. Unlike most women she knew, she never had detectable PMS, only a vague moodiness, so she was forever being caught off guard this way.

She stripped the bed, rinsed everything in the old-fashioned claw-foot bathtub, using the coldest water possible. It had always seemed magical to her how effectively cold water removed blood. She squeezed out the water until it ran clean, inspected her sheets and panties, and, satisfied that they were ready to go into the wash, loaded them into the stacked washer-dryer off the kitchen. The unit was tiny; a set of sheets and a pair of underwear were almost all it could handle. She then put on period pants, which al-

ways felt vaguely diaper-ish to her, but were undeniably effective.
O Brave New World.

*Uterine atony*, the doctor said.

*What?*

*Uterine atony. You lost almost three times as much blood as nor-
mal for a vaginal birth. You were lu—anyway, you're fine. But how
could you not know you were pregnant, Amber? When was your last
period?*

*How could you not know?* She would be asked that question
so many times the summer of 1997. Mostly by men. Men and her
mother. She could see why the men didn't get it, but she thought
her mother should understand how mysterious Amber's body was
to her, primarily because her mother had been determined to
make it that way. It was as if Amber were growing up in a fairy tale
and her mother thought that deeming something dark and forbidden could spare Amber some terrible destiny. Don't go there, don't
touch that, don't ask any questions. Did that ever work? Even in a
fairy tale? Sleeping Beauty touches the spindle, Rapunzel allows
the prince to climb her hair, Eve eats the apple. Okay, the last one
wasn't a fairy tale. Or was it?

It was hard for her, as a teen, to understand how odd Rona
was. Amber didn't have any idea what other people's parents were
like, not having the kind of close friends who might share such
information. Sure, she knew how babies were made, but it was
kind of like understanding how a car works. You put your foot
on the accelerator and it moves forward; you put your foot on the
brake and it stops. Steer into the direction of a skid. But when
actually going into a skid, did anyone have the presence of mind
to steer in that direction?

She had gotten her period relatively late, at age fourteen,

almost fifteen. She hated the lumpy pads, the adhesive wings that somehow got twisted and caught in her pubic hair. She yearned to use tampons, and she asked her mother to help her. Rona Deluca's face had twisted with disgust. "That's something every woman has to learn on her own." Amber had pleaded and Rona had finally agreed to stand on the other side of the closed bathroom door and shout the instructional manual to her. "Toward the small of my back? One foot up? Does it matter which foot? Wait—"

She had broken down in tears and Rona had said in disgust and frustration: "I knew more about my body when I was twelve than you do now."

"How," Amber had asked between her sobs. "How?" Her mother never answered.

Amber had done the math after discovering her mother's marriage certificate in a desk drawer. Rona had been eighteen when she married Amber's bio-dad—and six months pregnant. Amber was born ten weeks after her parents' courthouse ceremony. There was a photograph of this not-so-momentous occasion, notable mainly for the ridiculous shoulder pads in her mother's suit jacket and the happy couple's sour expressions. Her mother's father was already dead, and Rona's mother was as neglectful of Rona as Rona was of Amber, so Amber couldn't imagine who had insisted on the wedding. Her father's parents? They lived far away; she couldn't have even told you in what state.

Her father was considerably older than her mother, twenty-seven at the time, and there had always been some vagueness about how they had met. Amber remembered him only slightly. Tall, tired. Very tall and very tired. He left when she was three, and the wonder of it was that he had the energy to pack his things into the trunk of the car.

A year ago, she had decided to submit a spit sample to 23andMe to see what she might learn about herself, opting in to hear from any DNA matches that popped up. It turned out she had two younger sisters, out in Arizona. They exchanged letters and then the letters stopped abruptly. Amber assumed they had persevered past all the Google searches that yielded Depression-era tableware and found out who she was. She understood. Who would want "Prom Mom" as a sister?

Amber had hoped she might pick up some last-minute shoppers today. The day was bright and cold; she turned on her oven to help heat the drafty kitchen. January 20, 2020, seemed like an auspicious date to her, in terms of numerology, although maybe February 20, 2020, would be better still. She had a vague memory of twos being good. She didn't believe in numerology or astrology, but she didn't *not* believe, either. Anything was possible. Someone, something had to have a plan for this world.

She googled her way to a Refinery29 article on numerology and the current year. It would be a wonderful one, the article's expert promised, a time to achieve objectives. She supposed such articles always promised good, exciting things for the year to come, yet— she believed it.

"I REMEMBER," UNCLE Tony said to Joe via FaceTime, "when Martin Luther King's birthday wasn't a holiday. In fact, the city of Baltimore recognized it before the federal government did. Probably because of the riots. I remember when he was shot, I was on my way home from school—"

Joe had heard this story before, many times. By now, he was pretty sure he had heard all of his uncle Tony's stories. But he didn't mind. He had always been close to his mother's twin brother.

Which made having him as a boss tricky at times. His uncle loved him, but he kept forgetting Joe was a grown man, years removed from the teenager Tony had taken in for a year after high school.

"We're still on for next week, right?" Joe asked, once the story wound down. "In Houston?"

"Yes, although I'm not looking forward to it. Retail is really taking a beating. Except grocery stores. People don't want to buy their groceries online. Yet."

A grocery store. Joe wondered if he should be trying to find a small grocery for one of the open spaces in his shopping center. Better yet—what about an independent grocer, sort of like a year-round farmers market, with a coffee bar, maybe even baked goods made on-site—

"What brings you to the office today?" his uncle asked.

"If you're working, I'm working," Joe assured him. "I've got some things I want to run past you next week."

"I don't want to take on any more retail, Joe. Not in Maryland. It's just not my territory."

*That's right,* Joe thought. *It's my territory. And when I flip the place in North East, you'll see I knew all along what I was talking about.*

Joe would have come into the office even if he hadn't expected his uncle to check on him. It was too soon for another holiday just three weeks into the new year. He had roared into 2020 full of resolve. Not just resolutions—*resolve.* Flipping that Class C in Cecil was just the beginning. He was in good shape, but he could be in better shape still—six-pack abs instead of four, more definition in his calves. He played tennis only once a week during the cold-weather months, so there would be plenty of time to focus on weights. He'd try to use the Peloton that Meredith had given him, but he couldn't see how that would help him get more cut. Still, he had to log some hours on it, or she would be hurt.

And, finally—Jordan was behind him. She was a bad dream, he decided. He had lost his way. But that was 2019. Now it was 2020, and he wouldn't repeat that mistake. True, he had not broken up with her as definitively as he should have on Christmas Eve, but he had not initiated any kind of contact with her since that meeting and he was achingly polite when she checked in with him. He wished he could get away with ghosting her, but that was risky. Ghosting seemed an extremely civilized development to Joe. It's what he would prefer, he decided, if someone decided to end a casual relationship with him. Just stop. No explanations. Act as if you're dead. People owed less in the way of explanations than they realized.

He looked over the plans for Nottingham, the shopping center on which he had closed in September. There were two anchors, Modell's and Sizzler. That left four other stores, two of which were vacant. Jersey Mike's was ready to sign a lease on one of those; once he nailed down the fourth tenant, he would sell the whole thing, making a tidy profit. Of course, a lot of that would have to go back to where he had gotten it—the second mortgage on the house, his investment portfolio. He hoped to buy back into the market on a downswing. Assuming there was one. Meredith hated it when he noted that Trump had been pretty good for markets. She couldn't stand to admit he could do anything right.

Joe's office was a small suite of rooms just off the traffic circle in Towson—a reception area, a place for his assistant, his office, a seldom-used conference room. Joe was good at his job, but he couldn't quite get the stink of nepotism off him; everyone assumed his uncle allowed him to work from Baltimore because of their relationship. Which was true; it just wasn't the entire story. His uncle loved Meredith from the moment he met her and wanted to do whatever he could to help their marriage. If she was going to attend Johns Hopkins, then he was going to let Joe work from Baltimore, even though most of his firm's business was in the Southeast. Joe was on a plane to Atlanta or Jacksonville every other week.

Joe would have been happy to stay in Texas, but he had never told Meredith that. Although Meredith liked Trinity and the small corner of San Antonio it inhabited, she disdained Texas. Funny, because many of her criticisms—*provincial but doesn't know it, full of itself, football obsessed*—could have been applied to her hometown of New Orleans. Then again, Meredith didn't want to live in New Orleans, either. She had been even more adamant about that than Texas.

In the end, she had gotten into medical school at Columbia, Johns Hopkins, and Baylor. Joe, with a year left at Trinity because of his gap year at his uncle's home, hoped she'd pick Baylor, only five hours away, which might convince her to stay in Texas. He worried she would choose Columbia because she had an affinity for New York, a place Joe didn't like at all.

Johns Hopkins seemed the outlier among her choices, but when she settled on it, he understood immediately: She was pledging herself to Joe and what he wanted. *What she thought he wanted.* Joe wanted to work in his uncle's company in Houston. He wanted to sit in the box at Astros games, go down to Kingsville to hunt in the fall, drive a Range Rover, smoke the occasional cigar. He wouldn't live in The Woodlands as his uncle did—too far out—

and he probably couldn't afford River Oaks, but he wanted to live in the city, maybe near Rice.

Anyway, Meredith went to Johns Hopkins, and that was that, his future was sealed. He fooled around a little his senior year. Meredith all but encouraged him to. "This will be our last year apart," she said, and, like so much of what Meredith said, it felt as if an oracle had spoken, that he had no choice in the matter. It was, as she decreed, their last year apart. He dated enough to figure out what Meredith already knew: He couldn't do better. And, until Jordan, he had been relatively faithful—one-offs on business trips, once with a pro, not because he had to pay for it, but because he was curious about what it was like to pay for it. Then Jordan. Jesus, why had he messed up like that? Meredith would probably forgive him if he told her, but he wasn't sure he could forgive himself.

Say her name three times and Jordan, like the Candyman, surfaced. She was FaceTiming him. From bed.

"Hey, lover," she said. She was wearing a cute but not overtly sexy camisole with matching shorts, in a riotous flower print. Her hair was tousled; she was definitely going for an "I woke up like this" vibe, yet she had a full face of makeup. "Knew you'd be at work today, you striver."

Easy, in a text, to keep things clipped and neutral; harder face-to-face. Which was probably why she had ambushed him like this. He studied Jordan's bed, a place he had never been; they always met at the model. She had one of those beds with an upholstered headboard that rose so high he couldn't see the top. The fabric looked soft and creamy, but it also was tufted with little buttons, which made no sense to Joe. Wasn't the point of those headboards to provide comfort, so one could sit up and read? Not that Jordan was big on reading.

"Always something to do," he said. "Putting the final touches on the contracts for a lease at Nottingham."

An awkward silence. She stretched prettily, extending her arms behind her so her chest thrust up and out. He let the silence build and expand. She had called him. It was on her to state her business.

"When am I going to see you again?"

"Not sure. Things are hectic. Need one more tenant before I can put this place back on the market."

She pouted. "Well, I miss you."

*Say it*, he urged himself. *Say it. Tell her it's over. She clearly can't take a hint.* Instead, he blurted out: "Meredith and I are trying to have a child."

Her eyes rounded and he could tell that she was suppressing shock, maybe even outrage. Joe had told her they were child-free by choice. A left turn like this was a way of telling her that they were over. Without having to tell her they were over. Sure, it was a lie, but what of it? He was only trying to be solicitous of her feelings.

"Whose idea was that?"

"It was mutual," he said. "We got to talking about our resolutions for 2020 and we realized we are not, in fact, the same people we were twenty years ago. That we want something more, something that would give our life meaning."

Amazing, he thought, how sincerely he could argue for something he didn't believe. Part of what made him a good salesman.

"So children give a life meaning? What does that say about my life?"

"You're young," Joe said. "At your age, I had no desire to settle down, start a family. Give yourself time."

"Aren't you—isn't she—I mean, it's not that easy after forty, is it?"

"The doctors think we've got a good shot. We might have to do in vitro. We'll see."

It was hard to tell on the phone screen, but her eyes looked misty, as if filling up with tears. "Well, anyway, I just wanted to say hi. I'll see you around."

Good. She was a proud girl. Joe had counted on that. "See you around."

He wondered, for a moment, if his lie about a child came from some deeply Freudian place, a great truth spoken in jest. He was pretty sure not. There were plenty of people in the world. He never grieved for that barely-a-baby who probably wouldn't have survived anyway, given how premature it was. The planet was over-crowded. Hard to mourn the absence of someone who was dead before you had time to register the fact she was ever alive.

He wondered if Amber felt the same way. But then—Amber had weeks, months to acquaint herself with what was growing inside her. Meredith had been the first person—besides Joe's mother, and she didn't count—to say out loud what Joe had felt but never dared to say: *You were a victim in this, too.*

Still, he felt sorry for Amber. How could he not? No one wanted to be frozen in time, identified with the single worst thing they had ever done. Joe had feared the same fate for so long, shunning high school friends when he first returned to Baltimore. Even Meredith, as much as she loved him and supported him, had never quite understood that part of it.

Could he be a friend to Amber, offer her the kind of benediction that Meredith had provided him? Just check in on her from time to time? Would that make up for everything?

MEREDITH PULLED INTO her mother-in-law's driveway and sighed audibly, knowing she would be sighing inwardly for much of the evening ahead. How rich that her MIL was named Caryn, a homonym for the behavior for which Caryn Simpson had long been famous. Caryn Simpson quite possibly *invented* asking to speak to managers, a tactic that she continued to defend. "You work your way up the chain of command," she would say, "until you get the answer you want."

Meredith had heard Caryn give this speech numerous times and long before such a thing as a "Karen" had been established, if she was going to be fair about it.

Caryn also was exceedingly polite when trying to get her way, but it was a kind of politeness that fooled no one. Real steel magnolia shit, and Meredith had grown up among some of the steeliest magnolias around. Not so much her mother, who never conquered her inferiority complex at being the Baton Rouge country mouse who had moved to New Orleans. But her mother traveled in circles that included some true grande dames. Caryn could have hung with the best of them, although she wasn't quite as charming. She lacked the self-awareness, the hint of self-deprecation common to the Southern women Meredith knew.

"Oh, Eddie's cheddar biscuits," Caryn cooed, taking Meredith's reusable shopping bag from her and peering inside without asking. "And Otterbein cookies. You are so clever. Why bother to bake from scratch when the readymades are better than the results most of us can achieve."

She meant, *Better than you can achieve.* Although Caryn had worked before Joe was born, she had stayed at home until he was a teenager, devoting herself to the domestic goddess racket full-time, then returning to her job as a school social worker when he entered high school. That irony was never discussed: Caryn, so omnipresent in Joe's childhood, was tending to other people's children when her son got into trouble. Oh well, two teenagers intent on having sex would find a way to do it even with a parent under the roof, Meredith supposed.

"Is Joe here yet?" she asked, knowing he wasn't, or his Range Rover would have been in the driveway.

"He called and said he's running a little late. Said he had to stop someplace en route."

Meredith poured herself a healthy glug of red wine without asking, a daughter-in-law's prerogative, she reckoned. She would have happily put the biscuits into the oven to warm, or arrayed the cookies on a plate, but she knew Caryn was proprietary about her space.

It surprised her, when she met Caryn at a parents' weekend in Joe's second year at Trinity, that her new boyfriend's mother did not seem warmly inclined toward her. Meredith was used to being the kind of girl that parents loved. But she soon learned that Joe was Caryn's favorite of her three sons and, understandably, she felt protective of him. If it was a bit closing-the-barn-door etc. etc., so be it. A female had almost led to Joe's downfall, and now all females were suspect.

But Caryn's passive-aggressiveness only worsened with each passing year. She managed, with the sweetest smile, to be rude about so much. The house. (*Why do two people who are determined not to have children need such a large house?*) Meredith's shoes. (*I don't know, I guess I really am a slave to fashion, but I'll endure a little pain if it makes the outfit.)* Most of all, she could not help throwing little jabs at Meredith's ability to care for Joe on every front. Once, tipsy on her box pinot grigio, she had gone so far as to tell her daughter-in-law: "I hope you're keeping him happy in the one way that matters. Because nothing else counts for anything if—you know."

Meredith did know, thank you very much. Ah, well, Caryn was almost as rude to her two other daughters-in-law, although it didn't create as much of a bond as it should have among the sisters-in-law. Besides, they had children, teenagers around the same age as Joe when his life veered so crazily off track.

"How was your day?" she asked her mother-in-law.

"It was a day," Caryn said. "Since I retired, days don't have a lot of meaning."

Caryn was seventy-four. She had retired nine years ago. *That's a lot of non-meaning*, Meredith thought, but did not say. It was a trap. If she said that work was not important, Caryn would argue that *Meredith* certainly seemed to think it mattered. There was always this weird subtext bobbing beneath the surface, that Meredith should have a more minor career, one that allowed her to put Joe front and center the way that Caryn had done for her husband, dead for five years now. It was okay to have a small-*j* job, but not a vocation. Joe was supposed to be Meredith's raison d'être.

The thing is—he was! Meredith couldn't live without him. He was her everything *and* she had a job that she loved. Was that so hard to understand? She knew Joe had this fantasy that he would become so successful that she wouldn't "have to" work. It wasn't a fight worth having, because it didn't seem an imminent threat. He made good money, but their life cost a lot. He couldn't do it without her.

She bit back a suggestion that Caryn might volunteer or find a hobby. Caryn liked to complain. All one had to do was listen, and Meredith could do that.

Still, they both perked up when they heard a car in the drive. Joe was—not the glue, he didn't bind them together. He was whatever ingredient mellowed two battling flavors, created an unthinkable synergy. Was there such an ingredient? Meredith was a paint-by-numbers cook, following directions well enough, but not aware of how flavors melded.

"I stopped to buy bread pudding from that bistro on York," he said.

"I thought you said you wouldn't go there anymore because you know someone who got a bad oyster," Meredith said.

"Oh, I think it's okay as long as you order your oysters in season."

"That's what I kept trying to tell you," Meredith said.

"Bread pudding," his mother said. "The perfect dessert. Smart boy."

*February 2, 2020*

JOE ENTERED THE party and looked around warily. He assumed Jordan would be here; it was her boss's party, after all. It was where he had met her last year. Not that he was worried she would behave inappropriately. She hadn't reached out to him at all since he told her the lie that they were trying to get pregnant.

He wasn't much invested in tonight's game. San Francisco, Kansas City—neither team meant anything to him. He had a soft spot for the Tennessee Titans, dating back to their Houston Oilers days. But he always attended this party. He just wished he wasn't alone tonight. Meredith had a terrible cold, even by her standards. Her breathing was so shallow yesterday that they had almost gone to urgent care.

But she was better now and adamant that he put in an appearance. "I'm just going to stay in bed and watch Lifetime movies about women who kill their duplicitous husbands," she said. He had tried not to wince. He deserved such a fate. He had been bad. He wouldn't be, not anymore. He was going to be a good man, worthy of the woman who had saved him. *It's never too late to start being good.* Who had told him that?

Meredith, the night they had shared their most personal stories, that bonding ritual all young lovers do in the beginning, although Meredith's and Joe's stories were far from typical.

The party room was on the top floor of one of those new apartment buildings that Decca had been throwing up around the harbor, made to appeal to twentysomethings. Funny thing, a lot of the twentysomethings who wanted apartments in the city had jobs out in the burbs. They lived to live, these kids. Good neighborhood restaurants and bike storage were more important to them than—well, what had Joe wanted in an apartment when he was a twentysomething? Probably the biggest television possible. But he had married so young, starting down the path of true adulthood early. He and Meredith had been shopping for a house before they were thirty, unburdened by debt, thanks to boomer parents who had paid for their college educations. He felt so much older than people in their twenties. Even Jordan, at thirty-one, with all her single-minded ambition, seemed immature to Joe.

Speak of the devil. He watched her sidle into the room, resplendent in a bright gold top and tight black pants. A KC fan, then, or at least one for tonight. Was she from the Midwest? He realized he didn't know. He didn't really know anything about her, other than the fact that she had been Decca's number one salesperson for three years running.

*You're an old soul. Like me.* Meredith had said those words to him the first night they slept together, in her narrow dormitory bed.

*What makes you say that?*

*You just seem older than a typical freshman.*

*Well, I am. I'm a whole year older. I deferred admission and lived with my uncle's family in Houston, worked at his real estate firm.*

*No, I'm not talking about the fact that you're nineteen. You have—gravitas.*

He did not tell his story that night, but he knew immediately that he would confide in Meredith, and soon. He felt seen, in the best possible way. Someone was looking at him, all the way down. "I'm Looking Through You," the Beatles sang, and it was supposed to mark the moment that someone had disappointed you. But what if someone looked through you, glimpsed the darkness of your secrets—and *stayed*? God, he loved her. He was so lucky to have found her.

His phone buzzed in his pocket. JA: The bathroom here is quite large. A selfie of her in the mirror. She had taken her top off. Even her bra was black and gold. Jesus, was she testing him? He deleted the message and texted Meredith: How are you feeling? Can I get you anything?

No, I'm fine. Worst cold ever. I can barely taste anything.

The game had started. Joe was more interested in the commercials than in the action on the field. And not for their entertainment value. Joe was curious to see what the ads revealed about consumers right now—their aspirations, their dreams, at least as reflected by marketing research. As always, there were true consumables—snacks and beverages. Some money-related services—a mortgage company, TurboTax. Lots and lots of car ads. Those were all over the place. The ones that amused Joe the most were the big luxury SUVs that pitched themselves as good for the environment. Sure, let's go with that. *So who are we, the American people, in 2020? We are nice folks who want to eat chips, drive whatever we want to drive while feeling no guilt about that choice, and maybe manage our money better.*

Who was Joe in 2020? He was on top of the world professionally, or at least about to be. He was a good husband after his brief, um, lapse. Jordan was a slip, nothing more. He was only forty, allegedly the age at which a midlife crisis began, but maybe he had gotten that out of his system with Jordan. Yes, that was it. He had had his little breakdown and now he was done.

The Super Bowl Joe remembered best was the one during what he learned to call his gap year, living with his uncle Tony and aunt Inez in The Woodlands outside Houston. The night had been mild, even by Texas standards, and they had stood outside at halftime, smoking cigars by the pool. In the darkness, their cigars the only light, he had found himself saying: *She never told me a thing.*

*We know, son. Sorry   I shouldn't call you that. You've got a father, a good one.* Joe had understood in that moment that his uncle liked his father, but found him soft by his hypermasculine standards. Funny, his uncle was a Baltimore native, but he seemed more Texan than a lot of real Texans. Uncle Tony's life showed Joe that destinies were not fixed, that you could decide to be whoever you wanted. You just had to know who that was.

*She could have ruined my life.*

*She almost did. But trust me, no one's going to remember. You stay down here, go to Rice, or even Trinity. It will be 2002 by the time you graduate, and the world will be a different place.*

Boy, was it, and not in a way his uncle could ever have predicted. Yet watching the country rebound from the 9/11 attacks had been helpful to Joe. One day, people were saying things would never be the same again—and then, before you knew it, life was more or less the same again; they just never went back to letting non-travelers go past security at airports. Joe enrolled at Trinity, he met Meredith, he followed her to his own hometown, where she had started med school at Johns Hopkins.

No regrets, none, not a one. Well, Jordan.

He looked at the city of Baltimore, beautiful from this vantage point, all shiny lights and glittering buildings, reflections in the water. He would be a man and tell Jordan that he was done, that she had to stop coming on to him. He would be good. He *was* good, he had simply done a bad thing—an important distinction.

THE FIRST SUNDAY in February was mild, even by Amber's standards, and at midafternoon, she decided to walk to MOM's Organic Market. She wore a backpack, which would limit what she could buy, but she could not bear to have one of those carts, which she associated with old women. Besides, a body didn't need that much to get through the week. Almost everyone overbought groceries.

*A body.* She smiled at the echo of the Miss Margaret in her head. Miss Margaret was forever talking about what *a* body and *the* body required. It was a longer list than some might expect— certainly more than food, water, and shelter. A body required a good pillow. The body required hydration. A body should be shielded from chills. The body needed a chair that would not deform the spine. The choice of article mattered, although Amber had never worked out the rules and she suspected Miss Margaret was not consistent. Amber's working theory was that "a" body was specific to Miss Margaret's own needs, while "the" body was universal, true of everyone.

The grocery store, usually busy on Sunday afternoons, was a ghost town. "Super Bowl," the cashier grunted, and only then did she remember. Amber wasn't much of one for football. She had no team, she didn't follow the sport, although she did remember one Super Bowl in particular: the New Orleans Saints victory in 2010.

She had lived in the city less than a year, renting in the section known as the Irish Channel. She had not watched the game because it seemed like bad faith, jumping on the bandwagon. But when it was over and she began to hear the shouts, she couldn't help herself. She put on a coat—it was freakishly cold—and made her way to Magazine Street.

It was unlike anything she had ever witnessed.

People were everywhere, and they were the happiest people Amber had ever seen. The police drove along Magazine, narrowed to a single lane by the throngs, and their only response was to fly a Saints banner from the window of the patrol car.

Amber, standing outside the Rendezvous Tavern, saw two men circling each other in wonder. "We did it, brother. We did it!" They embraced. Normally she would have mocked two fans taking credit for what professional athletes had achieved on the field, but she was touched by their sincerity and vulnerability. What did it feel like to care so much about something over which one had no control?

New as she was to New Orleans, Amber had already heard multiple theories about how this city, unlike almost any other in North America, could celebrate without sliding into mayhem. (And even NOLA was not immune; there were acts of violence at Mardi Gras parades, but they were isolated, they did not subsume the event.) One lady Amber had met through Miss Margaret avowed that it was because there was no set closing time. "We don't turn all the drunks out into the street at two a.m., a recipe for disaster." The Rendezvous, for example, had lock-ins. Amber, an early riser, had walked past it many a Sunday morning, heard the rumble of voices, the cheery bleat of the jukebox.

"We're lovers, not fighters," others said of the locals. (They could not be held accountable for the mischief that tourists got up to.) The crowds on Magazine that night were sweet and gentle and nonthreatening, and Amber still couldn't last for more than fifteen minutes.

Agoraphobia seemed a counterintuitive response to her confinement as a teenager, but there was no doubt in Amber's mind that her problems had begun there, in Middlebrook. *How lucky*, everyone said to her. *How lucky you are that you're being treated as a juvenile.*

She had not felt lucky. The only break she caught at Middlebrook was the presence of an even more notorious girl during her time there, a pre-teen who had killed a stranger's child, an *actual* baby. That was how Amber thought of it. The baby who had died on prom night was barely a living thing. Her lawyer had argued that the autopsy was inaccurate, that the suffocation could have been a result of the prolonged birth, and the baby was only twenty-eight weeks. Even in a hospital, such a baby might not have survived.

*You're lucky*, they said, when she was sent to Middlebrook until her eighteenth birthday. *Sealed record. No hard time.*

It had felt hard to Amber. She had lived every moment, no exaggeration, in fear. And while nothing truly terrible happened to her, only some light hazing and bullying, almost two years of being in constant fear had damaged her, marked her as someone who would spend the rest of her life checking for exits, literal and figurative. It was yet another reason she loved New Orleans: the shotgun bungalows meant you always had a way to get out.

When Amber was released, her mother had told her she was not welcome at home and offered her a small amount of money, Rod's money, to start over. Amber found herself drifting south, to Eckerd College, the college Joe had once described to her as the opposite to Michigan. He wasn't there or in Ann Arbor—she had heard he switched courses entirely and ended up in Texas—but it made her feel close to him, her knowledge that he had briefly considered this school. She tried to write him twice—once in care of his parents' home, once in care of Trinity University. She didn't know what happened to the Trinity letter, which she had sent to the biggest dorm on a hunch, but the letter to his Stoneleigh address had been returned by his mother, with a lawyer's cease-and-desist notice attached.

She liked St. Pete. She worked two jobs—waitressing on Central Avenue, cashier at a boutique on Beach Drive. There was a beautiful poet, a local woman of note, who came into the boutique sometimes. The poet was crazy about the random folk art items that the store stocked. Amber was, too. They fell into conversation and Amber found herself trying to explain why she loved these pieces, but she didn't have the vocabulary for it. Visionary, outsider, naive—it was all new to her. The poet gave her books to read, a list of artists in Florida and Georgia. Amber began scouting, visiting and charming the artists, bringing her finds back to the shop. The artists liked her. They recognized Amber as a kindred spirit.

Amber also had a good eye, the boutique's owner said, but the store could take only a few of the items Amber acquired. Amber began selling her discoveries on eBay, then started a store on Etsy as that site was taking off.

Then she followed a man to New Orleans. Embarrassing, but true. Embarrassing because she didn't even like him that much; she was just restless and in need of a change. And if her internet-gleaned knowledge that Joe Simpson had married a New Orleans girl played into that decision—what of it? She genuinely liked what she saw of New Orleans in 2009. Four years after the storm, as she quickly learned to call it, the city struck a familiar chord in her. It needed love, wholehearted, unconditional love.

The relationship with the man petered out, and he moved back to Florida, but Amber was able to manage the rent on their place on Eighth Street. She met Miss Margaret, she settled in, juggling days at the gallery with a server's job at the Upperline, which she loved because of the art that crowded the walls. Basically, the same life she had in St. Pete, only now with college debt. A good life, in a city that felt as if it was meant for her.

So why was she here, picking over produce in an organic market in Baltimore on Super Bowl Sunday? Why was she covertly using social media to study the man who had contributed, albeit un-wittingly, to the demise of her dreams? She had a *life* back in New Orleans. Friends—Miss Margaret, some people from the Upper-line. Baltimore hadn't felt like home even when it was home.

She decided to make a meatloaf for dinner, a properly deca-dent one with cream and ground veal, from Judith Jones's *The Pleasures of Cooking for One*, her favorite cookbook. Ingredients gathered, she walked down Elm Street to the Wine Source, which somehow had found a way around Baltimore's liquor laws and was allowed to open on Sunday, although maybe all Baltimore liquor stores were allowed to open on Super Bowl Sunday? It had been quite a shock, after New Orleans, to be reminded of Baltimore's old-fashioned liquor laws. She picked a pinot noir and went home to make her dinner, eating her salad after the main, a custom she practiced because it was the closest she was ever going to get to living in Paris.

She thought about Joe. She thought about Joe all the time. She could see things from his point of view. She always could. Wasn't that a good thing, that level of empathy? He had been young, he'd had no idea what was going on. She hadn't been entirely clear what was happening, and to the extent that she could even confront the information that her body was trying to convey, Amber, the prize-winning extemporaneous speaker, had argued with herself: *I can work that out this summer.* The prom was everything to her. At the prom, Joe would see her, finally see her, and realize he loved her. Movies had promised nothing less. At a prom, a girl was finally seen as who she was.

The baby had denied her that. The baby, not Joe.

MEREDITH CHECKED HER temperature again: 102.7. She couldn't believe it, her second flu this season, and she had gotten the damn shot, she always got the shot. She was so sick she didn't have any appetite, so weak she didn't trust herself to go downstairs to get a glass of water. She wobbled to the bathroom and ran the tap, cupping water in her palm and lifting it to her parched lips.

She crawled back into bed with her tablet. Although she could have watched whatever she wanted on the large-screen television in the armoire opposite the bed, she preferred her iPad, propped up in a frame, inches from her face. Sometimes, when Joe was away on business, she slept with it under her pillow, listening to the rat-a-tat dialogue of beloved old films—*The Palm Beach Story, Bringing Up Baby.* It was not unlike how she had slept as a young teen with a Walkman tuned to her favorite oldies station playing the hits of the '70s.

Super Bowl Sunday had never meant much to her, not even that year when the Saints had won. She loathed football, thought it should be banned. The increasing evidence about the damage it did to the players' bodies made it indefensible, barbaric.

Meredith disliked a lot of popular things, and if she had too much to drink at a dinner party—rare, but not unheard-of—she was prone to hold forth about them. Football. Reality television. She also hated most true crime stories, and that included all those popular podcasts. It was the worst kind of voyeurism, grooving on the misfortunes of others, treating people's lives like they were nothing more than whodunits.

She clicked through the suggestions that Apple TV made based on her most recent choice, *Some Like it Hot. The Philadelphia Story?* Meredith identified almost too closely with Hepburn's character in that film, and not in a way that made her happy. She didn't consider herself brittle, although her mother had suggested, more than once, that Meredith found imperfection unforgivable. Untrue! She did not consider herself perfect; that was a word others wielded against her, like a cudgel.

"Seen it, seen it, seen it," she croaked to her tablet as she scrolled through the suggestions. God, it felt like a sodden animal was sitting on top of her, yet also inside her lungs. *What's Up, Doc?* No, she hated movies about men rescued from uptight women by charming weirdos. *Check into those relationships ten years hence and tell me how it worked out, bub.*

*The Philadelphia Story*'s Tracy Lord would probably feel the same way Meredith did about the depiction of uptight women, although Meredith could not be optimistic about the second union of Tracy and Dex, either.

The funny thing was, very few people knew that Meredith was capable of not only tolerating imperfection but extending true forgiveness, profound forgiveness. Joe had tapped that vein in her the night he told her about what had happened at his prom. *I never talk about this,* he said, *and I will probably never talk about it again.* He waited for her judgment, and when it didn't come, she was even more relieved than he was. This was love, she was capable of love, she could tolerate at least one person who had made a huge mistake. Joe made her believe she could be human.

He had been so sweet yesterday, when her fever rose to 104 and she was shaking all over. He had been on the verge of carrying her to his car and driving her to urgent care, something she was desperate to avoid. Still, she cherished his devotion, his solicitation. No one else dared to try to take care of Meredith. She wouldn't let them.

And just like that, his text appeared at the top of her screen. How are you feeling? Can I get you anything?

She texted back: No, I'm fine. Worst cold ever. I can barely taste anything. In bed with Cary Grant. (She had decided to watch *Charade*. It was closer to the experience of *Some Like It Hot* than anything Apple had suggested—lots of bodies falling, yes, yet never a death that anyone had to mourn. And at least Cary Grant knew he was too old for Audrey Hepburn and kept saying so.)

Lucky man, Joe replied.

# THE SONG

THE THEME FOR the 1997 prom at Towson High School was "Under the Sea," but the song was "Un-break my Heart." Often, song and theme could be conflated, but the decorating committee, headed by Susannah Caufield, could not see a way to create visuals from the Toni Braxton song, popular as it was.

One member had suggested that they make enormous paper hearts, "crack" them by cutting zigzag lines, and then put Band-Aids on them. But it was such a downer of an image. Then again, it was a downer of a song. The video began with a woman watching her gorgeous boyfriend, maybe husband, die in a bloodless motorcycle accident, but the song was clearly about a more pedestrian breakup. Toni Braxton was a Maryland girl, so there was some local pride in choosing her ballad, but the bottom line was that the girls wanted a slow song, a romantic one. Well, the girls with boyfriends did, and those were the girls who dominated the prom committee.

"Un-break My Heart" inevitably was the last song played, just before midnight. Susannah glanced at Joe, alone at their table. His date had gone upstairs, complaining of a stomachache, and never returned. That seemed to bother Joe not at all; his eyes were fixed on his ex, Kaitlyn, who had brought her bored-looking college boyfriend to prom, but danced one dance with Joe. Before Susannah let Zach lead her to the dance floor, she impulsively leaned over and whispered into Joe's ear: "They've all but broken up. But it's not like she could have found another date if she broke up with him before prom."

Pressed tightly against Zach, she wondered why she had violated Kaitlyn's confidence. Her loyalty should be to her best friend. Then again, Kaitlyn hadn't shown loyalty to Susannah when she dumped Joe on Labor Day weekend. They had been the best foursome, junior year, and they had big plans for senior year.

Then Kaitlyn had to go fall for some guy who worked at the beach pizza place where she worked. And while he was older, and fairly cute, he wasn't really that impressive. He went to Towson, for gosh sake. Was a sophomore at Towson really superior to Joe, who was going to go to University of Michigan and probably play lacrosse, although it would be at the club level? Susannah adored Zach, of course, but acknowledging the fact that Joe was the number one catch at Towson High was simply objective. She often had wondered if Kaitlyn had dumped him because that was the ultimate cachet, breaking up with the guy everyone else wanted.

Zach leaned in and kissed her neck. She sighed. Zach was not the smooth lover he imagined himself, but Susannah had never figured out how to elevate his game without revealing she had far more experience than he did. Susannah had known her share of college boys. Unlike Kaitlyn, however, Susannah had never mistaken those holiday and summer flings for anything meaningful. Vacation boys were strictly for fun. Fun and practice.

She surveyed the hotel ballroom over Zach's shoulder. She was particularly proud of the centerpieces, small glass globes with live goldfish. The advisor had objected, but Susannah had been adamant in her vision. "If elementary school fairs can have that game where kids win goldfish by throwing a Ping-Pong ball, I don't see why we can't have something similar." The advisor had asked what would happen to the goldfish after the prom. "Oh, there will be someone at each table who wants to take them home," Susannah said, hoping she was right. Not everyone went to the after-party. Some parents were stupid strict.

Not hers, bless them. Her parents were cool. When Susannah had started dating, her parents had sat her down and said they didn't worry about *her*, but they did fear driving impaired, country roads, outdoor spaces. They made a deal with Susannah that she would have complete privacy in their basement rec room if she brought her dates there. *Complete privacy.* Door shut, they wouldn't open the door or come down those steps unless the house was on fire.

At first, the boys were dubious, and Susannah didn't blame them. But by the time she started dating Zach, she had realized her parents were true to their word. They remained in their bedroom, two floors away, and she could do pretty much anything she wanted in the family rec room. Maybe they thought she would be too inhibited under their roof to have sex. They were wrong.

It was a source of friction that she and Zach were having sex, while Kaitlyn and Joe were not. "I'm just not ready," Kaitlyn would tell Susannah, and she tried to be patient with her friend, but she also felt there was a world of unspoken judgment in Kaitlyn's reluctance. It wasn't that big a deal. Go on the pill, make the guy wear a condom, and what could possibly happen? It was exhausting to listen to Kaitlyn agonize over this, like it was 1955 or something. And, again, a little insulting.

Then Kaitlyn went to Rehoboth and *cheated on Joe*. Really, Kaitlyn was such a hypocrite.

Still, Susannah shouldn't have said anything to Joe, whose eyes remained fixed on his ex. But Susannah didn't like Amber Glass. Who did? She was weird. Not an obvious nerd, but she missed the mark in some way that Susannah couldn't be bothered to pinpoint. Her clothes were okay, she was sort of pretty, but something was off.

*Un-break my heart.* Susannah had decided to break up with Zach at Thanksgiving. She was going to Dartmouth, while he would be at Ohio State, his dad's alma mater. He and Joe liked to joke about how they would be rivals now. She didn't want to end their relationship before leaving for college, because she believed it would boost her desirability to the boys at Dartmouth if she had a nominal boyfriend. Susannah was a practical girl who approached dating the way she had managed her studies. Do the required reading, prepare for the tests, but don't take any of it too seriously. She had big plans for herself. She wanted to work in politics, on campaigns. She wanted to be involved in policy. She wasn't sure, exactly, how one did that or what it meant, but she assumed she would figure it out.

"Jesus fucking Christ," Zach said.

"What?"

"Gorman. Fucking Gorman."

Gorman was Alfonso "Alfie" Gorman, center on the football team, the kind of guy who got just enough attention to always crave more. A circle had formed around him, chanting. Susannah couldn't make out what he was being exhorted to do, and by the time she realized what was going on, it was too late—Alfie raised the fishbowl to his mouth and drank its contents, fish and all.

Un-break her heart indeed. Well, that was one fish they didn't have to worry about finding a home for.

The dance over, prom over, but the evening far from over, people started filing out. Susannah thought she saw Kaitlyn squeeze Joe's hand. Later, she realized she was slipping him a note. Maybe that explained why Joe didn't try harder to get his date to open the hotel room door, or think to ask someone to let him in. Even Zach thought it was a little cold, Joe not trying harder to check on Amber.

She didn't see Kaitlyn again one-on-one until several days later. But when they were finally alone, at the end of a week when gossip hissed and fizzled through the school, a week of somber assemblies and teachers making concerned faces, she asked: "Did you give Joe a note? At the prom?"

"Would it matter if I did?" Kaitlyn asked.

"I've been thinking—if he thought he was going to hook up with you at the after-party, that might explain why he didn't try to check on Amber."

They were in Susannah's room and Kaitlyn lay back on the rug, fixed her eyes on the ceiling. "We didn't hook up, though."

"But if he thought there was a chance—maybe that's why he didn't do anything more than knock."

"So what?"

"And maybe the baby wouldn't be dead." There, she had said it.

"That's a lot," Kaitlyn said, "to put on me. And Joe. Okay, fine, I gave him a note saying I still cared about him. Because I do. I thought we could have fun this summer, hanging out. That's all. Don't make it into some big drama. He knocked on the door, she didn't let him in, she had the only key. What was he supposed to do?"

The two friends drifted apart that summer, and by Thanksgiving, when Susannah returned to Baltimore to break up with Zach, having already snagged a sophomore, it didn't even occur to her to try to spend time with Kaitlyn. They didn't have that much in common, not anymore.

*February 25, 2020*

MEREDITH SLIPPED FROM bed at five a.m. for what was slated to be a long day of consultations and surgeries, thinking: *Everywhere else it's just Tuesday*, then corrected herself: *Here* it's *just Tuesday.*

It had been five years since she had managed to spend a Mardi Gras in New Orleans, but she was missing it especially hard this year for some reason. She knew if she lived in her hometown, full-time, she probably would be someone who went back and forth, as so many old-school locals did—participating fervently one year, leaving town the next, grumbling about the tourists and the traffic disruptions. In a few hours, her parents would be setting up camp on neutral ground for Rex, putting out their chairs and their cooler near Washington Avenue, where they had friends.

Her day *here*, now that she was recovered from the flu, started with a thirty-minute ride on Joe's Peloton, which she was using more than he did. It saved so much time, doing her cardio in the basement gym, then enjoying a quick steam or sauna.

She had tried to pretend, when they first moved into the house, that this space wasn't really a *gym*. It seemed so showy, so over-the-top, to have a room dedicated to workouts, especially for two people with gym memberships. But here was not only Joe's Christmas Peloton, but a rack of weights, two yoga mats, a stability ball, and a set of TRX straps suspended from the ceiling. One wall was mirrored, and Meredith had considered adding a barre, but that seemed like too much. She chose her favorite ride, a Cody class that focused on speed in the saddle, and was pleased to clock a personal best. She was soaked with sweat, a healthy, virtuous sweat.

Their bedroom had an enormous bathroom with walk-in closets on either side, so she was able to shower and dress without bothering a still-sleeping Joe. She chose what was essentially her uniform—conservative yet figure-conscious knit dress, her Christmas diamond studs, low-heeled suede boots.

She usually wore a lab coat when seeing her patients, but not always. She liked them to see how good her body looked, knowing they would infer it was the result of the procedures they sought. It wasn't, not yet. As she aged, Meredith would, of course, avail herself of the services she provided, but so far, she was getting by with a little microdermabrasion, the occasional chemical peel, Botox for the two lines between her brows. *It's such a bait and switch,* Joe had said to her one time, *for a woman as naturally beautiful as you to be a plastic surgeon.*

Meredith didn't see it that way. Plastic surgery was a great equalizer. If people were going to be judged by their appearance—and they *were*, let's not pretend otherwise—why should they accept their genetic lotteries as fixed, unchangeable? We don't assume we have to stay in the income brackets into which we are born. We don't even have to accept the genders assigned to us at birth. The world was full of possibilities and Meredith approved.

The morning sped along in its usual blur of consultations, and she was on her last one before she knew it. There would be a quick lunch at her desk, then an afternoon of minor in-office procedures.

Strange—this patient, barely thirty, hadn't specified any particular surgeries; she was just prattling on about her job, how stressful it was. As the woman spoke, Meredith played absentmindedly with the sequined shoe on her desk, a throw from the annual all-female Muses parade, then immediately regretted it. No Mardi Gras throw was ever truly clean. She loved her Mardi Gras mementos, especially this shoe, so exquisitely wrought that it was an object worthy of admiration even to those ignorant of Muses and its traditions. Most people, seeing this shoe featured so prominently in her office, assumed Meredith had some sort of shoe fetish. Sometimes she did wish she could wear something like the four-inch spikes on this patient. Louboutins. Meredith had noticed the red soles when the woman crossed her legs.

She put the shoe down, making a mental note not to shake hands with this patient when she left. The young woman continued to stare at Meredith's hands, now coated with dust. How careless she must look to her. She fished an antibacterial wipe from her drawer and cleaned herself, then offered as a kind of apology: "They're insured; I should be more careful with them."

"The . . . shoe?"

"My hands. I felt silly, but—lots of surgeons do it. Insure their hands."

"Oh."

"Now, do you have an actual procedure in mind," she asked the woman, "or are you simply curious? It's okay to be curious, not in a rush to take action. Preferable, in fact—"

She groped for the name, couldn't find it, and there was no graceful way to open her calendar to goose her memory. Meredith was terrible with names and created mnemonic devices to compensate for this flaw. Only she had already forgotten the device she had coined for this potential patient. *Movie theater*, her mind kept prompting her, but what did that mean? Was she named for a local movie theater? Something Charles? Senator Whosis? Was she a state senator's wife?

"I just want to be my best self," the woman said. "It's not vanity. I feel like it's the opposite of vanity. I'm admitting that I could be better. Not perfect, but better."

It was the right thing to say—it was practically Meredith's credo, *better, not perfect*—so why didn't she believe that it was what this woman really felt? She could not detect anything on this young face that she could justify changing. Sure, if the woman wanted fillers in her lips, that was relatively harmless. But Meredith specialized in true surgical procedures. Lifts, rhinoplasty, breast reconstruction. Those who wanted Botox or fillers usually saw another doctor in the practice.

"I'm glad you know there is no perfect—"

God, it bugged her, her inability to remember names. If she really cared about individuals, shouldn't she be able to remember their names? She had been fascinated to read that President Clinton had, even as a young student at Oxford, kept index cards on the people he met, jotting down salient details. But the practice struck her as coldly ambitious. Self-serving, still not about the other person, not really. *Movie theater, snack.* Was her name Poppy? Sno-Caps? How she envied Joe, with his innate salesman's ability to remember not only people's names but key facts about them.

Of course, Joe had the advantage of actually liking people.

"There are doctors in my field who will take advantage of someone's insecurity," she continued. "They will agree readily to whatever the patients say they want. I prefer to start with asking potential clients to try the practice of the five 'Why's.' Do you know it? You keep asking why, which lets you burrow to the truth of what you truly want. I'll start by saying, *Why* do you want plastic surgery?"

"To be my best self?" Ah, Meredith saw it now. This one was all bravado, a thin shell of confidence covering a tender, nervous heart.

"Why do you want to be your best self?"

"Doesn't everyone want to be their best self?"

Meredith smiled to keep her words from sounding harsh. "Don't ask the question back to me. Answer it: Why do you want to be your best self?"

"I want to be the best at *everything*." She seemed surprised at her own reply. "I mean—I turned thirty-one last year and I don't feel as if I've done as much as I should. Work is going well, but— work isn't everything."

"Why do you want to be the best at everything?"

"Because I like to win?"

"Why do you like to win?"

A pause. "Doesn't everyone—" She recognized she was about

to make the same mistake twice. "Because it feels good," she offered sheepishly.

Technically, she had answered only four "whys" and her answers were barely answers, but the young woman had played by Meredith's rules. She liked to win—as did everyone, she was right about that. But being one's best self didn't equal winning. Did it? Meredith was introspective enough to *own*, as people liked to say now, her competitiveness. She definitely liked to win. But she wasn't sure that being one's best had anything to do with winning. Quite the opposite, she'd argue. One's best self didn't care about winning, didn't measure one's standing relative to others. One's best self took risks, and that meant—what did it mean?

"It's unusual for someone to come to me and not have at least some idea of what they want."

"I worry about my breasts," the young woman said, the words rushing out as if she was making a momentous confession. "They're fine for now. But they're big, they're going to sag. Maybe a reduction now would prevent that?"

Her breasts, in a snug coral sweater that matched her shoes, were large for her frame. Amazing how some natural breasts looked like bad boob jobs.

"Gravity cannot be prevented," Meredith said. "All breasts will sag eventually. It's the nature of the tissue."

The young woman looked horrified. Meredith sympathized. How many times had she declared her own body off-limits to certain age-related changes, as if it were simply a matter of making one's preferences known? As a child, she had announced she had no intention of having a period. In her twenties, she believed her metabolism would always run at the same pace. Now when she saw those ads for women who "leak" and tried to persuade you that adult diapers could make one feel confident and poised, she shook her head, adamant that incontinence could never happen to her. She had never been pregnant. Why should she leak?

As for menopause—no. She didn't need to worry about that yet. She was only forty. Menopause wasn't going to happen for ten, fifteen years.

"We're talking decades, to be sure. And if you exercise, the effect can be less noticeable. But real breasts do sag. Eventually."

"Is that shoe . . . significant?"

Meredith had not realized she had picked up her Muses shoe again, shifting it from one hand to another, sequins and dust coming off on her palms at an alarming rate. Maybe it *was* significant. As a pretty teenage girl, Meredith had never come close to being granted a Muses shoe. The all-female krewes of Mardi Gras tended to reward those who were underserved at the other parades. Girls like Meredith were showered with beads and throws by the men of Tucks and Orpheus and Bacchus. When she had been handed this shoe, back in 2015, she had been thrilled, but also worried that the masked bestower was saying, *You're heading toward middle age now. Here's your consolation prize. The men of Orpheus and Bacchus won't be as quick to drape you with beads.*

Then she remembered: Her mother's friend rode with Muses and she was on Float #15, sidewalk side. She clearly had recognized Meredith and bestowed this shoe on her. Her time had not yet passed.

"Oh, no. I mean, it's not significant to my practice or plastic surgery. It's a souvenir from home, from New Orleans. Have you been there?"

The woman nodded. "For a bachelorette party last year. It was fun. But—the city's awfully dirty?"

"In the Quarter, sure." She wasn't wrong. Meredith thought of the way the Quarter smelled in the morning, the yeasty fetidness of it, and felt a real pang of homesickness. But she never doubted her decision to move elsewhere after college. In New Orleans, she would forever be "the Duval girl," and she preferred to be Meredith Simpson, old-fashioned as that might seem.

"So you're married?" Meredith asked.

"What? No. Oh, it wasn't my bachelorette party. It was a friend's."

"Do you have a boyfriend?"

"I'm seeing someone, but it's fairly new."

"I hope he hasn't said anything or made any suggestions—" It was something Meredith worried about with her patients, insecure women responding to men's critiques.

"No, he's, um, very complimentary of my figure."

"Look, plastic surgery is complicated. I wouldn't have gone into the field if I didn't love it and believe in it, see it as a force for good. But I consider it my ethical duty to make sure that people really want the procedures they're seeking. And the vibe I'm getting from you is that you're ambivalent. You're young. You seem to have good self-esteem—"

"I try to."

"Great. Go home, sleep on this idea. Sleep on it for at least six months. It's not a small decision."

"But isn't winter the best season to have plastic surgery?"

Ah, another Googler. "There is no best time of year, simply pros and cons, depending on one's lifestyle. With any surgical procedure, there will be pain and recovery. Please promise me you'll think about it"—and then, just when she needed it most, the prospective patient's name came back to her—"Jordan." (Jordan Altman/Jordan

Almonds, that's why her mind had kept circling back to the idea of pale pastels, she was thinking about the candy.) "Would you do that for me? Jordan?" It was hard to keep the note of triumph out of her voice for remembering a name.

"Sure," she said. She didn't even offer to shake hands as she left, but then, Meredith's hands were filthy again.

AMBER STRUGGLED TO braid the three strands of what Betty Crocker had promised would be an "easy" king cake recipe. For all her experience working with Sculpey, she found the task challenging, but she had awakened this morning with the thought that Mardi Gras was here, and she had not yet had a single slice of king cake.

She could have flown back, although her rented bungalow was probably rented to someone else. (Miss Margaret was running a covert Airbnb of sorts in Amber's place, strictly by word of mouth, and the income was enough to cover Amber's rent in both cities.) She knew people who would put her up, couches she could surf. Even Miss Margaret, private as she was, would have gladly given Amber her spare bedroom. But she would pepper Amber with questions about her life in Baltimore, and what would she say? *I saw him, he bought a painting from me . . . and gave it to his wife. Who's beautiful, by the way. Beautiful and accomplished and generous.*

Her finished cake was far from perfect, but it was good enough. Now what? What to do with a cake whose raison d'etre was to be shared? She inserted a plastic baby once it had cooled, put it on a plate, and brought the cake to work. If she had a UPS delivery, she would give the driver a slice, explain the tradition. Maybe she could take slices to the other shop owners and managers in her little strip center, most of whom seemed nice. And she would make a reservation for herself at the French restaurant—no, not a reservation, but she would go to the bar at five, eat dinner there.

The gallery was doing surprisingly well. Funny, what happened when one was freed from need. If she had been counting on the gallery to sustain her, it probably would have been a catastrophe. But between her still-thriving Etsy business and her inheritance, she was without money worries for the first time in her life. She had assumed she would be operating in the red for the first year, but she was on track to break even in six months. It helped, having virtually no expenses. Amber had learned to live on very little years ago, and it was a habit that sustained her.

She left the cake on her desk, in the center of the gallery. She was beginning to organize her next show, which required taking several pieces out of storage. Shipping them would have cost far too much, so she had hired a young man on Miss Margaret's recommendation. He would drive a rented panel truck from New Orleans to Baltimore, then fly home on Southwest. Even at $1,500—the cost of the van, his time, and his one-way ticket—it was a bargain compared to the crating and shipping for six pieces.

Meanwhile, Horace Latham, a local contact, was helping her find more pieces in the mid-Atlantic. He had done time in the penitentiary at Jessup decades ago, when art therapy was common in the Patuxent wing. He was helping her tap into a network of artists throughout the region. Horace was an artist, too, but not a particularly good one, and he knew that about himself. "I'm a connector," he said. With Horace's help and her existing pieces, she would be able to mount an outstanding show.

Amber had been smart about amassing work by past and current inmates, contacting penitentiaries throughout the South over the past decade, chatting up staff and instructors. Older pieces, produced in programs that no longer existed, were more valuable, but through her networking, Amber had found a small group of contemporary artists producing consistently good work. Tricky to obtain, but worth it.

She had one ironclad rule—she would not reveal the circumstances of the artist's sentence, what he or she had done, how long they were serving, if they were, in fact, still serving. To Amber, this was the dividing line between art that happened to be created by the incarcerated and the campy thrill of owning something by a killer. Jodi Arias's "work" was objectively bad; no one would care about it if she hadn't murdered her ex-boyfriend.

No UPS deliveries today. The day was almost gone, and her cake remained intact. What would she be doing in New Orleans right now? She would be wearing a costume, of course, something she had labored on since Christmas. Oh, the year she had been a pineapple, her hair dyed green and sprayed into a stiff geyser on top of her head. Much as she hated crowds, Amber liked to parade on Mardi Gras proper. She wasn't much of a day drinker, but she was sure she would have a mimosa in hand if the weather were fine. She usually stayed out until four or so, then went home and made a game out of fashioning dinner from whatever was in the house, making sure to finish or dispose of whatever king cake was left. And although she kept it secret, she often spent the evening watching the balls, which, in terms of excitement, was maybe one notch above the burning yule log that some local television stations used to show at Christmastime.

Amber was fascinated by the society girls who participated in the old rite and wondered if it would survive much longer. In a world where so much was being questioned—rituals, words, monuments—how long could the Rex and Comus balls continue? Best she could tell, no one had bothered to challenge the tradition. Perhaps it felt insignificant, this implicit bit of Confederacy cosplay, a simple acknowledgment of how things were. New Orleans was *complicated*. Amber had been shocked by Zulu at her first Mardi Gras, the sight of Black people marching in blackface, and some white folks, too, which made her feel even squirmier.

At four thirty, she began slicing the cake, placing it on paper plates leftover from her last opening. She walked them to the hardware store, the florist, and the poke shop, explaining the tradition. Amber had no use for her neighbors on Puritan Street, but it made sense to be friendly with her work neighbors. She was more likely to need them at some point, or to have a moment when it was important that they have warm feelings toward her.

Her neighbors along the strip appreciated her offerings, but she did not dare take cake to the restaurant, of course. Too coals to Newcastle.

*I guess that's coals to Newcastle*, she said when Joe mentioned someone had offered him tickets to an Orioles game, not knowing his father's law firm did work for the team and got free tickets all the time.

*What?*

*Coals to Newcastle. You know, giving someone something they already have in abundance.*

*I've never heard that. I'm not even sure where Newcastle is.*

*England*, she said.

*How do you know stuff like that?*

*I read a lot. I read old books.*

*I read, too*, Joe had said defensively.

*I know. You're really smart. You're just not doing well in French.*

*I'm not doing well in any of my subjects.* Said with a perverse pride, as if Joe was enjoying being bad at something.

She had longed to ask him: *Is it true you have a broken heart? What does it feel like?* Never having been in love, she could not imagine what it was like to be out of love. She knew what songs said about it. But she didn't believe the songs. She wanted to learn about love from someone who had actually experienced it.

All but two slices of her cake distributed, she returned to the gallery. A man was ringing the buzzer. Joe. Had she willed him here with her memories?

"Oh," she said. "Hi."

"I was just in the neighborhood and I thought—my, um, wife, she wanted to know more about the artist. Do you have a brochure or something?"

"I don't think so. I might have a newspaper article in my files, but I didn't bring a lot of archival material when I set up here. It's in storage. Did you try googling Marian Baker's name?"

He smacked his forehead good-naturedly, then made the sign of an *L*. "I couldn't even remember her name."

"Why don't you come in while I look? Meanwhile, let me write the name down for you."

He handed her one of his business cards to jot down the name on the back. She offered him a slice of cake to occupy him while she was in the storeroom. When she returned, empty-handed as she had known she would be, he was holding a neon green baby figurine pinched between his thumb and forefinger.

"So with a king cake—" she began.

"I know," he said. "My wife is from New Orleans. It's on me to give the next party. But I guess that means next Mardi Gras season, right?"

"Your wife is from New Orleans?" she parroted, as if not having gleaned that information long ago. "I moved there in 2009. What part of town?"

"Calhoun, near Audubon Park."

"*Nice.*" She decided not to mention that she had lived not even a mile away by sheer happenstance. Had it been happenstance? Had Joe visited his in-laws, had they passed each other on the street?

"I guess so. It's hard to get to know a place, staying with your in-laws."

That struck her as true and hilarious, and she rewarded Joe with a laugh. And Joe, who was good at so many things, but not particularly funny, looked pleased, as he always had when she laughed at his jokes all those years ago.

"I'm going to stop in at the place on the corner, order an early dinner. You want to have a drink while I'm eating, catch up? I'd love to hear how you're doing. You've clearly got good taste, marrying a New Orleans girl."

The mention of his wife softened the invitation, made it non-threatening, as she had hoped it would. "Only a drink," he said. "I'm expected home for dinner."

They chose seats at the corner of the bar—easier to talk, less intimate than being side by side, leg to leg.

"Look, they have red beans and rice," Joe said. "In honor of Mardi Gras."

"I never ate crab cakes in New Orleans, and I'm not going to have red beans here," Amber said. New Orleans and working at the Upperline had made her serious about food in a way she had never been before. She was no longer the girl who tilted a bag of pizza-flavored Goldfish into her canned soup.

"I'm going to try it. If it's good, I'll get another order to take to Meredith."

So he was solicitous of his wife, maybe even uxorious. She would expect nothing less. Had Joe found a love that rivaled the one that had derailed his young life? Was that even possible, to love as an adult the way you loved as a teenager? People always seemed shocked at how young Romeo and Juliet were, but their ages were what made their story credible to Amber. You loved that way only once. If you were lucky. Or maybe unlucky.

He ordered the beans, while she chose a frisée salad with a poached egg. She drank a glass of white burgundy, he had a vodka martini. They talked about their lives since 1997. He began with Trinity University, meeting his wife. He could not go for more than a sentence or two without invoking his wife. Amber started with Eckerd, the job at the gift shop on Beach Drive, her eventual move to New Orleans, then back to Baltimore. To her ears, she sounded like a stalker, but Joe didn't seem to notice his connection to the places in her life.

"You really loved it there? New Orleans?" he asked. By then their food had arrived, and he dug into the beans with great gusto, despite having eaten all the bread. "It's only a matter of time before a storm succeeds in wiping it off the face of the earth, in my opinion."

"Just makes it all the more precious to me. It's hard for me to imagine leaving."

"Yet you did leave. You're here."

"I had an opportunity. My stepfather died. He left me some money. New Orleans didn't need another gallery, not like mine."

"How's it going?"

"Better than expected—" she began, only to have Joe interrupt: "These are *good*. You have to try them." Without waiting for permission, he slid his spoon into her mouth.

Dammit, they were good, creamy and spicy, with coins of excellent andouille sausage.

"Very good," she conceded. "Mine's better."

"Maybe you'll make it for me—for us, my wife and me— sometime."

"I'd be happy to bring you and your wife my red beans. If she's a true New Orleanian, her contempt is worth more than others' approval."

"Meredith would never criticize anyone's cooking." Joe grinned. "To their face."

"Oh, better still. I shall drop a casserole off at your house and you can bring the dish back to me and report on all the ways I am insufficient."

He was hunched over the small ramekin in which the beans had been served—they were meant more as a side or appetizer than an entrée—shoveling the remainder in. "You've really changed, Amber. In a good way. You've come out of your shell."

"People change a lot in twenty years, even if very little happens to them."

"Meredith knows," he said abruptly. "She's always known, almost from the day we met. I couldn't help myself—I just blurted the whole story out to her."

"Everything?"

"Everything."

Amber wondered if they defined "everything" the same way.

"Do you . . . tell people?" Joe asked.

"When appropriate." She did not bother to add that it had almost never been appropriate. Miss Margaret knew. An occasional man had proved adept enough at googling to find the truth, to unearth the Amber Glass beneath all that amber glass.

"We were good kids," Joe said. "But we were kids."

She knew the right thing was to nod, to accept the bond he was offering, but her mind couldn't help getting stuck on his words. *Kids.* Undeniably. She had been only sixteen, and a young sixteen. Even Joe, at eighteen, had been sheltered. But good? She could never claim she was good, and she envied Joe for being able to see himself that way.

She insisted on paying the check when it came, saying she was the one who had eaten a real meal. As Joe headed to the car with his bag of red beans and rice, she called out to him: "Do you want me to phone or email, if I find more information on the artist?"

He took a business card from his wallet, pressed it into her hand. "Calling or texting is best," he said. "I hate email."

JOE HAD BEEN FaceTiming with his uncle on his office computer when Jordan texted him that she needed to talk. Although he was alone, he turned his cell phone over and set it to silent. He had been avoiding her pretty successfully, with credible stories about work and commitments. He had seen her only once, at that Super Bowl party a few weeks ago, but suddenly she had started texting and calling again, several times a week. He still intended to tell her in person that there could be no relationship between them, but it was hard, figuring out where and when.

No more putting it off. He called her back when his meeting was finished.

"What's up?" he asked, heart in his throat.

"That piece of art you gave me for Christmas? A designer friend saw it and wants to know more about the artist, maybe buy some additional pieces."

He almost blurted out "Really?" then realized that he had pretended to like the piece when he gave it to her. "I don't even remember the name."

"Neither do I. It's unsigned," Jordan said. Was it? He didn't recall that.

"Do you want the gallery's name?" As soon as he made the offer, he realized it was a terrible idea. There was probably no harm in Jordan meeting Amber, but he had told Amber he was buying the painting for his *wife* and he didn't want to give the lie any additional oxygen. "You know what? I'll stop by there, see what they can tell me."

"You're the best," Jordan said. "When am I going to see you again?"

And there it was, and he was still a coward. He hated knowing that about himself. But it was wrong to break up with someone over the phone.

"Let's see what I can find out about your painting, the artist, and take it from there."

He could have called the gallery, of course, but in the back of his mind, he figured he would just wait a few days, do nothing, and then tell Jordan that the gallery hadn't been able to help him. The story wouldn't be credible, but that was to his advantage. Maybe Jordan would finally take the hint.

Yet when he found himself on York Road at day's end, it made sense to swing by the gallery, ask about the artist. *Marian Baker.*

Go figure, he had ended up handing his business card with the artist's name back to Amber when he said goodbye. But he never had a problem remembering names, at least not when he was motivated.

Amber really had changed. This woman was confident; she had a sparkle, whereas teenage Amber should have been in a rom-com about a girl who got a makeover, like that movie *She's All That*, which he had watched uncomfortably with Meredith in a San Antonio movie theater. The premise—popular guy claims he can make any girl popular—had been a little too close for comfort. Teenage Amber was *not* all that, she was never all that, and Joe choosing her as his prom date did not boost her status; it only made him look more desperate about Kaitlyn. It was one thing to turn his tutoring sessions into regular sex; he had no problem telling Zach how he was really progressing in French. But taking Amber to the prom crossed a boundary.

Still, it had seemed a small ask on her part, and he thought it would show Kaitlyn how little she mattered to him. Then he saw Kaitlyn, and then Susannah had to go and tell him that Kaitlyn missed him and—well, what happened, happened. He could never change it. But it was hard to feel bad about sneaking off with Kaitlyn, given the secret that Amber had kept from him.

It was almost eight when he pulled into his driveway, which, like the house itself, was A Little Too Much—and he loved it. Loved the iron gate that slid open so languidly, the heated pavement large enough to hold five cars, the porte cochere. Meredith's car was here, but she had gotten home only five minutes ahead of him. He knew because she had called him while he was in the car, asking what he wanted for dinner, and he told her grandly that he had arranged for dinner, and she would be happily surprised.

She was. Oh, she had some criticisms of the beans and rice, inevitably—"They're a teeny bit too highbrow"—but she ate them happily. And she had thought to order a king cake from Dong Phuong on the West Bank. He didn't really feel like another slice, but how could he explain that he had already had his quota of king cake?

They talked about their days. They understood the ins and outs of each other's jobs and found them genuinely interesting. Meredith could be catty about her clients at times, but she was generally just informational. Today, she was upset at her usual problem with names. "My brain fog has been worse than usual," she said.

"You've always been bad at names," he said.

"I know, but today, I couldn't make sense of my own memory tricks. Like this one patient—well, obviously, I shouldn't tell you her full name, that would be a HIPAA violation, but I told my-self 'movie theater' and then I couldn't remember what that was supposed to trigger. Eventually, I figured out it was one of the concessions, that it not only sounded like her name, but looked like her, too, pretty and pastel. And as she was leaving, it was all I could do not to scream out 'Jordan Almonds!' although her last name isn't Almond, of course, just a near homonym—Joe, what in the world? No, no, don't rub it."

An enormous forkful of king cake had fallen on the journey to Joe's mouth and tumbled down his favorite Ferragamo tie, leaving a trail of cream cheese and glittery sugar. He grabbed a napkin and began rubbing it heedlessly, mindlessly, despite knowing better.

"Give me that," Meredith said, "and let me see if I can rescue it."

*March 11, 2020*

MEREDITH WALKED INTO Wegmans, grabbed a cart, and studied her shopping list, downloaded from a prepper site. She seldom went to Wegmans, in part because of its Hunt Valley location, which felt dauntingly far, although it wasn't even fifteen minutes from her office. The store also was too vast for her comfort; she quickly became overwhelmed. The combination of high-quality goods—the meats! The fish! The cheese! The bakery!—and the abundance of all the usual crap—candy! Cookies! Canned goods!—was too much for her. Wegmans made her feel as if she were unworthy of it, like someone who went to Paris and saw only the Louvre and the Eiffel Tower. She was a Wegmans tourist, a bad one.

Convinced, however, that she needed to lay in at least three months of food and paper goods, she had steeled herself to confront Wegmans today. She clearly wasn't the only person on such a mission, based on the carts piled high with multipacks of toilet paper and paper towels. Meredith had grabbed her paper goods and cleaning supplies at Target yesterday. Today was about food. Food that was shelf stable, or food that could be frozen.

She started with soup. Joe had a fondness for Progresso, a legacy of his latchkey years, when he came home from school and made his own snack. Meredith had tried, without success, to wean him from this taste for salty canned goods, but now she was glad he was easy to please. She loaded a variety into the cart, focusing on the heartier ones—barley, chicken noodle, beef stew. She moved on to beans, even though she was a member of Rancho Gordo, picking up bags of black beans, kidney beans, and the prettiest red lentils. Red beans and rice would be one of their staples. Right, she needed rice, instant and basmati. Egg noodles. Flour. Yeast. Falafel mix—why not? The prepper sites she had consulted had also recommended loading up on salsa, hot sauce, mustard—anything that added flavor. Canned tuna, of course. But other tinned fish, too. Maybe she would finally learn how to make tuna conserva, one of her favorite dishes at Tapas Teatro, the lovely restaurant next to the Charles Theater.

She felt conspicuous in her N95 mask, but so be it. She couldn't risk exposure. "Aren't you overreacting?" Joe had asked her when he saw her heading out this morning. She had flushed with anger, until Joe had laughed and said: "I mean—you don't need to wear it in the car, when you're alone. That's all. I'm glad you're taking precautions."

Thank god they had a standing deep freezer in the basement. She began tossing meat into the cart—hamburger, steaks, ground turkey, sausages, whole chickens, chicken breasts. It was like preparing for a hurricane. No—it was the opposite. With a hurricane, if you stayed, you anticipated losing power; you would never stock your freezer. Meredith had ridden out many storms with her parents where they lived off nothing but gas station snacks and room-temperature booze. Well, she had the snacks, they had the booze.

What was she forgetting? Flour, although that had a shorter shelf life than canned goods. Sugar, brown sugar, even though she seldom baked. Canned chili. Bags of candy, why not? Bottled water, of course. Was she preparing for quarantine or a zombie apocalypse? Were those two things different? All those hours by Joe's side watching *The Walking Dead*. Maybe she should be shopping for a bow and arrow.

She almost started to buy new cookware, then stopped herself. This was another reason she didn't like to shop at Wegmans—too many consumerist sirens encouraging you to dash your shopping cart on rocks filled with things you didn't want or need. Her cookware was fine. She didn't need that twenty-four-piece food storage set, no matter how cunningly the pieces and tops nested and connected.

Life would be simpler if Wegmans sold booze, of course, but Maryland was so backward on that score. Good god, in New Orleans, you could buy perfectly acceptable wine in the Rite Aid, every day of the week. In the Baltimore metropolitan area, there was only one grocery store that Meredith knew of that had a liquor license, and it wasn't allowed to sell on Sundays. That was okay; she would hit up Total Wine in Towson tomorrow. Not that she and Joe drank that much. Not that they cooked or baked or ate that much. But they needed to be prepared. If only she could be sure what they were preparing for.

The bill was over $500, and it took her a long time to unpack once at home, ferrying frozen goods to the basement, converting a closet there to an impromptu overflow pantry. It was oddly pleasing to line up the cans and boxes and bags, taking time to alphabetize the soups. A memory tugged at her about how children loved things in abundance. Or was it the poor?

She stopped, determined to pin down the source. Ah, *A Tree Grows in Brooklyn*, when Frannie—was it Frannie or Francie? Meredith couldn't even remember the names of fictional people— sees the large collection of tightly rolled parasols that a neighbor has won at weekly costume parties that she always attends in a one-sleeved outfit. The one sleeve was to conceal a disfigured arm, burned in a childhood accident, but it was assumed to be symbolic, and that was why she always won. They had read *Tree* in book club; Brynn had slyly stretched the "prize-winning" requirement by arguing that the film version had received two Oscars. It had, although for acting, as it turned out. Meredith didn't care. She loved the book, which she had read in her teens and believed should be considered a classic.

"Don't you think," Wendy had asked at what seemed such a long-ago meeting, although it was only June 2018, "that your affection for the book also has a lot to do with your own situation?"

"What do you mean?" Meredith asked. "I didn't grow up in Brooklyn and I didn't grow up poor. Can't one admire a book without seeing herself in it?"

But, of course, she *did* see herself in Francie, the child of an alcoholic she loved fiercely. The other lesson of *Tree* was that you could be strong and unsentimental and live, or you could be soft and dreamy—and die young. Meredith knew which lane she had chosen.

She flattened her paper bags and put them into the recycling bin. She was ready. Whatever happened, she would be ready. Joe had thought she was overreacting, but he would be grateful for this food, this level of preparedness. The poor may like things in abundance, but, then, so do the rich.

AMBER CHECKED HER watch—almost two! This trip was eating up the entire day. But Horace had been adamant about stopping at the Dairy Queen on Route 50, and Amber was inclined to indulge Horace's whims. He was such a good scout. Amber had met him years ago, when she was in Florida and he was living outside Greenville, South Carolina. They had bonded over their Maryland roots and the other thing they shared, which was how they usually phrased it. "The other thing."

Sweet serendipity, Horace had moved back to Maryland about two years before Amber did. She had reached out to him in an email only to learn he was less than twenty miles away. He brought in some of his own work—fussy toothpick tableaux that were too meticulous for Amber—then told her that he knew other artists in the area. "People like us," he said. "You know." Amber knew. She told him to keep an eye and ear out, and now he was driving her to Belleville, Delaware, to see some sculptures that he refused to describe. "You really gotta see this guy's work to believe it," he said.

Horace cultivated an air of mystery. He even liked to imply that his associations with his former Jessup colleagues involved transactions more nefarious than art, but Amber assumed he was just trying to make himself interesting, as almost everybody did.

She had let him drive her car and she was trying not to fret over his speed as they turned onto the rutted barely-a-road that led to where Everett Hanover lived and worked. Horace, who was almost seventy, could be prickly about instructions of any kind, especially from a woman, even when he was driving that woman's car.

"Oh my god," Amber shouted. "What is THAT?"

Horace chuckled, proud of himself. "I told you. You have to see it for yourself. A photo can't convey how big they are."

That/It was a towering metal sculpture, a scarecrow made of cast-off objects, in the same vein of the "robots" one could find all over Etsy and eBay, but at a scale unlike anything Amber had ever seen. It was a folk-art Ozymandias, at least twelve feet tall, rising out of the sere late-winter landscape. As her eyes adjusted, she saw that there were other figures dotting the fields—one, two, three, four, five in all, utterly distinctive.

"They're *magnificent*," she said. "But how would one show them? Who would have the space to own one?"

"Don't get ahead of yourself," Horace said. "First we have to convince Everett to think about letting go of them at all."

There was no farmhouse on the acreage, only a wheelless mobile home on cinder blocks. The man who greeted them at the door looked like the human kin to his creations—tall, gaunt, full of sharp angles.

"Horace said he knew a woman who would want to meet my family," Everett said without preamble. "I'm not sure why."

"I'm an art dealer," Amber began.

He looked puzzled. "I don't consider them art."

"But that's the thing. You don't have to have formal training to be an artist—"

He held up a hand to quiet her. "I'm not saying that I'm not proud of what I do. I'm saying they're part of me. I can't sell them."

"What about loaning one to a museum?" Amber asked, following him into the trailer without being asked. If she found a way to get a piece in AVAM's courtyard, that would immediately add value. Certain collectors loved to buy things that had been featured in museums. "They're so beautiful. It would be nice if others could see them."

"I didn't make them for others," Everett said. He sat in the middle of a plaid sofa, leaving Amber and Horace to perch on uncomfortable chairs, part of a 1950s-era dinette set. He was not a good host, but, then—they were not invited guests.

"I get that," Amber said. "But that doesn't mean you can't share them with others. Let me ask you this"—the idea was developing as she spoke, there was no delay between her thoughts and her words—"what if we brought people *here*? What if your farm was the exhibit?"

"How would that work?" Everett asked.

She had no idea, only the belief that she could make it work if he said yes.

"I don't know," he said. "My experiences with people—did Horace tell you about me?"

"I know you were at Patuxent. Did Horace tell you about *my* background?"

Now she had his interest. "No."

"When I was sixteen, I gave birth to a baby in a hotel bathroom while attending the prom." Although Amber seldom told this story, she was precise in the details when she did—*The*, not *my*, prom. That was an important distinction to her, one that had often been lost in the media coverage at the time. "The baby died and I accepted a plea deal. I was in a juvenile facility until I was eighteen."

"They say I killed my child," Everett said. "My wife, too. I have no memory of it. All I know is I have no family now."

"So you made one."

"I made one," he agreed. "For me. But I wouldn't want people to know that part."

"Which part?"

"All of it, I guess. Can't I just be a man who builds scarecrows from things I find at the junkyard?"

"Of course you can," Amber said. "But don't you need money?"

"Who doesn't? But these things aren't going to make money."

"You'd be surprised, I think, at what even one of these sculptures might bring in. For now, let's just plan on getting people to see them. There's this concept called 'pop-ups.' Your farm could be a pop-up version of my gallery this summer. People going to and from the beach—they can stop and walk among the fields, admire your creations. If you have a friend who sells produce, they can set up here, too. It could even be a destination unto itself, a day trip from Baltimore and D.C."

"Beach traffic never wants to stop, in my experience, just wants to keep going forward, like a shark. But, okay, maybe. Who knows? Not even clear if the world is going to be here this summer."

"Oh, I don't think things are that bad," Amber said. "They'll get this coronavirus thing under control."

He looked at her, curious. "What's the coronavirus?"

Back on the highway, she said to Horace: "I liked him."

"I knew you would. But he lied to you. He never had a family. Killed three women, women he didn't even know. Prostitutes."

"Sex workers, Horace."

"*Whatever.* Truth be told, I don't even think he was crazy enough to be in Patuxent, he just knew it was to his advantage to fake being psychotic. Good artist, though."

*So he was worse than I was*, Amber thought, then regretted it. But it was a kind of scorekeeping she could never quite stop. Horace had served time for manslaughter, but he was blackout drunk when it happened, so she considered Horace her equivalent. Prom Mom was obviously worse than Cad Dad. Miss Margaret had once shot a man, but he was trying to break into her house. So on and so forth.

They headed west, Amber imagining corn in the desolate fields, people walking among Everett's creations. She would have to find a way to tell his story without revealing his past. Maybe she would borrow his own myth: He lost his family and created a new one. It was true enough, and true enough was a perfectly good standard in art, which still tolerated a certain amount of mythmaking.

She dropped Horace off at his house in Linthicum, then decided to run by the gallery before going home. She found a business card lying on the floor. She recognized it instantly as Joe's, and when she saw what he had written—well, her heart, in full defiance of her head, began to beat double time.

"YOU EVER GO there?" Joe asked his assistant, Bobbie, as they drove past the sign touting "attractions" for MD 272. "Plumpton Park Zoo?"

"Never heard of it," she said.

"I thought you grew up here."

"I grew up in *Maryland*," she said. "My 'here' isn't your 'here.' I'm from Howard County. Did you go to the Howard County Fair when you were a kid?"

"Why would I go to a county fair when the state fair was fifteen minutes from my house?"

"Exactly," Bobbie said. Joe had no idea what she was talking about. Joe frequently had no idea what Bobbie was talking about. They were thirteen years and a galaxy apart.

If the zoo hadn't been in the opposite direction on MD 272, he might have insisted on stopping there. Plumpton Park Zoo wasn't just any small zoo. It was a perfect oasis for little kids, scaled to them, unlike the Baltimore Zoo, and never mind the National. Plumpton Park Zoo had been a sacred place in Joe's childhood. Pop-pop, his father's father, had lived up here in Cecil County and taken him every year until he outgrew it.

"I wonder if zoos will even exist in fifty years," Joe said.

"The planet's not going to exist in fifty years," Bobbie said. "But if it does, it's people who are going to be in zoos."

A lot of his conversations with Bobbie seemed to go this way. Joe definitely felt a generation gap, even more pronounced than the one between him and Jordan, who wasn't that much older than Bobbie. Or maybe it was just that he was continually surprised at how little deference Bobbie paid him. When he was coming up, he dutifully affirmed his bosses' points of view. He could not imagine saying to his uncle Tony, *Your here isn't my here.*

He liked Bobbie, though, despite, or maybe because of her sass. He felt—not fatherly, not brotherly, but sort of uncle-y. He was her uncle Tony, or aspired to be. Despite the circumstances that had led to it, Joe had nothing but fond memories of his gap year in Houston. What he learned in his uncle's office when he was eighteen had been of far more use to him than the four years at Trinity. Not that he ever regretted Trinity, because he had met Meredith there. Still, college was more of a credential than a utility, a conversational lubricant. *Where did you go to school?* Although in Baltimore, when someone asked that, they were curious only about your high school.

Anyway, it was his ongoing desire to impress his uncle that had encouraged him to take the flier on their destination today, Nottingham Ridge, a Class C shopping center in North East. For years, Joe had been pushing to do more local deals. His uncle insisted he didn't see any potential in the mid-Atlantic—too built up, too union friendly. So Joe had decided to find a property on his own and flip it in order to prove to his uncle that the Baltimore office could be a true division of the corporation, not just a nepotistic convenience.

He had snapped up Nottingham Ridge last fall for $3.2 million—ten acres, four stores, one currently vacant, but the anchor, at 27,000 square feet, was a Modell's Sporting Goods, and there also was a freestanding Sizzler. He was meeting today with a local who wanted to put a used bookstore in the smallest space, the one that had housed the old-fashioned candy store that Joe's family had always visited after going to Plumpton Park Zoo. That had been a magical place, full of little barrels of candy, sold by the ounce. It had gone out of business years ago, only to have its business model replicated by a chain that charged an outlandish per-pound price. Scale was everything if you wanted to make money off penny candy.

"God, it feels like forever getting here from the city," Bobbie groused. "How come I can get to the Pennsylvania border in less than forty minutes on I-83, and we've been in the car almost an hour now and we're still in Maryland?"

"People forget how sharply 95 angles to the east. But, again, that's why this is a good investment. People want to shop locally.

They don't want to drive up to Wilmington or over to Newark all the time. Cecil County deserves something special."

"People don't want to drive *anywhere*," Bobbie said. "They want to stay at home and have stuff brought to them."

"Not everything can be delivered."

"Name one thing I can't have sent to my home."

"A haircut."

Bobbie made a rude noise, like a buzzer on a game show. "Sorry, there's an app that lets you book salon appointments in your house."

"Even in Baltimore?"

"Even in Baltimore."

"Sounds like a great idea, opening your door to strangers with scissors."

"Look, when you're used to dating apps, asking a stranger to cut your hair is nothing."

It was a familiar, low-stakes argument for them. Low-stakes for Bobbie, at least. She didn't have $3.2 million invested in a shopping center in a relatively low-density county. She had not sold a substantial chunk of her stock portfolio to underwrite that purchase.

And she had not taken out a second mortgage in order to make an all-cash offer, which was the only way Joe had been able to secure the shopping center at a bargain price. Bobbie didn't even own a house. She lived in an apartment with a month-to-month lease, while trying to pay down her student debt as quickly as possible. "I need to be nimble," she said. But she never said why.

Still, Joe believed in Nottingham Ridge. It had needed a little sprucing up, and he had provided that. He was excited that a local wanted to open a non-chain outlet and was prepared to give the guy a deal on the rent, at least for the first year, and by the second year—well, that would be the new owner's deal to make. He was sure one of the companies that specialized in Class B and Class C centers nationwide would want his new and improved Nottingham, which would, in turn, convince his uncle of the potential a *true* mid-Atlantic office could have. The reports of the shopping center's demise had been greatly exaggerated.

He was surprised that the guy who met him at the store was Indian.

"Joe Simpson," he said, putting his hand out. "But I could have sworn your name was Dave Patterson."

"It is," the man said, offering no explanation for his dark eyes and complexion. Joe knew no one had to explain their origins these days, but it still felt deceptive somehow. North East was a bit of a backwater. People might not want to buy books from someone they suspected was Muslim. God, he hoped the guy wasn't going to specialize in religious texts.

Of course, any kind of bookstore seemed counterintuitive in this day and age—that was where Amazon had started, after all— but a used bookstore that also sold vinyl records could become a destination, he supposed.

They walked through the property one more time. Its last tenant had been a dry cleaner, and there was still a faint chemical whiff. But the walls were freshly painted, the floor refinished, and it stood ready to become the backdrop onto which this guy would project his dream. That's what Joe loved about commercial real estate. It was all about dreams.

"How did you get the idea to open a bookstore?" he asked, simply making conversation.

"Do you know about the Curmudgeon down in Marley Station?

Moved in there in 2015 and it's still going strong, despite the mall's problems. It's a good model. They've focused on history, especially the Civil War. I've been collecting books on World War I and World War II all my life, so that's going to be my core audience."

*If you say so.* But the man's credit checks had come back strong; he had cash reserves. Maybe social media marketing and word of mouth would get him through. The location was convenient to I-95, although not as close to the interchange as Northeast Plaza, which had a fucking Walmart. How it pained Joe that no one could reach his little oasis without driving past that behemoth first.

When they signed the lease, Joe realized his confusion. "Oh, *Dev*," he said, looking at the man's name. "I thought you said 'Dave.'"

"That's how my name is pronounced," he said. "Dave."

Joe almost started to say, *Are you sure?*, then realized how ridiculous he would sound, arguing with a man about his own name. "Anyway, welcome to Nottingham Ridge. I hope you'll be happy here. What are you going to call your bookstore?"

"The Curiosity Shop."

"Inspired by Dickens?"

Dev looked surprised. "Wouldn't have pegged you as a Dickens reader."

"I'm not these days. But I was an honors student once upon a time. I cracked a book or two." Said with friendly self-deprecation, but Joe found himself wondering: *What had happened to that Joe, the one who had read challenging books for pleasure?* He read mostly nonfiction these days, usually about money or markets.

He took one last walk around the property. The lines on the parking lot had been repainted, the lights upgraded. He had calls scheduled with two big firms next week. With the right combination of tenants, a place like this could be a community's heart. Sporting goods, a bookstore, a Sizzler, a Jersey Mike's. He remembered how important the little center on York Avenue was to him as a child, how exciting it was when he was granted permission to walk there for ice cream or meet his friends for duckpins. Sure, you could get everything brought to your door nowadays, but that was no way to live. Malls might be on the way out, but shopping centers still had potential.

The drive home was a slog, the news so dire he turned off NPR south of Aberdeen. He dropped Bobbie at their office in Towson and found himself on York Road. All roads lead to York Road. He decided to stop at the faux Tudor shopping center, telling himself that he wanted to see if he could feel whatever emotions it had stirred in him as a child, a teen. He needed to be reminded that shopping wasn't strictly utilitarian, that it could feel like a journey or a quest.

But what he was really feeling was nostalgia for the boy he had been before Amber Glass tore through his life. Did anyone remember *that* boy? His mother, although she was so disciplined in never referencing the events of his senior year that it felt like a kind of amnesia. Zach, but he was not someone who dwelled on the past. As for Kaitlyn—the suburban matron who had attended the twentieth reunion had seemed like a stranger to Joe; he could barely muster the most basic conversational banter with her.

*Amber. Amber knew me, that me.* He had told Amber things he hadn't told other people. That he thought about joining the Peace Corps. That he still read Green Lantern comics.

He glanced in her windows, but the gallery was dark; she wasn't there. If he could be a friend to her now—wouldn't that be a kind of redemption? Could he rediscover, through Amber, the boy he had been? And if he found him, wouldn't that make it easier for him to be good now? But also, wouldn't he be doing something nice for Amber? A win-win.

He took out his business card and dashed off a quick note: *Never did get those red beans and rice you promised. Scared?* He added a winking smiley face.

*April 5, 2020*

MEREDITH KNEW IT was not supposed to be a competition, finding a place to walk on Sundays, yet their new ritual had already taken on a sense of gamesmanship just three weeks in. This Sunday, it was her turn to choose, and Joe was second-guessing her as they drove to the northwest corner of the city, commenting on the sketchy neighborhoods they passed en route.

"I don't know, Meredith," he said. "There's probably a reason that this park is famous for dead bodies."

"Don't be racist, Joe."

"I'm not a racist."

"I was describing your speech, not your identity. I had a patient who lived over here. You remember—the burn victim."

She could tell Joe did not remember the sweet boy who had

needed multiple surgeries, and whose life had been documented in a moving series in the *Beacon-Light*. Meredith had participated only on background, refusing to be photographed or interviewed on the record. While his family had been happy to waive the child's confidentiality and privacy, Meredith could only remember herself at the same age, dealing with illness, although not disfigured. *Disfigured*. Her mind played with the word, poked at it. Should one say "differently figured"? How was disfigured different from disabled?

It was the third weekend since the governor had issued the stay-at-home advisory. Meredith was uneasy about how things would play out with the virus, and as a cancer survivor, she had to be extra careful. That was part of the reason she couldn't volunteer to help with the rising caseloads, although Joe had urged her to get the antibody test to see if February's flu had been COVID. Reluctantly, she had started shopping online for the fresh food that she hadn't been able to stockpile. She did not like other people picking out her produce, and she missed the serendipitous impulse purchases. Obviously, she wouldn't dream of going to the gym, thank god she had the Peloton.

But other than those accommodations, she didn't mind being at home. True, her income had taken a hit; there wouldn't be a lot of elective surgery in the coming weeks. But she and Joe had a cushion of savings, and she enjoyed having him to herself. She was grateful, however, that their house was large enough to afford them privacy during the day.

Even with a big house and an enormous yard, they needed to get *out*. They had walked last weekend at Lake Roland, formerly Robert E. Lee Park. (Joe groused about what he called the "mania" of renaming, but Meredith thought it was progressive to recognize how harmful these tributes were.) The paths there had been a little crowded for Meredith's liking—everyone was desperate to get out, apparently—so she had done some research online and found this lesser-known, lesser-used trail.

Joe could not conceal his amazement when she parked the car on the side of the once-public road that had been barricaded to traffic. She really had unearthed a wilderness space in the heart of the city. The Gwynns Falls Trail was a decommissioned road, at least through this stretch, pitted but wide, surrounded by trees. Even if they were to see another person, Wetheredsville Road was broad enough to allow them to socially distance.

They walked hand in hand, masks at their chins, but they encountered almost no one beyond an occasional runner or hiker. It was an overcast day, and the light had a gray-green quality. A stream was rushing over rocks at the bottom of a ravine, similar to the pink noise Meredith preferred when trying to sleep, not that it helped. Nothing could help her when her body was determined to be insomniac. That's how it felt, as if her body were a tantrum-ming toddler.

"How long do you think this is going to last?" Joe asked.

"It depends," Meredith said, "on how people behave."

"I think things will be back to normal by July first."

"You do? Why is that?" She couldn't tell if Joe had facts she didn't have or was just being his usual optimistic self.

"The curve is already flattening," he said. "We're not Italy, for god's sake."

"We're also not China or South Korea," Meredith said.

"Goddamn right."

"I mean—in a pandemic, stricter, um, regimes, have an advantage. Our love of personal liberty, the emphasis on states' rights—

it's not like we can build a wall around the states that have laxer rules and keep people out."

"Summer will change everything," Joe said. "I wish you would get the antibody test."

"Why?"

"Well, because I'd like to know. Because if you had it, I probably had it and was asymptomatic, which would be a good thing."

"I'm not going to waste time on a test when—"

They heard a loud crashing noise coming from the woods. Joe hugged Meredith to him, and how she loved him for that instinctive gallantry. Three deer burst onto the old road, not even ten feet from them, and Meredith, to her embarrassment, screamed. The deer ran as if they were being pursued, although nothing followed in their wake. They vanished as quickly as they had appeared, white tails bobbing in the distance. Joe and Meredith had to laugh at their own disproportionate shock and fear.

"I hit a deer with my car once," Joe said. "Did I ever tell you that?"

"No!" Meredith said. Together for more than twenty years and there were still secrets, new stories to share.

"I was driving up to the reservoir. It was a hang, you know, when I was in high school. A place to drink beer, smoke dope, take girls to see the submarine races."

Earnest Meredith needed a moment to decipher *submarine races*, but when she got it, she smiled.

"It was spring, early. On the cool side. The deer were moving, especially at dusk. A huge buck came out of nowhere and I was lucky to be young, lucky my reflexes were good, because I saw him out of the corner of my eye and I braked, so he careened off the driver's side fender—"

"'Careered,' although you probably mean 'carom,'" Meredith said.

"What?"

"Never mind, I'm being pedantic, keep going."

"I mean, if he had gotten a few more inches, he would have come up over the hood, his hooves could have shattered the windshield—it could have been so much worse for, uh, me."

She picked up on his hesitation. He wasn't alone in that car. Gallant Joe. He didn't want Meredith to be jealous of some girl riding in his car almost twenty-five years ago. Was it Kaitlyn? She had finally met the love of Joe's early life at his reunion three years ago, and Meredith had not been impressed. But, if Meredith was honest, that was part of the reason she had encouraged Joe to go, because she suspected that even if Kaitlyn had aged well—she had *not*—it would still dispel whatever lingering memory Joe had of her as his perfect young love. Meredith didn't worry about other women. She worried about the *fantasy* of other women, the imagined perfection of someone out of reach, or merely new. Meredith was everything to Joe, but she could never be new.

"What happened?" Meredith asked.

"The car was drivable, so I went home. My parents didn't believe me at first. Well, my father didn't believe me. He thought I made the whole thing up. My mother had to show him the blood and the hair embedded in the fender—"

He shuddered. Joe couldn't stand the sight of blood. Even a cut finger was too much for him.

"Anyway, my dad insisted that I get in his car and show him where it had happened. Because there would be a deer corpse, right? And when we got there, there was no deer, and my dad was yelling at me, saying I was a liar, and then this hillbilly who lived on the road ambled by and said, 'Don't be mad at your son. If you want some roadkill deer, you gotta move fast up here. Nothing stays on the road for long.' Some Baltimore county redneck probably was eating venison for weeks, thanks to me."

"Don't say 'redneck,'" Meredith said, hugging him to undercut the correction. She understood all the layers of Joe's story—how fraught his relationship with his father had been, which had made his early death, at the age of fifty-five, more painful, not less. She had liked her laconic father-in-law.

Their walk over, they used their phones to find a fun place to eat and landed on a pit beef stand over on Johnnycake Road. "Oh, Jesus, I have to piss," Joe said, so Meredith told him to find a place to relieve himself and waited in line to order. An enormous rat scurried from the restaurant while she was in line, but she wasn't deterred. *Consider it a kind of recommendation*, she told herself. She didn't mention it to Joe, because he had a virulent fear of rodents. Bugs, too. The food, which they ate at home with beer, was outstanding, and she felt justified in her deception by omission.

After lunch, she went to her office and Joe wandered off into some part of the house so they couldn't even hear each other if they shouted. In her head, she heard Joe's mother's frequent complaint: *Why do two* childless *people need such a large house?* Meredith had always detected a note of envy. Parents were supposed to want their children to have a better life, but maybe not-that-much-better. Anyway, she was glad for its spaciousness, happy that they had six bathrooms, that she had an office in the basement.

About three p.m., Joe wandered into her office, where she was scrolling through various plastic surgeons' Instagram accounts; she really needed to up her game on social media. "I'm restless," he said. "I'm going to get a coffee at the Starbucks drive-through, maybe take a drive."

"You'll be up all night," she said, knowing he wouldn't. Joe could down an espresso at ten and go to sleep at eleven. So unfair.

"You want anything?"

She understood that he preferred not to have company on the drive, that he was restless and antsy. Much as she missed her work, Meredith could live inside this cocooned life indefinitely. But it was hell for a sociable soul such as Joe, who loved being around people. "No, I'm good. Enjoy your drive. Dinner at seven?"

"Let me check my calendar and see if I'm free," he said with a smile.

AMBER WAS IN the drive-through line at the Starbucks on York Road when she saw what she now recognized as Joe's Range Rover two cars behind her. It was a hard car to miss, once you knew to look for it—and she realized she had been looking for it everywhere. Dark green, with showy silver trim, and that dumb vanity plate. On impulse, when she paid for her order, she said to the barista: "See that green Range Rover two cars back? I want to pay for his order, too." She then took her milky latte and pulled into one of the parking spots, curious to see what Joe would do.

A few minutes later, he backed into the space next to hers, then motioned that she should roll down her window.

"Not exactly six feet," she said.

"Call me," he said. "I gave you my number. Do you still have my card?"

She had both his cards: the one he had given her when he stopped by to find out Marian Baker's name and the one he had slipped under her door almost a month ago. They were side by side in her wallet. And she had entered his number in her phone the night he gave her his card for the first time, listing the contact as

JS. But she shook her head. Let him wonder if she had even seen the note about the red beans and rice. Smiley face indeed.

"This is fine, I think. Sitting like this," she said. "Although I've started wearing masks when I shop. Better safe than sorry, right?"

He sipped the coffee, the coffee she had bought him. "Here's the thing. I think my wife had it, back in February. She had a flu unlike anything I've ever seen, and I'm used to Meredith getting sick. If she had it and I didn't get it—I was either asymptomatic or I'm immune."

She couldn't decide how she felt about this information. Was it a flaw in the otherwise perfect Meredith, or something that made Joe love her more? It was Amber's observation that men liked women who needed to be cared for. And maybe that was part of the reason she never lasted long with any man, because she had, by necessity, learned to take care of herself when she was still a teenager.

"Is that even possible?"

"Who knows? No one knows anything." He pointed to the mask at his chin. "But I do this for her, because she's a doctor and she's worried."

"Even when you're driving?"

"Oh, I'm headed to—an appointment."

"Are you still meeting face-to-face with people?"

A long, contemplative sip of coffee. "We're still winding down a few deals, and some things have to be done in person. In fact"—he glanced at his watch—"I'm going to be late if I don't get moving. Nice of you to buy me a coffee. I'll have to return the favor one day. I've become pretty dependent on this drive-through. The stuff we brew at home doesn't cut it. I head over here every morning, first thing, about eight."

"But it's not—I mean, you don't still live near here, do you? In Stoneleigh?"

"No. I could never talk Meredith into that." He grinned. When Joe smiled, he reminded her of the sunny, lovely boy she had known in high school. "Do you live around here?"

And although she hated people who didn't answer questions directly, Amber wasn't ready for Joe to know where she lived. She would not make the mistake of revealing too much about herself to him. Not again.

She said: "Even though I can't keep the gallery open, I still visit it every day. Art gets sad if people don't look at it."

"*What?*"

"It's true. You know the thing about whether a tree falling in the forest makes a noise if no one's there? Well, unseen art isn't art. So I visit my gallery. I have a particularly great show up." She paused. "It's art by incarcerated people."

"What, like sketches by Ted Bundy?"

"No, no one famous. And I never share the stories of their crimes. They're artists who happen to be in prison. Their crimes don't define them."

An awkward silence, or maybe it was just silence and she was reading too much into it. "Gotta go," he repeated. "Maybe I'll see you on the other side of this thing, come summer."

"You think it will be over by then?"

"Early July. Count on it."

On her way home, she stopped at the Wine Source in Hampden. She was too lazy to grocery shop today, but she could cobble dinner together from the food they sold in the little gourmet shop—jamón ibérico, fresh bread, cheese, olives. As for wine, she decided a tempranillo was the only sensible accompaniment to jamón ibérico.

In the aisle dedicated to Italian and Spanish wines, she recognized Zach immediately. He was studying a shelf of Italian reds, indifferent to how much space he was taking up. Just look at how he was standing, how oblivious he was that people could barely get by him, that someone else might want to buy a Nebbiolo on this cool spring Sunday.

Emboldened by her mask, and her belief that Zach wouldn't recognize her even if he could see her entire face, she edged past him and then, from a distance of six feet, which put her within reach of the Spanish reds, turned back and said, "Zach Trowbridge?"

"Yeah?" He didn't turn his head and there was a wariness in his greeting, as if he had reason to believe that not everyone was glad to see him.

"We were at Towson High School together." That earned her a blank stare. Oh, how wonderful. "I'm a couple of years younger."

All true. Two years younger, although only one year behind him.

"It was a big school," he said. There was no note of apology in his voice. Unlike Joe, Zach had never been known for niceness. She remembered him at Baskin-Robbins, drawing out the *cherry* in Cherries Jubilee and studying her chest, while Joe looked pained and uncomfortable.

"It sure was. I bet this happens to you a lot—people remembering you, and you don't have a clue who they are."

"Well, the ads—"

"Ads?"

"Before I sold my law firm, I did my own television ads. People love to quote them back to me." He managed the trick of looking sheepish and angry at the same time. What a jerk. Of course, she had spent only one evening in his company, and, given how it had ended, she had not dwelled too much on his behavior at dinner and the dance. But she never doubted that he was a prick then, and she was sure he was a prick now.

"What kind of law firm?"

"Personal injury."

"Wish I'd known," she said. "I could have used you. I do not lack for personal injuries."

He looked confused. "I'm still an attorney. My firm's just part of a larger one now. What was the nature of your personal injury?"

*You should know. You were there.* "Oh, it's ancient history at this point. All's well that ends well." She wished she had a third cliché to complete the hat trick.

He was frankly studying her now, which she enjoyed. Amber dressed up even for basic errands. Miss Margaret always said a gallery owner should be a walking advertisement for her gallery. Amber tried to look put-together, deliberate, wherever she went. For a Sunday afternoon trip to her gallery, she was wearing velvet leggings with flats, a body-hugging black sweater, and a patterned denim jacket, bold black flowers on a white background.

"Did we run in the same circles in high school?"

"Oh, no." Again, true. Zach may have been Joe's best friend, but Amber and Joe had been their own circle. Can two points make up a circle? "This has to be a secret," Joe would say when he took her by the hand and led her to his bed. "They won't let you tutor me anymore if they find out what we're doing, and I need your tutoring." At the time, she would have sworn Joe said, *If they find out we're in love,* but she accepted now that Joe had never said those words. Even when he sent off his college applications and he no longer needed her help, he said it still had to be a secret. *My mom's a snob, Amber. She likes you okay, but if we were boyfriend and girlfriend, she would object. Besides, I'm going away next fall. We don't want to get too serious.*

Amber couldn't help being serious, though. That was her problem, then and now. She was serious.

Zach said: "I'm sorry, I didn't catch your name."

"I didn't give it."

She let the silence between them build, maintaining eye contact. She could lie and he would never know. She could tell the truth and it would be meaningless. He did not know her. It was never her name that people remembered.

He grabbed a bottle that someone on the staff had labeled a "No-Brainer." "Well, nice running into you—"

"You were friends with Joe Simpson, right?"

"Joe?"

"Joe Simpson."

"Yeah, I know Joe. We hang out." *Hang out*, as if they were teenagers still.

"He's really changed, don't you think? Since high school?"

Zach was studying her face now, and she was grateful for the mask. True, her eyes, her namesake eyes, could have given her away, but she bet Zach had never paid any attention to her eyes.

"Look, my wife's waiting, we're having a barbecue—"

"A little chilly. But then, it's been such a cool spring. What a year."

"Yeah. Anyway—"

"I just had coffee with Joe. He seems to be doing well. Maybe we should all get together, talk about old times? Are you in touch with Susannah?"

He knew then. He began backing away from her, but his path wasn't straight and he bumped into the endcap of rosés, almost knocking a few from the shelf. He turned and disappeared around the corner. She continued to shop placidly, settling on a bottle of tempranillo. Like the one that Zach had chosen, this, too, was considered a no-brainer.

"WHY ARE YOU wearing *that*?" Jordan demanded when Joe arrived at the model home.

"What—oh." He removed the mask that was dangling from one ear. "I wore it to use at the drive-through, didn't even remember I still had it on."

"On your way here?" She seemed hurt, as if his decision to grab a quick latte at a Starbucks was a betrayal.

"I was just killing time. You said four. I didn't want to beat you here and then have to sit in the driveway. That would have looked suspicious."

Assured, she kissed him. "I think everyone's overreacting. It's like the flu."

"I don't know," he said. "Meredith says—"

"Meredith. Did *she* tell you to wear a mask?"

"Jordan, she has comorbidities."

He felt a little fake, using that word, which he hadn't even known a month ago. He did think people were overreacting, but given Meredith's past, he was inclined to appease her on this score. Meredith wasn't scared of dying. She was scared of getting really sick, being a burden to anyone. She didn't want to get the antibody test because she didn't want to know that she hadn't had COVID; she wanted to believe that she had faced it down and kicked its ass. The funny thing is, he would kill to have Meredith be just a little more dependent on him. To let him provide for her.

"I don't think I knew that. Is she a diabetic or something?"

"She survived childhood leukemia."

"Oh goodness, that's like forty years ago."

"More like thirty, Jordan. She was ten."

"Why did I think she was so much older than you?"

"I don't know. We're the same age, but she was a year ahead of me at college, because I deferred a year." It was not the first time he had alluded to his delayed college attendance—and it was not the first time Jordan had failed to ask a follow-up question. Which he used to think was for the best. He didn't want to talk about why he put off college for a year. Still, her incuriosity irked him.

Although, come to think of it, he didn't ask her a lot of questions, either.

"Do you want anything to eat or drink or—"

He did, actually. He was ravenous and hopeful that she had brought food, as she often did. But given that she had been hurt about a cup of coffee, he wasn't going to make the mistake of admitting his hunger. He was supposed to be hungry for her. Not that long ago, he had been. "That can wait," he said.

She led him to the owner's suite, the first place they ever had sex. Well, actually, they had been in the en suite bathroom. What a revelation she had been, at once wild and vulnerable. That first time had been fast and dirty, completely outlaw. That had been the attraction. But today Joe would be tender, romantic, even. He was going to leave her with a lovely memory because this was over, truly. Finally. Coronavirus, however serious or not, was an ideal reason to end an affair. He would tell her that they had to stop seeing each other for health reasons, Meredith's in particular. By the time this was over, she'd have moved on.

Today, when they were done, she curled into his side. "I feel so close you."

"To quote Groucho, if I were any closer, I'd be behind you." Meredith had taught him to love the Marx Brothers. He felt a pang. He owed Meredith everything. Thank god he wasn't going to do this anymore. Not just Jordan. No more extracurricular sex whatsoever, never again. It was never too late to start being good.

"Silly." She gave his forehead a fake swat. "I mean that even though we don't spend that much time together, I feel really bonded to you."

"That's the oxytocin talking."

"What?"

"It's a hormone. The theory is that it facilitates bonding, makes women less likely to stray."

"You know the wildest things," Jordan said, her eyes shining with admiration. "How do you know these things?"

"I read a lot." Meredith had told him about oxytocin, early in their relationship, lying in bed, wrapped around each other. They still had sex, good sex, Joe and Meredith. Not as often as he would like, but still plenty and still quite good. His only complaint was that sex never seemed particularly *urgent* to her. She knew it was important and she was attentive to it, but sometimes he felt like part of her routine, another piece of exercise equipment, like the Peloton she had given him for Christmas and now used as often as he did. He imagined Meredith keeping a log of metrics for each of their "sessions." Energy burned, calories burned, whether she had achieved a personal best.

He felt a wave of tenderness for this young woman next to

him. They were not even a decade apart, but the age difference seemed enormous to him. It was 20 percent of his life, 25 percent of hers. They were, he believed, different generations, but maybe not. They *felt* like different generations, but that could be the difference between a man who married his college sweetheart at twenty-five and was now forty and a woman who had just turned thirty-two—oh, fuck, he had not given her anything for her birthday. But that was okay; that was preferable, in fact. It established that he was not serious about her.

He was not serious about her.

And then, as if she could read his mind: "I love you."

Fuck. No. How to play it? Funny. Keep it light. "No, you don't."

"I think I do?"

"Again—oxytocin. It's probably evolutionary. The sex is really good. Your body—your mind—is trying to make sense of it."

"Are you saying"—he could tell she was trying not to cry—"that you don't care about me?"

"Of course I care for you. You're amazing. A man would have to be crazy not to care about you. But I'm married. I never withheld that information. I"—why was it so hard to say?—"I love my wife. She knows me as no one else does. I would never leave her. I was clear about that from the start."

He did not add: *You only got me back out here by freaking me the fuck out with that visit to her at work.*

He could almost feel the calculations thrumming through her body—*give this, take that, settle for this.* God, her body. It was exquisite, a Barbie doll body, and every inch of it natural.

"I do love you. And I don't think I would feel that way if I didn't believe you loved me, too."

*If only you could. If you really knew me, you wouldn't stay. No one could love me. Only Meredith.* That was why she was extraordinary. He loved her for knowing him, but it frightened him, too. Meredith's love for him was so unconditional that it felt like a condition. Was that even possible?

*It's a paradox, Joe.* A young, high voice, speaking to him from the past. Dust motes floating in the air of his bedroom, dim in the afternoon light. *Let me try to explain it again*—silencing that voice by putting his mouth on hers, tired and bored of lessons, eager to be the expert, only to be amazed, again and again, by what *that* girl knew via sheer instinct.

"I don't know when I can see you again," he said. "This thing, this coronavirus—my wife's comorbidities. It might be summer before it's safe. I can't see you anymore, Jordan. It's not right."

"It's just a flu," she said.

"Probably," he said. "But I can't risk her health, Jordan. I mean—if anything happened to Meredith because I was doing something I shouldn't—"

He listened to his own words. *If anything happened to Meredith because I was doing something I shouldn't.* For more than a year now, he had risked just that. Meredith probably could handle his infidelity. But she would be hurt because they were both so invested in the idea of Joe not making mistakes anymore. Meredith wanted Joe to be good for his own sake. He was happier when he was good. He was, he was.

"We'll talk, right? We'll touch base. Maybe go for walks?"

"Sure," he said, although they had never done any of those things and he knew they never would and assumed she did, too. Jordan would continue to call and text him for a little while, but only to save face. She would learn to accept that he could no longer see her. He was working at home now, and Meredith's practice was closed for the foreseeable future. Every time Jordan reached out, he would be a little slower in replying, citing the circumstances, and he would make sure that his messages were bloodless, without a scintilla of flirtation. By the time life was back to normal—July? August at the latest?—she would have moved on. She was young, in search of excitement.

That night, he wrapped himself around Meredith. He didn't need sex, but she seemed to assume he did, and that was fine. Thank god he could perform after the exertions of the afternoon. Here was the love of his life. *His life.* She had saved him, but he had saved her, too. Those who had known Meredith in her youth couldn't stop treating her as if she might break. Yet she was strong enough to be with him. She knew everything about him and accepted him as he was. He did the same for her.

Meredith took his face in her hands. "Where are you? You seem so far away."

"Here," he said. "I'm here, love. Forever and always."

*May 1997*

# THE LIMO

CHARLEY COULD TELL right away that these were going to be good ones, parents *and* kids. The dad and the son came out to see the limo, go over the fees and the rules. The kid was bright-eyed, clearly an athlete, but he wasn't a jerk or two-faced. The father looked like the dad in an insurance commercial—calm, kind, gray at the temples, just enough wrinkles to look wise. This wouldn't be one of the dads who carried a cooler out to the car at the last minute and tried to sweet-talk Charley into turning a blind eye. This kid would respect the limo.

On prom night, there were only two couples, which simplified things, but the boy was adamant that he didn't want to do a group pickup, everybody at one house. In fact, he asked for something odd—could Charley pick him up, solo, take him to his date's house, then pick up the second couple at that girl's house. The company had a firm limit of three on pickups and encouraged prom-goers to meet at one house. But Charley couldn't remember an arrangement quite like this. The first boy's parents wouldn't be able to take any photographs except of their own son, tall and handsome in a tux. They seemed okay with that. The mom shot almost an entire roll of film while the boy looked increasingly uncomfortable. Solo photos of boys—that was unusual in Charley's experience.

Once in the limo, he kept the partition down—another sign of a good kid—and said, "It's not very far, Mr. Fuller."

"You can call me Charley if I can call you Joe, Mr. Simpson."

"Sure—Charley." He didn't seem all that enthusiastic about the night. When they got to the girl's house on Regester, with that freak show of a front yard, he seemed desperate to rush through the photos. There almost weren't any photos, in fact; the girl's father had to remind her mother to take photos. "With what?" she said. "You know I don't have a camera." But she scavenged around and came up with a dusty disposable, possibly a souvenir from a wedding or a birthday.

Charley quickly figured out that this was one of those just-friends dates, but the second couple highlighted how platonic the first one was. Another athlete, dark-haired and slim—lacrosse or soccer or baseball, no football for these two—and his date was so gorgeous that it made Charley uncomfortable. A grown man should be able to look at a teenage girl without feeling like a pervert. Still, what a contrast. It wasn't that the first girl wasn't pretty, but her dress was loose and long, her makeup and hair subdued. This girl looked like she was going to the Oscars. Slinky dress with a plunging neckline, blonde curls piled on top of her head. The second they were in the car, her boyfriend was cuddling her, cozying up to her, even as she said, "Stop, Zach, you'll smudge my lipstick."

Their prom was at the Towson Sheraton, where they also had rooms for the night, one for the boys, one for the girls. Allegedly. The sleeping arrangements were none of Charley's business. The plan was to have the dinner and dance at the hotel, then go to a downtown club that was offering a booze-free after-party. The boys had parked their cars at the hotel earlier that day, so Charley would bring them back here at four and be off the clock.

The hours during the dance itself were the best time to nap, maybe talk to the drivers he knew. The chaperones were watching the doors, making sure no one tried to sneak out to the limos or their personal cars. That would happen later, downtown. Charley had no doubt that the dark-haired boy and the hot one would ask if they could sit in the car for a while. By then, she wouldn't be so worried about her makeup.

When the dance ended at eleven, only three kids got into the limo.

"Where's your date, Joe?"

"She got sick, Charley. She said it was the dinner, but we all ate the same thing and we're fine. Crab ravioli. She went up to the room and never came back down."

"Did you check on her?"

"I knocked on the door, but she said to go on without her. She's so sick, she doesn't want to be too far away from a bathroom."

Charley took them to the club, which was near the Inner Harbor. May was a wild card in Baltimore, but this night had turned out perfect, balmy with a pleasant breeze off the water. Charley was old enough to remember when McCormick's had been downtown and you could smell cinnamon in the air. Now even the spice factory had decamped for the suburbs. You couldn't pay Charley to live in the city, although he had grown up in Remington. Dirt, crime—he was very happy to be out in Perry Hall.

About three a.m., a couple approached, but it wasn't the dark-haired boy and his date. It was Joe with a pretty little blonde.

"This is Kaitlyn, Charley. She's an old friend and we have a lot to catch up on and it's so noisy in there. Is it okay if we sit in the limo for a bit?"

"Fine, Joe." He walked a little ways from the car, kept his eyes on the harbor, gave them their privacy. They wouldn't be let back into the after-party once they had left, but it was almost over anyway. Joe walked the girl back to the club, though. He was a gentleman that way.

In the limo en route to the hotel, the kids drowsy and quiet, the inevitable letdown settling in, Charley heard Joe say to the couple, "You know what? I don't feel so good, either."

"The curse of the crab ravioli," the other boy said. Charley heard a funny little sound, a snore, and figured the girl had fallen asleep.

"Two people puking in the same room, that will be fun."

Charley decided to join in. "Remember, if you puke in the limo, you pay the cleaning fee!" They laughed and Charley was glad they realized he was joking.

A 20 percent gratuity was included in the rate, but these boys had parents who knew how things were done, made sure they tipped on top of it. $100, pretty nice.

"See you at the reservoir?" the girl asked Joe, yawning.

"I don't know," he said, clutching his stomach. "Let me see how I feel."

Charley watched the trio walk toward the hotel. The girl had taken off her high heels, and they dangled from her hand while she leaned on her date. He assumed it was alcohol, not crab ravioli, that was affecting all their gaits, but they hadn't consumed it in his car, which was all that mattered to him. He didn't want to be young again, not really, but he didn't think youth was wasted on the young. These were good kids, and nothing he read about them after that night would change his mind.

*May 9, 2020*

**THE PING OF** her phone woke Meredith at six a.m. A text from WA, Wendy Asher.

Charmin and Bounty back in stock at the Canton Target as of last night. Limit 1 to a customer. BUT—if you go to Harris Teeter in the same parking center, they also have limited supplies. Both open by 7 a.m. Remember the electronics dept. hack.

Meredith slid from bed as quietly as possible, not wanting to disturb Joe. In her dressing room, she pulled on her version of pandemic comfort—Everlane cashmere sweatpants, Athleta sports bra layered under an oversized white shirt, an Everlane hoodie over the shirt. But when she stepped outside, she was shocked to realize how cold this May morning was. She had to return to the house for her peacoat.

The roads were empty, and not just Saturday empty—almost Christmas empty. She would reach the shopping center well before the stores even opened. "Siri," she instructed her phone, "find a Starbucks near me with a drive-through." It sent her to the one on York Road, near Joe's childhood home. She got a venti black coffee and finished it in the Canton Crossing parking lot, waiting for the store to open. At least twenty other cars were there as well. Was everyone on the hunt for toilet paper and paper towels? Or was a Target run simply one of the few things to do as the stay-at-home advisory and this strangely cold spring dragged on?

She was the third person through the door when Target opened, but the store filled up quickly. She decided it was best to seem nonchalant about her goal, as if that would be to her advantage, as if the paper products would be impressed by her studied indifference. She detoured through the home goods, where she enjoyed sneering at the products offered through that HGTV family's brand, checked out wrapping paper, picked up some Bliss face masks.

Only then did she allow herself to push her almost empty cart toward the corner where household paper products were kept. The shelves had clearly been restocked last night, as Wendy's intel had indicated; there were no gaps at all. She calculated which large pack yielded the most paper, took her allotment of one each. There were only two cashiers on duty, and the lines at checkout were already all the way back into women's clothing. Not the longest she had seen, but nettlesome. She headed to the back of the store, to electronics, picked up a charger—one could always use another charger—and checked out with the clerk there.

"I see you know the secret, too," a dark-haired man behind her in line said conspiratorially, brandishing his own charger. She winked, meaning it to be jovial, nothing more. The man's eyes quickly went to her hands, covered in fingerless gloves, presumably scanning for a ring.

"It feels like cheating, doesn't it?" he continued. She didn't find his choice of words coincidental. Who did this? Who cruised a strange woman buying toilet paper at Target at seven a.m. on a Saturday? Meredith took no pleasure in this kind of attention. In fact, she found it offensive. She turned her back on the handsome stranger.

Rinse, lather, repeat at Harris Teeter, only she went straight to the paper goods aisle and there was no secret checkout section, no flirtatious man. Now she had two large packs of paper towels and toilet paper to add to her cache in the basement.

The funny thing was—Meredith had yet to experience a true shortage of anything. Once, only once, she couldn't find her favorite brand of dishwashing capsules, but that was it. She had seen empty spaces where yeast had once been, but that didn't bother her, because Meredith seldom baked. Yet whenever someone in her group chat shared a tip about paper towels or toilet paper, she practically salivated. Pavlov's housewife.

Back home, her latest bounty of Bounty stowed, she realized it wasn't even nine o'clock. She stripped down to her sports bra and her leggings, got on Joe's Peloton. Oh, that was something else she couldn't get—an actual bike! She was on a waiting list at two different stores and kept searching for used ones online. It was an unfamiliar sensation to Meredith, not being able to jump the line when she really wanted something.

She stacked her Peloton rides—30–15–5. She already had 180 rides, but she didn't approve of the credit she got for the 5-minute cooldowns. It felt like cheating.

*Cheating.* She thought again about the man at Target. What made him think she was available? She supposed she should be flattered, but she was anything but.

IF ONLY I *could play golf.*

It was, if not the first thing Joe thought when he had awakened alone on an unseasonably cold Saturday in May, pretty close to it. The idea shocked him. Nothing would make Meredith angrier than Joe embracing golf. He honestly believed she would be more likely to forgive infidelity than golf. People thought she was joking when she said she hated golf, that she had forbidden Joe from ever taking up the sport, that it was her one dealbreaker.

She meant every word of it.

He had never minded before, but he felt an idle yearning for it now. At least golf would be a reason to leave the house, to move with purpose. The day was too cold for tennis, but golf would have been possible. God, he needed to get out more. Their weekend walks weren't enough for him, and, although he didn't want to tell Meredith, he *loathed* the Peloton. He used it just enough to make her happy, but he also resumed running outside, saying he did it for the vitamin D. That was good for only thirty minutes or so. He needed to *do things*, to be around people.

Their Sunday walks were sweet, truly, especially the way they kept trying to surprise each other with new locations. Tomorrow, he was going to take Meredith to a park in the shadow of I-95 on the south side, Al Kaline Field, named for the Detroit Tiger all-star who had grown up in the neighborhood. They could make a loop around the field, then continue south to Covington Park, cross under the Hanover Street Bridge, walk down toward the Sagamore

Distillery. It wasn't open for visitors right now, but it's not like Joe wanted to visit a distillery on a Sunday morning.

Tomorrow also was Mother's Day, Joe reminded himself. They would make dutiful calls to their respective moms, and Joe would leave flowers on his mother's doorstep, maybe yell-talk to her from the end of the walk. His mom was in her seventies. He couldn't risk being in her house.

Meredith was always strangely touchy on Mother's Day, given that it was her choice—their choice—not to have kids. The holiday annoyed her. "People want too much credit for reproducing," she had said to him more than once.

Joe didn't necessarily see it that way, but he had never regretted their agreement to stay childless. Joe didn't want to be a father. Technically, had he been a father? He thought about that from time to time. Did impregnating someone make you a father, or was that something you became during a child's life? Did you have to show up to be a father, toss a ball, attend activities, coach Little League?

By that standard, his own workaholic dad hadn't been much of a father. And since his father's death, Joe had grown even closer to Uncle Tony, worked so hard to impress him. How that year in Texas in his uncle's house had changed his life. He had fallen in love with Texas, which led to enrolling at Trinity in San Antonio and falling in love with Meredith—who had brought him back to Baltimore.

Life is funny. He said the words out loud to fill the overwhelming silence of the day.

"What's that, honey?" Meredith said, coming into the room, sweaty and salty from her workout.

"Just thinking about the circumstances that led me to meeting you."

"Oh, that party we had for incoming freshmen, where your roommate spilled punch on me."

"Sure," he said. Then: "Come here."

"Oh, no, Joe, I'm so sweaty and gross—"

"I like it." He did.

"Let me shower—"

"Only if I can shower with you."

"I guess I can allow that."

The shower was huge and, in Joe's opinion, made for sex. Sometimes, he felt that the entire house had a vibe to it, as if the previous owners had designed it so they had lots of places to fuck, inside and out. The shower had two showerheads, positioned so two people could be entwined, yet still receive the full force of the spray.

Two people. *Such a big house for just the two of you.* Two people. *You're never going to have children?* It was just going to be the two of them, until—when? One thing to find one's one and only, another thing altogether to be confined for an indefinable time with one's one and only.

"What are we going to do today?" Meredith asked.

What indeed. Saturday stretched before them, cold and stark. They walked on Sundays. Then, in the afternoons, he met up with Amber at Starbucks. He did not realize until this moment that the Sunday coffee with Amber had, like the walk, become a weekly ritual—one he increasingly looked forward to. For a space of no more than an hour, sitting inside his own car, talking on his phone, he was his seventeen-year-old self again. It made no sense, but Amber was the only person who allowed him to forget what had happened. She, too, wanted to be who she was *before*. On their phones, stealing glances at each other—they were now what they had never been, two teenage friends, lying on their beds, talking on their phones about everything and nothing.

Why couldn't two friends drink coffee on a *Saturday* afternoon? Especially the coldest May Saturday in history?

He just needed to move, go somewhere, anywhere.

THIRTY-TWO DEGREES ON the second Saturday of May. Amber, in a fit of homesickness, called Miss Margaret and asked her about the weather in New Orleans.

"Is Baltimore making you boring?" she replied. "If I want people to ask me about the weather, I'll go to Ralphs and look for the dullest clerk, stand in his line."

"There's a record cold snap here," Amber said. "I'm not used to wearing a coat in May."

"Do you have plans for today?"

"Not exactly."

"What does that mean?"

"I'll go to the gallery. I usually do, on weekends. Even if I can't open, I like to be there, turn the lights on, sit behind my desk. I've ended up selling a piece or two to people who stop and window shop, then get in touch with me via my Instagram."

"You can't open?"

"No, we're under a stay-at-home advisory for now, but Virginia has already lifted its restrictions on retail, so I think it's only a matter of time before we do as well."

Miss Margaret made a harrumphing noise, but it was hard for Amber to figure out if she disapproved of Maryland being closed or Virginia being open. Louisiana had looser regulations than either state. It also had a much higher positivity rate. In hindsight, Amber was glad she had missed Mardi Gras this year. What a petri dish that must have been.

"Is your Joe one of your window shoppers?"

"Not *my* Joe," she said, glad that Miss Margaret was someone who would never FaceTime, or she would have noticed Amber's reddening cheeks. She tried to keep her voice steady, in its usual register. "He's married, I told you. Happily, to all appearances."

"Happiness," Miss Margaret said, "is generally an appearance. But you see him? You talk to him?"

"We've been having coffee together."

"How does that work?"

"We go to a Starbucks with a drive-through, get our drinks, and then park our cars side by side, talk on our phones. It's right across from the gallery."

Another undecipherable grunt from Miss Margaret.

"He's nice, Miss M."

"So you're saying he's changed?"

"No, he was always nice, actually. That's the thing—he was always nice."

*Does this mean I'm your girlfriend?* she had asked Joe the third time they had sex. She had bled the first time, which had freaked Joe out, although he'd had the foresight to put a towel on his bed. He had asked Amber to take it with her, folded up in her backpack. She brought it back, freshly laundered—*and he had sniffed it.* As if he were afraid of some phantom scent remaining behind.

"I'm not ready for another girlfriend," Joe told her, not unkindly. He was honest with her from the start. "I need to go slowly. Kaitlyn really did a number on me."

"That's okay," she said. "I don't need to be your girlfriend. But what should we call this?"

"Our secret," Joe said.

She assumed he would fall in love with her, eventually. How could he not? She was so willing, so available. And not only in terms of her body. She never criticized Joe. Even during their tutoring sessions, when she had to correct him, she did it as gently as possible. She helped him with his college applications. "Is Eckerd your first choice?" she asked. "No, that's more of my safety. But if I get into Michigan, my mom's going to push me to go there." She researched all the schools to which he applied, confident that she could get in anywhere Joe did. She had better grades and a more-rounded list of extracurriculars, although she didn't play a sport. Money was her only problem.

But once Joe's applications were submitted and the first semester was behind them, his grade in French secure, they no longer had a reason to be together. She kept waiting for him to miss her. He didn't take up with anyone else, she noticed. He had told her the truth. He wasn't ready for a girlfriend. Poor Joe.

*Poor Joe.*

It was late April, twenty-three years ago, that he saw her walking down York Road and fell in step beside her. He asked if she wanted to stop by his house. She did and she didn't. Aware of the weight she had gained, she managed to keep most of her clothes on, then, just as he was about to enter her, she rolled away from him and said: "If we're going to do this, I think you should take me to prom."

"Jesus, Amber—"

"Have you asked anyone else?"

"No, but—"

"Ask me. Ask me and—" She tentatively put her mouth on him. His ex didn't do that, either. Joe had mentioned this a time or two. She stayed there, became bolder, then pulled away again. He had always needed her. But that had never been acknowledged.

"Amber—"

"It doesn't have to mean anything, Joe. But I want to go, and you don't have a date."

"Yes," he said. She returned her mouth to him. "Yes, yes, YES."

He was a good person. He didn't renege on the promise she had extracted from him under duress. No one would have faulted him for changing his mind. But he didn't change his mind, and that had to mean something. He rented a tux, he picked her up at her house, he brought her a beautiful wrist corsage. *Ranunculus.* He was the one who told her to bring an overnight bag, who outlined the whole evening—after-party, watching the sun rise over Loch Raven, breakfast at the Towson Diner. He was not prepared for how the evening deviated from that simple plan.

Neither was she. But while she felt betrayed by her body on one front, she felt her mind had saved her, taking whatever memories she had and shutting them behind an impenetrable wall. The public defender had suggested hypnosis at one point, and it marked the only time that Amber had spoken sternly on her own behalf, saying she'd rather end up in an adult prison than be forced to remember anything.

Her mother had asked only how much it might cost.

The strange thing about that summer was that Amber and Joe were never together, except in the newspapers and tabloids. Yet she felt linked to him, and it made sense to her that they were now friends again. Again, or maybe for the first time? She could never decide.

They had been meeting for coffee every Sunday for a month now. Sitting in their cars, windows up, speaking through their Bluetooth devices. He was nice. She had not been wrong to care for him. She had not come back to Baltimore to be reminded of this fact, but here the information was, and what should she do with it?

Miss Margaret, uncannily prophetic as ever, seemed to read her thoughts. "This is not why you went back there. To fall for him again."

"I haven't *fallen* for him again," Amber said, feeling truthful. She was truthful. She had not fallen for him again, because she had never gotten up from her first fall. She had not known it was possible to love someone who had hurt you so terribly. The fact that Joe wanted her as a friend, that he spoke to her of how much he loved and admired his wife—that only made him more attractive to her. He was a good man. And a good man, etc. etc.

She made her excuses, got off the phone, went to the gallery. By four, she was about to close for the day when she saw a figure at the glass, tapping. Joe. He mimed getting coffee—at least, she thought that was what he mimed—and she nodded happily. Their ritual was so new, she kept expecting it to end as suddenly as it had started.

"How are you doing?" she asked, when they were parked with their drinks.

"How is anyone doing?" he said. "Stir-crazy. Worried. This is going to kill the economy."

Amber did not tell him that her sales in her Etsy store were up over this time last year. People, forced to stare at their own four walls, suddenly wanted to put new things on those walls. She was trying to think of a gallery show that somehow spoke to the moment. Nothing too on the nose—she didn't want to deal with images of illness or plagues. Maybe something about "the view from inside," a playful take on that Magritte painting.

"It requires a different kind of creativity, living this way, that's for sure," she said. "I know a lot of people are cooking, doing crafts. But I don't feel particularly urgent about those things. I feel as if this is an opportunity, while all our lives are paused, to ask if we're really where we want to be."

"Are you?"

"Yes, I think so."

"I'm not," he blurted out. She could see him only in profile, but he seemed shocked by what he had said. "I mean, I'm happy, of course—"

"Why 'of course'?"

"I'm healthy, I have a good job, no one I know is sick, I have an amazing wife."

She noticed Meredith was the last thing on his list.

"Just think," she said, keen to change the subject, "if someone had tried to show us 2020 when we were kids. Imagine this moment—you and me, in our cars, talking. We wouldn't be able to make sense of it. There was no Bluetooth then, no smartphones—"

"No drive-through Starbucks on York Road, that's for sure. I don't think Starbucks had even made it to Baltimore when we were in high school. No one we knew drank coffee then. Now middle schoolers go to Starbucks."

"We would be like, 'Why are they in separate cars, parked like that?'"

"It would look covert to us."

"Covert?"

"Like we're spies. Like we had a secret."

She waited a beat. "Don't we?"

He divined her meaning. "I haven't told Meredith about our conversations because she wouldn't understand. No one could. I barely do."

"True." She waited. When she was younger, clumsy and inexpert, she had made the mistake of making demands, pushing for answers and definitions. *Am I your girlfriend now? Will you take me to the prom?*

"Amber," Joe said. "I'm sorry. About that night. I was so stupid."

"You didn't know," she said. "I barely knew."

"But if I had been more insistent about checking on you, if I hadn't just gone away when you didn't come to the door at the first knock—"

"Let it go, Joe."

She sipped her coffee, felt the past ebbing away. If you wanted to have a future, you had to let go of the past.

"Have you been tested?" Joe asked. A curious jump in logic, but she understood the segue. All roads led to COVID these days.

"No. No reason for me to, and the test is hard to find. You?"

"No, but Meredith did and she was negative, so I guess I am, too."

"Hmmmmm." She wasn't sure it worked that way.

"Still, Meredith is immunocompromised, so I have to be careful."

"Of course."

"But eating outside, six feet apart—that's okay with anybody."

"Yes, I think so."

"Do you have a backyard space? Maybe we could sit there sometimes, when the weather is better."

"I have a little yard," she conceded. "And it has to get warmer soon. Please tell me it's going to get warmer?" As if she had not lived here, as if she needed Joe to explain a Baltimore spring to her.

"The Preakness was supposed to be next weekend," Joe said. "I always go. Good seats, with—well, with some old friends." Amber had a hunch whose name he wasn't saying. "Anyway, it's canceled, but Meredith has a virtual conference. She's going to be at her office all day, doing Zoom meetings. Since the governor released his 'Road to Recovery' last month, it's pretty clear she'll be back at work soon. I'm just happy that malls can reopen."

Amber thought of the large house on L'Hirondelle. Surely a woman could find enough privacy there to attend Zoom meetings. Why did she have to go to her office? Maybe Meredith had secrets, too.

"I guess we could sit in my garden at five thirty p.m.," she said, "and toast the race that's not happening. Or watch an old one on YouTube, confident we've bet on the winner. Sitting six feet apart, of course."

"Of course," he said. "Have you noticed that no one really seems to know what six feet is?"

"Aren't you about six feet?"

"Six feet one. So just imagine me falling at your feet. That's what I do."

"You imagine falling at my feet?"

She meant it as a joke, but her tone failed her. She stared straight ahead through her windshield, color rising in her cheeks, as bold as the glimmers of the sunset starting to flame to her right. She was facing south; Joe was facing north. They seldom made eye contact during their coffee meetups, their eyes fixed on the horizon as if they were driving.

She heard a tapping noise—Joe had rolled down his window and was knocking on hers with his left hand, motioning her to roll it down. The tap was the sound of his wedding ring striking her window.

"I'll bring the wine," he said, meeting her eyes. "Unless you actually like those godawful black-eyed Susans."

She held his gaze.

"I'm sure whatever you bring will be fine."

# PART II

# AFTER

*What was he thinking?*

*November 3, 2020*

"I HAVE TO shower."

Amber watched Joe roll away from her and head to her bath-room. His back was admirably muscled. He was leaner, a little longer, than the boy she had known, star athlete that he was. That boy had a round, almost cherubic face. He was sweet. Joe was still sweet, and their time together was achingly similar to what they had known as teenagers—secretive, hidden from the world.

Only this time, she was as invested in keeping the secret as Joe was.

She had confronted him that first night he came to her house. They were drinking wine under the stars in her backyard, and while no one else was out and about, Amber was always mindful of the fact that there was no real privacy in a place like Stone

Hill. The neighborhood might be hidden from the world at large, but that made it extra clannish. It was a hard place in which to be a private person. Luckily, Amber had done the work of establishing herself as standoffish long before Joe showed up. Still, outdoor conversations carried. Even indoors, despite the thick, old stone walls between the little duplexes, some sounds could be heard.

"I love Meredith," Joe kept saying that night. "She's the love of my life, my soulmate. She *saved* me. But sometimes I wonder if it's, well, natural."

"Love?" Amber parried.

"Monogamy."

"So you've cheated." Stated flatly, not judgmentally. Amber wasn't naive. Strange and unique as her bond with Joe was, she had known when he suggested this meeting what the subtext was. Men didn't ask to come and drink wine in a woman's backyard out of mere friendship. And the men who made such suggestions were seldom first-timers.

"Not in a meaningful way," he said. "Just sex. Very casual. And I know you're going to laugh, but it made me a better husband."

She didn't laugh.

"Meredith thinks I'm *good*. She thinks she made me good, by loving me and believing in me after I told her, well, everything. Most of the time, I want to be the person she thinks I am. Other times—I want to run away."

"Maybe you're just a little stir-crazy. These are strange times."

"Don't you get lonely? You don't see anyone."

"What are you, an apparition?"

He laughed. "A cup of coffee, drunk in separate cars on weekend afternoons. Now a glass of wine outside. That's not a lot of human contact."

"I don't require a lot of human contact."

Amber turned her own words over in her mind. Were they accurate? Yes, actually, they were. Her old life, in New Orleans, had involved plenty of people, and she thought she had liked it. She loved Miss Margaret, she enjoyed her coworkers at the Upperline. When she had first arrived in Baltimore, she had expected to be lonely, but there was so much to do, between selling Rod's house, settling his estate, and starting her gallery. She hadn't had time to be lonely.

Then everything shut down and she had felt—*peace*. It was restful, not being around people, keeping contact to a bare minimum. Of course she was horrified, too. The rising death tolls, the damage to the economy—what was happening to the world at large was almost beyond comprehension. But she hoped, when this was over, assuming what that might look like, assuming it would ever be over, that she would never forget how happy she was with her own company, how little she required from other people.

"It's bad for people," Joe had said under the stars back in May, "to be denied human touch. Like, it can make you literally sick."

He had hitched his chair closer, lowered his voice. She wondered what his move would be. Would he put his hand on her knee? Try to kiss her? All, of course, in the spirit of kindness, his concern over her solitary life. She decided to ask him directly.

"Do you want to touch me, Joe? Are you going to make a pass at me for strictly humanitarian reasons?"

He had been hunched forward, arms resting on his legs, hands clasped. Now he reared back almost as if trying to avoid a slap, although Amber was still, contained, one hand holding her wine, the other resting on her thigh.

"You always said the oddest things."

"Did I?"

"Well, they seemed odd to me at the time. Not like other girls, for sure. I am sorry, Amber. I'm sorry you didn't get to do the things you planned to do. I'm sorry for everything."

Everything. This was the second time he had used that word. How did Joe define "everything"? She considered pushing him, making him acknowledge that he had been awful to ditch her on prom night and chase after his ex, that he might have been able to help her, maybe even save the baby, if he had been more insistent on checking on her.

But this apology was good enough. It unlocked something in her that she had been trying to contain—and she kissed him, knowing where it would lead. Knowing they had been on this path all along, from the first time she saw him, maybe from the moment she decided to rent the vacant store.

Later, in her bed, she said, "We shouldn't do this again," and Joe agreed. It was a coda, an epigraph. They could both move forward now, go back to having coffee together.

Only they couldn't, it turned out. For the length of that strange, surreal summer, her bedroom was the only place that felt normal, whatever normal was now. Perhaps because the affair had started in the after-time, it would end organically—in what, the after-after time?

"How did you get out of the house today?" she asked Joe.

"I told Meredith I had to vote."

Oh, right. Election Day. Her stomach lurched. She was nervous about the outcome. "I voted absentee."

"Here or there?"

"Here. I registered here when I applied for my driver's license."

"I'm not even sure why I should bother. Not like my vote is going to change the outcome in Maryland."

She realized she had no idea for whom Joe would cast his vote—and maybe it was better that way. Could he—? She would not be the least bit surprised to learn he had voted for Trump in 2016. Misogyny was a hell of a drug. But would he do it again, after the last four years? If she asked and he told her—no. Don't ask, don't tell. The outside world had nothing to do with them.

"I feel like it's going to be a long time before we know who won," she said.

"Probably." Joe was dressing now. "Don't forget to get tested."

"I won't."

Joe had explained to her early on how dangerous it would be for his wife to be exposed to COVID. Amber felt he was a little paranoid, but she also liked the idea that one could be ethical while cheating. It set them apart somehow. They were not like other people who cheated. Joe cared about Meredith, and Amber cared about what Joe cared about. This wasn't an affair, per se.

Amber had realized, almost from the beginning, that she did not want to take Joe from Meredith. She had no desire to be a wife. How wrong she had been, back in high school, to yearn to be part of a public couple. The secret life she shared with Joe was better than any relationship she had known. And in a time as odd as this one, it was a comforting ballast, something to keep her rooted. For a few hours or so, once or twice a week, she felt as if she and Joe were the last two people on earth. Then again, it was easier and easier to imagine that there could be just two people left on earth.

She was still wearing her silk dressing gown when she sent

him on his way. But once he was out the door, she showered and dressed as if she were going in to work. She then began churning through her email, which was voluminous. Eight months into the pandemic, her business continued to thrive. People stuck at home wanted new things to see, to hang. This didn't just happen, of course. She cultivated her customer base, sending out weekly emails. She put on virtual shows. She learned to use TikTok, much as she loathed it. (She didn't dance, that was for sure.)

And then there had been media attention, because of the pop-up at Everett's farm. In a summer where there were so many things people could not do, an outdoor gallery of larger-than-life scarecrow sculptures had attracted far more attention than it would have normally.

Yes, he had been reluctant to sell his pieces. But when a D.C. lobbyist for whom Amber arranged a private showing offered to pay $12,000 for a new scarecrow for his St. Michaels mansion, Everett decided he would be open to working on commission. He could not sell his "family," the original pieces, but he could make new pieces and part with them.

Still, he had doubts. "I've never worked to anyone's specifications before," he said. "I have to make what's in my head." Amber assured him it would be all right, that the only thing that would be dictated beforehand would be price and size.

That had been July. They had sat, six feet apart, of course, in old-fashioned metal lawn chairs set up in front of his trailer. They each had a glass of iced tea, but neither one drank, because it was odd, slipping their masks off and on. They probably could have taken their masks off altogether, but Everett was in his seventies, and Amber had to be careful. Again, because of Meredith.

"Let me make a movie about you," she said, knowing he would

never understand the concept of Instagram, much less TikTok. The short videos she made created more demand. And yet—Everett's past was never mentioned, and she was simply "the Baltimore gallery owner" who had found him. She had rewritten his narrative. And hers.

Email done, she turned her attention to QuickBooks, for her most-loathed task. No matter how hard she tried, the accountant still had to reconcile multiple errors every month. But the main thing was, her bank account was robust. Everett's new work had netted her $30,000 so far. (She required payment in full before Everett would even start a sculpture, and he worked very fast, almost too fast—Amber often waited several weeks to deliver the new sculptures, fearful the buyers wouldn't value them if they arrived too quickly.) Ironic. Here she was, sitting on the fat nest egg of Rod's inheritance, but she almost didn't need it. There was so little to spend money on when one lived at home, venturing out only to the grocery store, maybe ordering clothes online. What a strange time.

She hoped it never ended.

Of course, she wanted people to stop dying, she grieved for the broken families and ruined businesses. But this quiet, secluded world was peaceful. She liked the simplicity, the lack of choice.

Joe did not. She could feel his constant restlessness, his need to move. When they weren't in bed, he paced back and forth without even realizing it. He had upped his running—going from three miles a day to six, sometimes running as much as ten miles on the weekend. He spoke about training for half or even full marathons. But when would there be races again? When would there be vaccinations?

She ate a quiet supper, consciously avoiding the news. There would be a president-elect when she woke up tomorrow. She could wait. If there was one thing Amber knew about herself, it was that she could wait.

JOE FELT FOOLISH, standing in line to vote, not that the line at his polling place, the fire station on Falls Road, was particularly long. Why hadn't he heeded Meredith's advice to vote absentee? If there was ever a year not to vote in person, this was it. He wasn't even going to bother with the down-the-ballot races. Just mark his choice for president and head home.

The weird thing is, he still wasn't sure who he was going to vote for.

He had voted for Trump in 2016, although he never told anyone, not even Meredith, especially Meredith. A person's vote was private. Besides, it had seemed harmless. He couldn't stand that woman, that smug know-it-all, and it's not like it mattered how he voted, not in Maryland, which had always gone for the Democratic candidate in Joe's voting lifetime. Reagan might have carried the state in '84, come to think of it, but Joe would have been in diapers then.

Now, in 2020, given all that had happened—why was he conflicted?

Money. He was worried about money.

He had been doing okay before the pandemic. But the past eight months had taken a toll. Which would be okay, if it weren't for the balloon mortgage on the house and the fact commercial real estate, in general, was in a trough. Nottingham Ridge, which he thought he would unload by late spring 2020, languished on the market, the most snakebitten project of his life.

The bad luck had started when his biggest anchor, Modell's,

had filed for bankruptcy in March *the very day he signed his final tenant*. Then, two months ago, Sizzler had filed for Chapter 11, although it swore the franchises wouldn't be affected. Meanwhile, Joe couldn't claim any Paycheck Protection Program money, because he was doing all this on the side, hoping to impress his uncle. It was a slow-motion car crash, except there would be no airbag to soften the blow. Quite the opposite—he was going to be smothered by that balloon payment if things didn't turn around by spring.

Meredith didn't realize how much they owed. She would be shocked, maybe even outraged, to learn that he had stripped their house of its equity and unloaded whatever savings they had outside of their retirement funds. Meredith and Joe had known few big blowups in their lives together, but they always involved money. Money and real estate.

Maybe he was selfish, but he had to vote for the man who would deliver the best economic outcome for him. Only who would that be? The stock market, historically, had performed better under Democratic presidents. But maybe that was because Democrats were voted in when times were bad and market corrections were inevitable. The economy had been going pretty well under Trump, at least before Covid. Then again, Trump had screwed over homeowners in states like Maryland, where they could no longer receive tax credit for their state income taxes. Would Biden reverse course on that? Joe wasn't sure.

His head hurt. As did his groin and his back. Amber wore him out. He had never met a woman so intent on pleasing him. It wasn't the sex, per se, that kept him coming back, but the way her face lit up when he arrived at her door. He could do no wrong in her eyes. Meredith, much as she loved him, didn't look at him that way. He supposed it couldn't be otherwise in a relationship of more than twenty years. Still, Amber's eyes, her face—it was like a drug.

He assumed the thing with Amber would end, almost naturally, when the pandemic lifted. When would that be? Spring of next year? Or maybe the end of this year would bring a natural end to it. When the pandemic stopped, he would stop. He had wanted to stop after Jordan, truly. Even when he had proposed sitting in Amber's garden and drinking wine on what should have been the Preakness, he hadn't intended anything other than maybe a slightly flirtatious conversation.

And here they were, six months later.

Alone at last in the booth with his ballot, he stared at his choices. Did it really make a difference? How had he grown so cynical? Joe had been passionate about politics as a kid, thrilled at Clinton's victory in '92, although he had disliked *her* even then. He had even briefly imagined a political future for himself. He had the personality, everyone said so.

*Fuck it*, he said, thinking he was inside his own head, but a muffled laugh from a nearby booth seemed to indicate he had spoken out loud—and was not alone in his dilemma. He marked his ballot for the Libertarian candidate. It was high time this country had a vice president with the middle name of "Spike."

Now, whatever happened, at least it wouldn't be Joe's fault.

"I DON'T WANT to watch the returns," Meredith told Joe after dinner. "It's too stressful. They probably won't know anything tonight anyway."

"I'll watch downstairs, then," he said. "Let you go to bed."

He rubbed her neck and shoulders. It had been another long

day for her, mostly surgeries. Now that her practice was open again, they had been deluged, as other practices had been, with requests for procedures to fix what people had noticed about their faces on their endless Zoom calls. She was glad to be busy, gladder still that she was exhausted. Maybe it would help her fall asleep with relative ease.

The nightmare of 2016 was still vivid to Meredith. She had been so excited about what she had thought the day would bring. She had even worn a pantsuit to vote that morning. After dinner, she had sat down with Joe, wine and computer in hand, ready to watch the needle on the *New York Times* web page declare Hillary's victory by ten p.m.

Then—she still got upset, thinking about it. She felt as if something had been taken from her. Was there not to be a female president in her mother's lifetime? Or maybe even *her* lifetime? Why did women have to wait so long for everything? She understood, intellectually, that people of color had it much harder than white women. She may not have known or understood the term *intersectionality* four years ago, but she did now. She had educated herself on the way that white supremacy elevated white women, how even liberal white women such as herself might not realize the extent to which they had been favored over minorities. So, no, she would never say it out loud, but—seriously, when the fuck was she going to get her female president?

She took a long soak in the tub and got into bed with *All the Light We Cannot See*, but she kept sneaking glances at her phone despite herself. Dammit, Florida. She honestly didn't think she could make it another four years. But what was the option? For the first time, she understood how people could get drawn into—and then ground up in—the wheels of fascism. It wasn't so easy, leaving a life, the only country one had ever known. How did one do it, where did one go?

She put her phone under the bed, where she would be able to hear the alarm in the morning, assuming she slept. She decided to think about Thanksgiving. Although they usually visited her family in the even years, they couldn't risk the trip, but that didn't mean they would go to her mother-in-law's, either. It would be just Joe and her this year, which she secretly found wonderful. Could Meredith do squab? Could she find squab? Maybe potatoes lyonnaise and an oyster stuffing? Did one stuff a squab?

*Squab* was her last conscious thought. She woke to a world without a president-elect, a world even more uncertain than the one she had known twenty-four hours earlier.

*December 23, 2020*

THE NEW ORLEANS skyline is not particularly impressive, especially when approached from the east, but when Amber saw the city rising from the bayou, her breath caught in her throat and her eyes brimmed with tears.

It had been risky to travel, even by car. But she didn't want to be alone over the holidays. She didn't resent Joe's obligations toward Meredith. She remained content within their bubble. She *preferred* the bubble. It was a cozy place to be heading into this dark, scary winter.

But she had missed New Orleans. "My Darlin' New Orleans," as the song went. In her Florida years, alone and largely aimless, Amber had yearned for Baltimore only because she was essentially an expatriate. When you're kicked out of a place, it's hard not to see it as Eden. Exiled from her hometown, the city she had once been determined to flee, she longed for it because she knew nothing else.

Then she discovered New Orleans, and now she was a bigamist, destined to be homesick wherever she was. In a way, it helped her understand Joe's dilemma. He loved Meredith and he wanted Amber. He couldn't choose.

But who was Baltimore and who was New Orleans in this scenario?

She had made it to Chattanooga the first day, a little more than halfway. The hotel had made a tepid effort at decorating for Christmas, which made it more depressing than ignoring the holiday all together. Amber had been spending Christmas alone for years. December 25 meant nothing to her. What she was missing was the *feel* of winter in New Orleans, which wasn't really winter at all, despite the occasional cold snaps. The nonstop party, party, party feel of the city, long lunches rolling into dinners, sometimes punctuated by house parties. She had assumed, in the stupidly hopeful fall of 2019, that she would be going back and forth all the time, if only for the gallery. Had she known that everything was going to go to hell right after Mardi Gras, she would have made sure to visit last February, maybe even conquered her fear of crowds to show up for Muses and take her shoe from Miss Margaret's hand.

If the skyline had failed to make her break down in tears, her rented bungalow did the trick. "I could have gotten you so much for a holiday rental," Miss Margaret had grumbled when Amber asked her to keep the Christmas week unbooked. "If you miss the food here so much I could just FedEx you some. Or you could check into a hotel if you're doing so well." But she couldn't imagine staying anywhere but her Irish Channel shotgun. Amber walked through the rooms. Fourteen months. She had been gone for fourteen months. The house had missed her, she could tell. She didn't really believe in ghosts, but this house had a soul, it felt things. Two cities, two houses, one man, and not a single one really belonged to her.

"I'm so glad they've moved back to this location," Miss Margaret said as they settled into their table at Boucherie that night. "That place around the corner was so sterile."

"Didn't they used to do a brisket braised in Dr Pepper?" Amber asked, studying the menu.

Miss Margaret looked at her over the rim of her gigantic bright green reading glasses. "We're in the middle of a global pandemic, my dear. We all have to make certain sacrifices."

"I don't care as long as they still have the Krispy Kreme bread pudding and the Thai chili chocolate chess pie. Do you remember that party—"

"Oh, yes, with the local girl who got so incensed about the fact that you said you liked Boucherie's chess pie and she said your opinion was meaningless because you didn't know that chess pie had been a staple in New Orleans public schools."

"I love how people get mad about food here. Really mad. In Baltimore, someone might take offense if, I don't know, you don't like steamed crabs or pit beef, but that's about it. People don't fight about it."

Miss Margaret took a long sip of her vodka martini. Amber was having a Sazerac. She didn't particularly like rye-based cocktails, but she was feeling sentimental. "And how is Baltimore? Are you almost over that nonsense?"

Amber assumed the "nonsense" was Joe and she regretted ever

confiding in Miss Margaret, but she had needed to talk to someone in the early days of the affair. Was it even an affair? That word didn't capture what was happening between her and Joe.

She decided to answer the question she wished she had been asked, a tactic taught to her by none other than Miss Margaret. "My business is great, successful beyond my wildest dreams. You know, I think I assumed I would fail and come back ho—here, with my tail between my legs."

"You were going to say 'home.' You can't fool me. You know where you belong."

"No," Amber said, "I don't, actually. Not anymore. I don't know where I belong and I don't know who I am."

Miss Margaret didn't say anything right away, and Amber's sentence took on more poignance than she had intended. Miss Margaret had long known where *she* belonged. She had arrived at Tulane in 1984 on a baseball scholarship, but when she found herself at home in New Orleans she also realized she could be at home in herself, and that self wasn't the right fielder for the Tulane (men's) baseball team. She changed her major to art history, went through surgery the summer before she got her MBA. A gallery owner on Magazine Street had mentored her, then Miss Margaret had mentored Amber. Now here they were, equals in a sense, although Amber understood she would probably never have Miss Margaret's terrifying certainty and confidence about all things, including herself. Especially herself.

"You know he's not going to leave her, right?"

"I don't want him to."

"What do you want, then? Of all the people to take up with—"

"No, don't you get it? He's the perfect person to be with, in this way. He knows the worst thing about me. Good god, he's *forgiven* me. I mean—that was his baby, even if he never knew the baby existed until it was dead. And he's never had a child. Sometimes, I think that's my fault."

"Maybe he's just shooting blanks now," Miss Margaret said.

Amber glared at her.

"I'm sorry, it's all very confusing. Is this, well, redemptive for you? Restorative? I can't see it ending well."

"I can't see the ending at all. I mean, I know it will end. It has to end. If I had to guess, they'll roll out the vaccine by the end of next year and life will go back to how it was, more or less."

"Did you exchange gifts for the holidays?"

"No. I can't give Joe anything because, well, where would he keep it?"

"Doesn't keep him from giving you something."

Amber wished that idea had not already crossed her mind.

"I know her parents," Miss Margaret said. "Inevitably. It's such a small town. They're liver specialists. Liver specialists who drink too much. It was hard on them, that thing with their daughter."

Amber tried to make a face as if this was new information to her, and some of it—the drinking part—actually was. She was pretty sure she had found out everything there was to find out about Meredith Duval Simpson online. Joe had told Amber repeatedly about her childhood cancer, how she believed it had destroyed her parents' marriage, how she hated the fact that they had stayed together for her, how it had affected their finances, despite their relatively good incomes.

"I miss this place so much."

"Then move back. If you've had success there, you can replicate it here."

Amber shook her head. "No, there's too much overlap with

Anton Haardt's place, and the rents here are fierce, even now. I can't believe there's a West Elm on Magazine."

"And that, my dear, is the most New Orleans thing you've ever said. Next thing you know, you'll be lecturing me about chess pie."

Their entrees arrived and they fell on them happily.

JOE MADE IT to Midtown by noon, which was pretty good, considering that he had left Baltimore at eight thirty and permitted himself a stop for coffee at Maryland House on I-95. The tricky part had been getting out of the house for eight hours—three and a half hours for the drive up, an hour to do his business, and three and a half back if he was lucky. He finally told Meredith a semi-truth: He had to go to New York because the lender on Notting-ham needed a notarized document *today*. She had not asked too many questions, a sign that she probably saw through his ruse. Meredith knew that Joe went to New York to buy expensive jew-elry, relying on Zach's brother Xavier who had married into one of the old diamond families. That's why Zach's wife, Amanda, always had the best jewels, something Meredith had commented on more than once.

It seemed like a lifetime ago that Joe, sick with guilt over the affair with Jordan, had driven up here to buy Meredith her Christmas earrings. Go figure, he was now nostalgic for that pre-COVID time, fraught as it had been. But at least he hadn't been hemorrhaging money a year ago. Four months. He had four months before he had to pay off the mortgage, probably by taking out a new mortgage. And he couldn't apply for COVID protec-tions, because he hadn't gone through a federally insured lender, instead relying on Zach's *other* brother, Yardley, who was a payday lender. And why had Joe chosen Zach's brother? Because Yardley hadn't required Meredith to sign the documents in front of him, which had allowed Joe to forge her name. A federal offense on top of everything else.

His stomach roiled. The financial problem could be solved, somehow. He could go to his uncle, metaphorical hat in hand, and explain what he had done. Commercial real estate was taking a beating, but his uncle was big enough to weather it. He'd bail Joe out, buy Nottingham Ridge, albeit at a bargain rate. Not exactly Joe's dream scenario, but his uncle loved him and his uncle would forgive him.

Meredith? He didn't want to find out what she would do if she discovered he had risked their house, wiped out their savings, and forged her name.

Obviously, the only thing to do was to buy her a way-too-expensive bracelet to go with last year's earrings.

At least traffic was light in the city and parking abundant. He slid into a garage only a block away from Rothstein's, walked quickly down 47th Street. A year ago, when he bought the earrings, not even batting an eye at the $75,000 cost, he had treated himself to lunch at Sushi Yasuda. He couldn't do that, not today.

Xavier was waiting for him. He was actually the youngest of the three Trowbridge boys; after Zach was born, his mother decided she wanted a trio of XYZ, even if it was really ZYX.

"And were the earrings successful?" asked Xavier, who had waited on him last year.

"Indeed. Now I need a bracelet to go with them—that's the problem, right? You have to keep topping yourself."

"What were you thinking of?"

"Well, diamonds, of course. But with a bracelet, I don't think cut and clarity matter as much, right? It's more about effect. It just needs to sparkle."

Xavier immediately understood what Joe was saying: *I don't want to spend as much as I did last year.* But Joe was insulted by the items that he began pulling out of the case. Tennis bracelets. Meredith would never wear anything as ordinary as a tennis bracelet. She would be offended by these. *Joe* was offended, even though he was the one who had intimated that he wasn't looking to spend a lot.

"I guess I'll know what I'm looking for when I see it," he said, wandering down to the next case. He noticed a ring that looked like a black cat—a panther, presumably—then his eyes moved across a row of antique-looking bangles, far more Meredith's style.

"What about this?" he asked, pointing to a bangle with yellow and white stones.

"You have good taste," Xavier said, something he probably said a dozen times a day, something he would have said to a guy who liked the tennis bracelets Joe had just rejected. It was business; it wasn't personal. "That's an estate piece, Bulgari. White and yellow diamonds. Because you're a friend I can let you have it for— $60,000."

An enemy would probably also pay $60,000. Joe's eyes drifted back to the panther ring and its glowing gold eyes. "Are those yellow diamonds, too?"

"Yes. That's a David Webb and it's a good price, only $9,000."

*Only $9,000. What world are you living in, man? Are you selling a lot of jewelry this year?* Joe found himself wondering what sales were like for luxury items this fall. Probably dismal, but then again— what if you were just happy to be alive, not one of the 300,000 dead so far? Homes were selling so quickly that real estate agents barely had to stage them. Who would have predicted that?

"How about $60,000 for the two?"

"Sure," Xavier said, and Joe knew he could have gotten them for less. But it was too late. He took out his AmEx—he had called ahead about the purchase and gotten approved; he was a good customer, never missing a payment. So far.

"Would you like them wrapped?"

"The bracelet, yes. The ring—that's for another, um, occasion."

"Smart man, buying ahead for Valentine's Day." He winked, and Joe saw a world of knowledge in that wink. Xavier had probably seen a lot of men buying two pieces of jewelry right before Christmas, one expensive, one not quite so much.

He was home in time for dinner, despite stopping at a Roy Rogers outside Philadelphia. The chain had been a favorite of his as a teen, and he thought it would make him happy, a roast beef sandwich, a holster of fries dipped into a combination of ketchup and barbecue sauce. But all it did was add more stress to his constantly churning stomach. How could he have spent so much? Because he still believed he would sell the shopping center, that it was only a matter of time before a tsunami of cash rolled in.

Meredith was bustling around the kitchen, happy and carefree. He almost envied her ignorance. He felt, well, like a virus crossing the doorstep, capable of destroying everything. He hugged her, forgetting the boxes, and she laughed. "Is that a present in your pocket or are you just happy to see me?" Nervous that she would reach in and pull out both boxes, he grabbed the longer one and handed it to her.

"You knew where I was all along, didn't you? I can never get anything past you."

"Christmas Eve is tomorrow."

"I can't wait," Joe said. "Open it now."

She did, and her eyes made it clear: He had chosen wisely. "Where will I wear such a gorgeous thing? And when?"

"Whenever we're all vaccinated, I guess." He looked at the bracelet on her left wrist, held her hands in his. Meredith's hands were beautiful. Plain, of course, the nails kept short and square cut, with only clear polish. But the fingers were long and dexterous. She was so careful with her hands, her precious hands. She had to be. They were literally six-million-dollar hands.

He squeezed them gently, then drew her to him and kissed her.

MEREDITH LAID THE new bracelet in a velvet-lined jewelry drawer in her dressing room. She should probably take it to the bank and put it in the safe-deposit box, although burglary seemed a remote risk. Still, maybe a small safe for the closet would be a prudent investment. They had security cameras, of course, and an alarm system, although they were careless about using it. Alarm systems were to Meredith and Joe's life what seat belts had been to their parents: precautions used only in certain circumstances, with indifference to actual risk. Her parents once told her they never wore seat belts for trips around town, only on long drives. Similarly, Meredith and Joe seldom engaged the alarm system if they were going out for just an hour or so. It was used for work-days, out-of-town trips. They did set the "stay" function every night, but only because Meredith was prone to hearing things go bump in the dark.

Why had he spent so much money? He couldn't be having a good year. The commercial real estate sector hadn't been particularly robust before the pandemic, and he hadn't been able to travel for work, because they agreed it put her at too much risk. (Even though Meredith was sure she'd had COVID in February, she could get it again. And she never did get around to taking the antibody test, so she didn't actually know.) He was a canny one, her Joe. She had been struck when she met his uncle how much more Joe seemed to resemble him than he did his own father. He, too, had that salesman personality, an authentic interest in people.

She loved the bracelet, but she felt let down. Christmas was over and it wasn't even December 24. What was there to look forward to over the next two days now that she had gotten her gift? Christmas Eve dinner and—nothing.

Joe's mother had made a last-minute appeal to carry on the tradition of her Christmas open house. In fact, she *was* carrying on the tradition, which made Meredith insane. So irresponsible. Joe was caught in the middle, inevitably—until Meredith told him that if he went to his mother's, he would have to quarantine for fourteen days before he could come back into the house. She was a doctor, in surgery every week. She owed it to her patients to be as careful as possible.

And, okay, she hated that open house, with football on the television and her nieces and nephews so hopped up on Christmas. Of course, they were grown now, in high school and college, yet still irritating to her. She was happy to be spared a year off. Was that so awful?

Meredith sat at her dressing table and brushed her hair a hundred strokes, a practice she had recently started after seeing a video online. Everything came full circle. Brush your hair, don't brush your hair, brush your hair. Use ten products on your face, use cold water and olive oil, use fifteen products on your face.

The holidays, even when scaled down for the pandemic, felt normal, a break from the political turmoil of the past six weeks. *May you live in interesting times*—was that a blessing or a curse? Probably both. The times were too interesting for Meredith. What was the line of poetry about the great beast slouching toward Bethlehem? Come to think of it, had she really understood that poem, in college or now? Christ was born in Bethlehem. What did it mean for a beast to be heading there? Was it a deliberate allusion to Satan or—? Meredith liked poetry, but she didn't really understand it. She always felt poets were laughing at literal-minded readers like herself, their pretty words a joke at her expense.

Joe was downstairs, watching television. They should make love tonight, they hadn't been together for at least a week, but she was so tired as of late. She was tested regularly for COVID at this point, so she knew that wasn't the problem, but she had never experienced a fatigue like this. With life's busyness for the sake of busyness stripped away, she should feel as if she had more time. Outside work, no one expected anything of her. The book club had tried to meet via Zoom, but it was wholly chaotic and they had given up. Then they had tried cocktails via Zoom, and that was even *more* chaotic. She muted herself midway through and no one even noticed.

Joe had been such a good sport about her work schedule, her ability to return to an actual workplace while he remained stuck in the alcove off the kitchen. Maybe she should relent and let him go to his mother's house on Christmas Day. They had gifts for everyone. And it would be something to *do*. According to the forecast, the day was going to start out mild, and Joe's mother had a firepit on the back terrace. It would truly be in the spirit of the holiday to let him go. Or, better yet, to go with him, as long as they stayed outside. In fact, if she went with him, she could make sure he stayed outside.

She went downstairs to tell him about her change of mind and found him staring at his computer in the kitchen nook. He started at her appearance and, she couldn't help noticing, closed the file he had open. A series of charts and numbers, it was probably work-related.

"I'm sure Mom will agree to do things outside," he said. Meredith wasn't. She was already anticipating a dozen little arguments and wheedles. *Of course we can watch the game, right? If people mask? When they're not eating?* Caryn would complain that some food couldn't be set up outside because she used chafing dishes. She would use the grandchildren, grown as they were, to get her way. *The kidlets are practically blue from cold.* It would be a series of—could you call them microaggressions? No, that was a corruption of the term. But Caryn would wheedle, wheedle, wheedle, needle, needle, needle. That was her way.

Still, it would make Joe happy, and that was what Meredith did: She made Joe happy. She made Joe happy and she made Joe good.

*January 8, 2021*

"YOU HAVE TO understand," Joe told Amber, "people are really angry."

They were in her kitchen, having their customary snack—cheese and meats from the Wine Source's deli section, a glass of wine for her, a beer for him. She did not want to talk about the events of two days ago. She did not want to talk about news in general. That was the outside world, unconnected to them. She thought Joe understood the division by now.

"But, you don't agree with them, right?" she asked carefully. "About the election being stolen?"

"I think he squeaked it out. Live by the electoral college, die by the electoral college. But, man, some hinky stuff happened. You have to admit that."

Did she? Amber felt the only thing she needed to do was steer this conversation toward a different, safer topic. Her sense of Joe was that he wasn't a particularly online person. But maybe he was online in a way that wasn't visible to her. It had slowly become evident to Amber that her social media life was not like others'. For her, everything was about commerce, driving customers to her virtual and real-life galleries. Bereft of family and friends, she moved differently than most through virtual spheres and had not understood that others were congregating in private groups, fomenting and fuming. Gah, it was like high school all over again—cliques and codes she couldn't quite decipher, interior worlds to which she was not invited.

She still didn't know for whom Joe had voted. Nor would she ever ask. That was "out there" stuff. It had nothing to do with them.

"Did you see that infographic, the one that allowed you to calculate when you might be vaccinated? Apparently I will be one of the last adults in Baltimore City to get a jab. Probably in autumn. I literally daydream about what I might wear the first time I go somewhere post-vaccination."

As a conversation topic, COVID wasn't much of an improvement over the election, but it was the best she could do.

"Meredith was in the AstraZeneca trial."

"You mentioned that before," she said. Although she felt no jealousy of Meredith, she hated it when Joe invoked her name.

"We're not doing well," he said abruptly.

If he thought this was what she wanted to hear, he was wrong.

"I'm sorry. I know the pandemic has been hard on some marriages."

"That's part of it. She gets to go on, living a more or less normal life, while I feel cooped up and my projects are stalled. Yet she still expects me to cover the lion's share of our bills."

"That doesn't seem right."

Her words were carefully ambiguous. It didn't *seem* right. But she also meant that she didn't assume she was getting the full picture from Joe. From what Amber knew of Meredith—quite a bit—she appeared generous, at least with her time. Would she really be a your-money, my-money kind of person?

"I admit, I haven't out-and-out asked her. But that's because she gets so stressed about finances. I did tell her that I thought the house was too much for us."

Amber nodded, familiar with the house on L'Hirondelle Club Road, although she had never seen it in person. It was set far back from the street, up a long curving driveway, and there was a sliding iron gate that was always closed. She had found photos online, though, a virtual brochure from the bankruptcy sale back in 2009. It had a port cochere. A fucking port cochere. She had told Miss Margaret about the port cochere and she had voiced exactly what Amber was thinking: *You have to be a special kind of asshole to have a port cochere.*

"We should downsize. For a lot of reasons. Our carbon footprint alone! But Meredith would never consider it."

"Joe, why are you telling me this?"

He crumpled his beer can, a local brand, Duckpin, which she stocked just for him. "It's on my mind. Sorry. I try not to bring my troubles to you."

"I don't mind," she said, surprising herself. "And if I can help you, I will. Not financially, but if I can help you brainstorm—"

"My tutor," he said.

"Still teaching you a few things, I guess."

He took her in his arms. "Still waters run deep. I don't think I really understood that saying until I met you. You can keep a secret, Amber. Most people can't."

She knew he meant it as a compliment, yet it made her unhappy. Amber was so good at secrets that she had managed to keep one from herself, and that had cost her so much.

"I'd do anything for you," she said, surprising herself. More surprising still, she realized she meant it. "Anything."

MEREDITH WAS GLAD she had an afternoon of surgical appointments. The other day's events had jangled her nerves. It would be a relief to focus. And she especially enjoyed jaw contouring, the final surgery scheduled for Lisbette, a trans woman who had already had her forehead, eyebrows, and nose done.

Lisbette was thirty-seven, tall, and broad-shouldered. According to the information gathered at intake, she'd had her bottom surgery seven years ago and it hadn't been a good experience. In fact, she had brought a suit for malpractice—a successful one, always unnerving. But Meredith, after reviewing the case, decided that Lisbette was right to pursue legal action. Luckily, she had been able to find another doctor who could correct the errors made in the original vaginoplasty. Still, the experience had left her gun-shy around surgeons and she had delayed her facial surgeries for almost five years.

"You're already a beautiful woman," Meredith had assured her at the consultation. "But if you want a more traditionally 'feminine' look, why not? Your face should be *your* face."

This is what she did: She helped people find confidence.

This woman, who had entrusted her face to Meredith—what had her life been like, *before*? Was that question even allowed? Meredith was unclear about whether life before the transition was something that was not to be discussed. She liked to think of herself as an inquisitive person. But she also valued politeness, and that was a tricky combination, getting trickier all the time. How did one express curiosity about others without violating boundaries?

Meredith preferred a quiet surgical suite—no music, only essential conversation. If she were honest, she felt a little godlike, hovering over her patients. Better than God, in a sense, as she was improving on his work. It didn't matter if the patient was a woman such as Lisbette or a boy in Guatemala. In fact, it didn't matter if the patient was a vapid Valley housewife who wanted a brow lift. Meredith loved them all. To her way of thinking, you had to love the flawed in order to improve them. No, you had to love the *flaw*. People were not flawed; they simply had them. Everyone could be improved.

Surgery over, she headed back to her office at Greenspring to confer with her office administrator. God, she was just so tired, and the parking lot was still quite full going on dusk. She had to park at the far edge. She had just reached the doors when a young woman overtook her. "Dr. Simpson?"

"Yes?"

"You might not remember me—and I'm wearing a mask now, but I met with you last February?"

*Movie theater*, Meredith's brain prompted. "Jordan," she said. "Jordan Altman." The woman's candy pastel theme remained constant. Today she was wearing a pale blue fuzzy coat, large and shapeless, but her exquisite legs were on view, in pale stockings that ended in the kind of high heels Meredith could never wear, also pale blue. She looked a little like one of those new-fangled Peeps.

"Yes, well, if you want to schedule another consultation, please go through my office manager."

"I called, but she said I wouldn't be able to get in for weeks."

"We are quite busy." She kept her tone sympathetic, but she was annoyed. This young woman was clearly used to getting her way. *Sorry, dear, but sometimes even beautiful women have to take no—or not now—for an answer.*

"I really need to talk to you. You see—"

"Please, call my office manager." Polite, but firm. "She keeps the schedule. I go where she tells me—there's no use in trying to go through me."

The woman seemed on the verge of tears. She blinked rapidly. Her eyes were only a shade darker than her coat and shoes. "I'm sorry," she said.

"It's a difficult time," Meredith said as gently as possible. "We're all emotional. But, please—don't rush at someone in the twilight. It's unsettling."

She went inside, talked to Susie, looked at tomorrow's schedule, decided not to mention her little stalker outside. What could have made that young woman so urgent, after almost a year? Granted, everyone was getting squirrelly, and if she was doing a lot of Zoom calls, she might have become obsessed with something else no one else really noticed—a slightly droopy eye, a bulbous chin.

Meredith headed home, listening to NPR for all of five minutes before she switched to a mindless oldies station. She couldn't take any more bad news, she just couldn't. Sometimes, she felt guilty about her relative comfort and safety in a world where people were dying by the thousands, daily. Then she resented feeling guilty. No one's life was perfect.

JOE WAS IN his kitchen office nook, studying his accounts. Over the past ten months, he had come to regret his generosity in giving Meredith the "real" office on the lower level. Easy to be magnanimous a decade ago when he couldn't envision working from home. Now he felt as if he was serving time in this alcove. When he was forced to do Zoom meetings here, he felt emasculated by the backdrop, a shelf full of decorative teapots that Meredith's mother had foisted on them, all shaped like various fruits—an apple, an orange, a pineapple, a strawberry, another pineapple. *Teapots.* As in, tempest in a.

The decor was the least of his concerns right now. The numbers that stared back at him told a stark story, the same story, every day. He was in a hole, with almost no hope of getting out. The news was full of the attack on the Capital, stories of alleged economic insecurity that had driven people to commit unspeakable acts. No one was more economically insecure than Joe and yet here he sat, happy to accept the results of the last election, rooting for a return to normalcy, whatever it would take to get him out of this hole.

He looked around the kitchen, through the windows, into the deep, dark backyard. Even if he could sidestep the coming catastrophe of the balloon note or unload Nottingham Ridge before May 1, the house would continue to be an albatross, month by month. Maybe he could persuade Meredith to downsize, only he wouldn't put it in those terms.

However, if he offered her a cool alternative—he began search-ing Zillow for the kind of place she used to want. Downtown, maybe a condo. There was a pretty nice penthouse apartment in Locust Point at a strangely attractive price point, especially given how fast residential properties were moving right now. Must have some invisible defect, mold or a sordid history, or—

And just like that, as if his phone could read his mind, or, more likely, as if his computer was feeding his phone cookies even as he browsed, he received a spam text: Are you thinking about a new house?

Then he realized the sender was *JA*. Jordan Altman.

She followed with a selfie, a Safe for Work selfie, thank god, just her in a blue coat, her face somber. She was standing outside the Greenspring Valley professional building that housed Mere-dith's practice. Safe for Work, but Not Safe for Joe.

*Everyone's an insurrectionist now,* Joe thought. Like the former president, Jordan had lost a contest but believed she could still change the outcome if she threw a big enough tantrum.

His fingers were nonplussed; he had no idea how to reply. Text bubbles on her end, then: We need to talk.

OK. When?

Joe felt eerily calm. She clearly hadn't said anything to Mere-dith yet, because Meredith would have called him immediately—and said what? Of that, he wasn't sure. Told him to get the fuck out? Where would he go? The last thing he needed right now was the expense of a hotel room, even a cheap one.

If Jordan did tell Meredith, maybe it wouldn't be the worst thing. He could confess to everything, get it all over with. Would she forgive him? He wasn't sure. Twenty-plus years ago, he had told Meredith the worst thing he had ever done and she'd had no problem forgiving him, even defending him against his own guilt and second-guessing. Meredith considered guilt a waste of time and energy. But Meredith had not been hurt by Joe's actions as an eighteen-year-old. Would she be as magnanimous now that she was the victim?

*Play for time,* he advised himself. *Meet with Jordan, find out what she wants.*

Then: *And tell Amber. Amber will know what to do.*

What about Tuesday? he typed.

Fine, she replied. See you next Tuesday.

She actually added a winking emoji.

*January 12, 2021*

AMBER PULLED INTO the drive-through pharmacy at a Walgreen's in Southwest Baltimore, on Hollins Ferry. Not one of Baltimore's best neighborhoods, which was probably why she had been able to schedule a COVID test here. Since the holidays, tests were harder and harder to find. But Joe was adamant that she test every week—Meredith and her precious immune system—and she was a pro by now. Get in the drive-through line, get the kit from the dispensary window, pull over, swab each nostril, drop the kit into a depository, and she was on her way in under ten minutes.

What if a test were to come back positive? Seemed unlikely. She went almost nowhere, did almost nothing, and she was fine with that. Walking down the Avenue in Hampden, she felt zero yearning when she saw people eating and drinking in the makeshift outdoor spaces. Some people were even comfortable eating indoors these days. Good for them. Amber did not need to join their ranks. Seeing Joe twice a week was all the contact she required, it turned out.

But suppose her test did come back positive, when she had no symptoms? And what if she simply decided not to share that information? What if she gave COVID to Joe and he gave it to Meredith and—she died? Would that make Amber a killer?

Good god, why was she even thinking such thoughts? What was wrong with her? Besides, Joe kept telling her that Meredith had COVID last February and had been vaccinated in the Astra-Zeneca trial. So why did Amber have to keep getting tested?

Unfamiliar with the area, she took a wrong turn and found herself going back and forth under I-895, trapped in a series of ugly streets with pretty names: Daisy, Magnolia, Violet. Eventually she found her way to Patapsco Avenue in Baltimore's Brooklyn, a place she dimly remembered, although she didn't remember it as a depressing jumble of dilapidated rowhouses and abandoned restaurants. There had been a seafood place here that Rod loved, one that served fried green peppers dredged in confectioners' sugar. She thought she spotted it. If so, it looked on the verge of collapse, the large crab mural from her childhood covered with a slapdash coat of bile-green paint that was now chipping.

She had so few specific memories of her stepfather, it seemed unfair that one could be undone this way. Frankly, it still bugged her that she had jettisoned his geese at the real estate agent's instructions. She should have kept them, used them in the gallery.

When she finally found her way to a street that took her back into the city across a low-lying bridge, she was astonished at how beautiful Baltimore appeared from this vantage point—the vast expanse of water to her right, the skyline ahead. Cold as the day was, there were even men fishing along the bridge.

If she got COVID and gave it to Joe and then Joe somehow gave it to Meredith—yes, maybe Meredith would die. But so could Amber. Or Joe. Or Amber and Joe. It would be almost like a parody of Shakespeare, all those bodies in a heap, no one getting what they wanted.

She headed to the gallery. She had some pieces to send out. A woman in California had bought one of her larger works, an exquisite painting by Mary L. Proctor. But the shipping was costly, and Amber was determined to defray the cost as much as possible. She had found a local handyman who was going to help her crate it. She would then use a freight company that would be relatively inexpensive as long as the buyer agreed to have it delivered to the foot of her driveway, not inside the house.

"Hey, this is really cool," the handyman said, walking around the piece, which had been painted on an old door. It featured a curvy woman, her dress a collage of broken crockery, and the inscription: *A woman got to love herself / if you don't who will?* Although Amber was ambivalent about artists who claimed an allegiance to a higher power, she loved the work of the Rev. Mary L. Proctor, and this was one of her all-time favorite pieces. She had priced it high, hoping it wouldn't sell for a while. The woman was so round and full, pulsing with life in her dress of broken crockery, possibly ascending to heaven, although that was unclear. Maybe she was just jumping for joy.

"Isn't it? I'll miss her," Amber said.

"It must be hard," he said, "letting go of things you love."

"Yes. Yes, it is. But if I don't, I won't have a business for long. The way I see it, everything in my life is on loan."

---

JORDAN HAD WANTED to meet at the model, but Joe said he didn't have time to drive that far out. She was confident enough in her power over him to challenge him—*How are you so busy these days?* But she acquiesced and agreed to meet in the parking lot at Wegmans.

"It's only another ten miles or so," she said, getting into his front seat. "You didn't save yourself much more than ten, fifteen minutes."

"One way," he said, then reminded himself he was not here to fight with her; quite the opposite. Jordan was intent on making trouble, and Joe needed to shut that down. Why had she surfaced all these months later? What did she want?

But he knew not to begin that way. He said instead: "How have you been? I admit, I've been a little worried about you."

"You have?" As he had expected, the sentiment, this basic claim of caring about her, made her brighten. God, she was just a kid, beneath her swagger. A brokenhearted kid. How had he ever mistaken her for a libertine, out for some harmless fun? "Do we have to keep our masks on?"

"We're inside and my wife—"

"I remember." Eyes lowered, like a naughty girl. "I went to her office last week."

"Yes. I recognized where you were in the photo you texted."

"I didn't mean to scare you. I just—I had to see you."

"You didn't scare me. For one thing, if you had actually spoken to her—"

"I did."

"But you didn't tell her anything. About us." He wanted to say *about me*, but that would be offensive. To her, they were still an us.

"That wasn't why I went to see her. Not exactly."

"Another consultation?"

She started. "How do you know about that? She's not allowed to share that kind of information, is she?"

"I guessed. She described the encounter with you last year, but not your name. I recognized the description of you." He didn't tell her that was when he knew he absolutely had to get away from her, that she was getting dangerously crazy. At least COVID had been good for something.

"No, not a consultation." She bit her lip. "She convinced me at the first meeting that I don't need anything, not now."

"No one's ever said otherwise, Jordan. You are gorgeous. It was never in doubt."

"Then why are you with someone else?"

It took him a beat to realize she wasn't referring to Meredith.

"What are you talking about?"

"You said we had to break things off because you didn't want to cheat anymore, that you were trying to have a baby, that you had to be more careful than other people because of your wife. But you're with someone else. Have been for a while."

"You're mistaken."

"Remember that painting you gave me? I liked it, but I wanted—what do you call two of a kind? A diptych. So I called around, figured out where it was from, and went to the gallery to see if they could tell me where I could find more of that artist's work. Your car was out front. I rang the bell, but no one answered."

*Did you hear that? No. It's the door. No you're wrong, turn over. There it is again. Well, if it's the door, then whoever it is left.*

"You're mistaken," Joe repeated.

"Your car was there."

"I was at the bistro, picking up food to go."

"I waited. I saw you come out—and I saw her lock the door behind you."

"I might have talked to her about renting a larger space—"

Jordan shook her head, tears welling in her eyes at the memory. God, if Jordan could cry over discovering he had been untrue, what would Meredith do? "I found out where she lives, that woman. I've seen your car outside her house several times. But also—I found out *who* she is."

Again he needed a beat.

"Meredith knows all about Amber, Jordan. What happened. She's known for years."

Jordan was shaking her head, trying to stem her tears, biting her trembling lip.

"You mean, she knows what happened back in high school, at your prom. She doesn't know what's happening *now*."

"Jordan—the pandemic, my business—it's been a really difficult time for me. Truthfully, I think I'm having a bit of a breakdown." Making excuses, but the moment he said it, the words felt true. He was losing his mind. Who wouldn't be? He had put everything he loved at risk. He was on the verge of losing his wife, his house, his reputation.

"I was going to tell your wife, last night. I was so hurt. But then I realized it wouldn't do any good. I still wouldn't have what I wanted."

"What do you want, Jordan?"

"To be with you."

"I don't see how—"

"How can you sleep with her, the woman who killed your baby?"

It was an unanswerable question. "Look, we were young, and she had no idea what was going on—"

"Do you love her?"

"No," he said. He wasn't sure if this was true, but he was sure it was what Jordan needed to hear.

"Then why are you with her?" A fair question. If only he could answer it. Even the parts he could articulate would only hurt Jordan more. How could he explain how he felt when he was with Amber? It was as if flunking French was the only mistake he had ever made. He was in his boyhood bedroom, with the vintage travel posters, and he was adored. No one got to be adored in adulthood. Not in adulthood, not in marriage. Meredith loved him, he never questioned that, but it had been a long time since she had adored him. Even Jordan would stop adoring him eventually. But that fact would be of no comfort to her now.

"A mistake," he said. "Like I said, I think I'm having a breakdown. It would be a mistake for us to resume, Jordan. And terribly unfair to you."

"I could probably sell this story? To TMZ or someplace. The affair between Prom Mom and the man whose baby she killed. What did the papers call you back then? Cad Dad?"

He was sure her heart wasn't in the threat. Pretty sure.

"That's not fair, Jordan. Amber never did anything to you. And you can't blackmail someone into loving you."

She started to cry in earnest, awkward in a mask. "But you did love me, right? Which means you could love me again, if you just let yourself try. Like you said, you went a little bit crazy. Everybody's crazy after the past year. But we started before the craziness. So you were sane when you were with me. I'm the sane choice. *Not* her."

"You're not the sane choice if you're stalking me, stalking my wife, threatening to tell her something that would hurt her badly."

She rubbed her eyes with the back of her hand, spreading streaks of mascara across her face. How lonely the past year must have been for her. Joe had thought he was going stir-crazy at times, but he had never lacked for company. "I'll be good this time, baby. I promise. Just come back to me. Be with me. Only me. I love you so much, I'd do anything for you. Joe—I'm so lonely. I miss you."

What could he do? He took off her mask, then his, and kissed her.

MEREDITH HAD STOPPED at the French bistro for take-out, hazarding a guess as to what Joe wanted, because he wasn't picking up his phone or replying to texts. He had probably let the battery die again. Joe's phone was forever dying because he was one of those people who never closed a single app and always had his Bluetooth and Wi-Fi on.

Interesting—the gallery was still here a year later. She would not have bet on *that*. It had seemed an unlikely match for the neighborhood. She glanced through the windows: *Self Portraits: How Visionary Artists See Themselves*. It reminded her of a shop on Magazine Street, back home, one that was almost never open.

*Back home.* Had she really referred to New Orleans as *back home*? She had been gone for almost twenty years now. And she didn't really miss it. She would have been "the Duvals' little girl" if she had gone into practice there, even with her new surname of Simpson, which she had been happy to take for so many reasons. She would forever be "the Duval girl" and all that entailed.

Besides, Joe would have been miserable in New Orleans. The city's social pace would have been too much for him, and he would never have understood the layers upon layers of hierarchies, a veri-table mille-feuille. Meredith barely understood it. And to the ex-tent that Joe did grasp the pecking order, he would have been baffled and angry by how impenetrable it was. Joe had yet to meet a situation or a culture where his good looks and sweetness didn't let him cut the line.

She picked up a roasted chicken and frites, a foolish choice. French fries, even the best ones, needed to be eaten hot, at the ta-ble. She dipped her hand in the bag as she drove. Soon, her fingers were greasy, and she had nothing on which to wipe them. Best to eat them all, to pretend they never existed.

Home. No Joe, unless he had pulled his car in the garage, which seemed unlikely. They both preferred to park under the porte cochere except in truly foul weather, which wasn't really a problem when you had a heated driveway. Where was he? What could he be doing? She knew he got a little stir-crazy sometimes, but where did someone go on a Tuesday night in January?

Once inside, she texted again: Where are you? What are you do-ing? She deleted the second sentence. That wasn't her style. She never showed any jealousy. She felt it sometimes, but she never showed it. Who didn't feel jealousy?

Idiots. Idiots are the only people who don't experience jealousy.

It hadn't been love at first sight for Meredith and Joe, but it had been desire at first sight, at least on her part. Joe looked like a certain genre of New Orleans boy, a preppy, handsome jock. *Never saw the Duval girl landing that kind of boy. Remember when she was bald?* Because that's who she was, forever and ever in New Orleans, the bald Duval—and that was what people said *within* her hearing. God knows what they said behind her back.

Alone in the kitchen, the chicken in the oven to keep it warm, the onion soup simmering in a copper double boiler, she indulged in her secret shame, yacht rock, the soundtrack of her parents' pre-Meredith life. She knew the songs from the radio stations on pre-set in her parents' respective vehicles. Her parents were almost proudly indifferent to New Orleans music and never listened to WWOZ, which was fine with Meredith, but it had been embarrassing as a teen to have friends in the car when her parents, especially her dad, began singing along to soft rock ballads. "Isn't that one of the most romantic songs you've ever heard?" he asked Meredith and her friend Lainey once, and it wouldn't be correct to say she wanted to kill herself, because she felt she was, in fact, already dead from the sheer shame of it all.

Then, in the summer of 2019, which seemed like such a rosy memory now, they had gone to a pool party and someone had been playing the yacht rock channel on Sirius. Meredith disliked it reflexively—at first. The concept was obnoxious, nonsensical. Who wanted to be a lockjawed rich person, the judge from *Caddyshack*? But as the songs wove their way through the afternoon, they made her nostalgic on her parents' behalf. This was the soundtrack of their courtship. As sexist and even creepy as the songs might be—so many stalker-ish vibes—they also had a perverse optimism. More precisely, these were songs about the power of romantic love, its ability to transport, to hurt, to heal, to destroy. Her parents had been the type of young couple about whom people said: *Oh, they were MADLY in love. They were CRAZY for each other.*

Meredith had robbed them of that. Her parents were too polite, too loving, to ever tell her as much, but their drinking was all the evidence Meredith needed. They had everything. And then they had her.

She knew this because her father's mother had been happy to say what her parents never would. *Oh, you just drained them, baby. A real one-two punch.*

They had been sitting on the back porch, screened against the bugs. It was May, Meredith's high school graduation week. Her grandmother was staying with them, having driven down from Baton Rouge. She didn't really approve of Meredith's mother. She had never said as much, yet Meredith instinctively understood this, always had. She wasn't sure why, if it was simply the natural jealousy of a mother for her only son, her only child, or if Granny Duval had a more specific grievance.

"I think they're okay," she had said timidly.

Her grandmother was drinking rum and Cokes, but they were mainly Coke, and watery with melted ice. They were sitting in the dark, although Formosan termite mating season was over and the chance of a swarm was small. Still, Meredith preferred sitting in the dark on the back porch, a beloved place full of old, mismatched wicker furniture. Their yard wasn't anything special and no one in the family had a green thumb, but it was peaceful, birds splashing in a concrete birdbath.

"If you love someone, really love someone—if you are head over heels, do not have children," her grandmother said. "Children kill that kind of love."

"But you had Daddy?"

"I never had that kind of love, so I had nothing to lose. But those two, when they first met—the shine on them. They got greedy. They thought they could have it all."

*Did my own grandmother just wish me into never existing?* No, Meredith realized, because Meredith hadn't cost her grandmother anything.

A little over a year later, when Meredith met Joe at Trinity, she remembered her grandmother's advice, such as it was. And when she learned that Joe never wanted to have children, that was more important to her than the reason he was determined not to be a father, chilling as that story was.

Her grandmother's cruel prophecy stayed with Meredith. And over the years, as she watched friends' marriages dissolve into part-nerships that seemed to be all about schedules and travel teams, she decided her grandmother had simply told a truth no one else wanted to say out loud. When she listened to yacht rock, she was imagining her parents as they were in their twenties, young and in love, unaware of the catastrophe that they would engender, their own little Frankenstein's monster. And, as so many teenagers yell at their parents, she yearned to scream back across the decades: *I didn't ask to be born. The things that happened, they weren't my fault!*

Even if she had been able to say those words aloud, she knew her mother and father would have claimed they loved her, that they didn't blame her for what had happened. But they probably did.

When Meredith found her person, she knew what she had to do. Or not do, as the case may be. No kids. Never, ever take him for granted. Don't undercut him in front of others. Keep the shine, whatever it takes.

*Whatever it takes.*

She heard Joe's car in the drive and jumped to turn off the radio in the middle of "Smoke from a Distant Fire." Yacht rock was her secret vice. So why, when Joe appeared in the kitchen, did she feel as if the song were still playing? He seemed preoccupied and absent, his eyes clouded. Smoke from a distant fire, indeed. But no, there was no joy, no yearning. Whatever was preoccupying him was making him unhappy, weighing him down.

"Everything okay?" she asked.

"Of course! Just had to drive up to North East to check on something. Roast chicken, but no frites? Did you eat them in the car, you naughty wench?"

She hung her head in mock shame, smiling at how well he knew her, how well she knew him, and at how they forgave each other everything.

*February 5, 2021*

**"WHAT ABOUT THIS?"**

Amber's hand hovered over the track pad of her laptop and she felt a sharp, almost out-of-body jolt of déjà vu. She had been in this position so many times in the past year, this literal position—hunched in front of her laptop, despite her preoccupation with posture, fingers of her right hand curled over her track pad, almost as if poised above a finger bowl, not that Amber had ever used a finger bowl. Her right hand was like a bird of prey—from finger bowls to hawks, that was quite the jump—always ready to swoop down and click on the link for the shoes, the dress, the vintage bracelet, the sassy pillbox that would change her life.

Odd, because she did not think of herself as a shopper. Amber had lived in small, rented spaces her entire adulthood. Her wardrobe was the result of sales racks and meticulous tailoring. Years ago, she had read about Diana Vreeland's "uniform" and chosen to create her own: Hoop earrings, vintage bangles, multiple chains, although never all three at once. Sleek monochrome dresses. But between the quiet of the pandemic and the sensation of having money for the first time in her life, she had become quite the little consumer without realizing it.

"Really?" Joe asked, squinting down at his phone. "It looks small."

"Click on the photo that shows what it looks like on a model."

He did. "Still looks small."

"I've ticked all your boxes here, Joe. Affordable, but special. Romantic, but not obvious. Trust me, vintage Elsa Peretti is the way to go."

"Vintage," Joe said. "Sometimes I think that's just a euphemism for *used*."

She was surprised by his tone, given that he had presented her with that perfect David Webb ring that she now wore every day, a new part of her uniform.

"Don't you own antiques?"

"Not really," he said. "They didn't really suit the house. The ones that were big enough for the scale of it tended to be very fussy. Carved."

Amber was in her back room at the gallery, while Joe was in his office. They were Zooming, their preferred method of contact. A phone log, a text—those were things that someone else might see. No one, not even someone as jealous and unpredictable as Jordan, would think to check a Zoom history. This was now the only "room" in which Amber and Joe saw each other, and it would remain this way, Amber had decreed, until they figured out what to do about Jordan.

Joe, to his credit, had told Amber everything as soon as possible. She had not been angry or hurt. Joe before May 2020 owed her nothing and Joe after May 2020 was required only to be honest. What he owed Meredith—that was between Joe and Meredith. Her more pressing concern, when Joe confessed, was to figure out how to keep Jordan from hurting them, hurting *her*. The only possible solution, for now, was that Joe must resume the affair.

Joe had been shocked, argumentative. If anything, the mere fact that Amber had issued orders swiftly and confidently seemed to bother him. *Didn't he have a say? How could she—Why should he—?* But Amber was adamant. She would not risk being in his physical presence until it was safe. Not in her home or her office, the two locales that Jordan had already stalked and staked out. Also not in a hotel or his office or (Joe had proposed this once) in a car in the parking lot at a remote city park.

So here they were, a week out from Valentine's Day, planning on what Joe should give his wife and his lover for the holiday. Joe had confessed to Amber that his usual MO with gifts was to spend extravagantly on Meredith, but that he couldn't afford to go crazy right now.

"What about Jordan?" Amber had asked.

"The only thing I ever gave her," he said on a rueful laugh, "was that painting from your gallery. She liked it."

"You say that almost as if you didn't?"

"Oh, no. I loved it. I just didn't think her taste would be, um, evolved enough to appreciate it. She's pretty basic."

Picking out Meredith's gift had been fun. Amber had a sense that while she and Meredith did not have the same taste, they had complementary ideas about what was fashionable, desirable.

But she also enjoyed showing Joe the bargains one could find shopping for used items. Elsa Peretti never went out of style, and Amber was pleased with an offering she had found on 1stDibs for only $1,600. Two interlocking circles in 18K gold, signifying a forever love.

"Definitely offer a little below asking," she advised Joe. "Say, $1400."

"Shouldn't we at least go for one of her heart necklaces?" he asked.

"No, that's too obvious. The circles are much more romantic."

"Okay," he said, thumbing his bid to the seller.

"Now, with Jordan, we can pick out something more, um, traditional." She went to TheRealReal site and pulled up the designer filter, began ticking the more obvious ones—Chanel, Cartier, Dior, Tiffany. Here, the box would matter almost more than the item itself.

"No rings," Joe said.

"Understood," Amber said.

"And no hearts."

"Why don't you google 'Chanel jewelry' under shopping and see what comes up?"

He did. "This stuff costs more than what I just spent on Meredith!"

"Search for earrings. And specify logos. You'll find something well below $500."

Joe was slower at this than she was. While she waited on him, she unconsciously pulled at the David Webb ring, which she wore on her right hand. She almost felt sorry for Jordan. Who knew better than Amber the feeling that one could persuade, argue, bully one's way into being loved? But Jordan had indirectly threatened

Amber, which was something she could not forgive. She had endured much, clawed her way back to a kind of respectability. That was not for Jordan to take from her.

She could probably survive the fallout from her affair with Joe being made public. Heck, she'd probably end up with her own miniseries on Netflix. But it was *her* story, her life, and no one else had a right to use it for their own purposes.

Strangely, she also felt angry on behalf of Meredith, the one person in this tangle who hadn't done anything to anyone. Amber had been given all the information. Amber had made a conscious choice. Meredith remained in the dark, oblivious and innocent.

But Joe loomed above them all, even herself. She had to take care of Joe. She owed him that. She had failed him once, in her ignorance and her denial. By refusing to acknowledge what was happening, she had risked both their futures. She wouldn't make that mistake again. Short term, she could do this. Short term, she could do anything. What did that even mean now, short term, long term? Amber had no idea.

"You're using your office address, right?" she asked Joe. "For mailing. You pay for Meredith's gift and I'll pay for Jordan's, which I'll have shipped to me, then I'll use TaskRabbit to have it dropped off at your office."

"Okay, but who's going to help me pick out a gift for you?"

She smiled, stealing a glance at herself in her Zoom box. She wondered if Joe took as much care with his appearance as she did for these calls. Probably not. She even hooked up her ring light. She tried to make eye contact with him to see if he was looking at her, but one could never really tell where someone was looking on a Zoom call.

"Give me two gifts next year," she said.

———

JOE LEFT THE always-empty office—Bobbie still worked from home, of course, and had made it clear that she intended to continue doing so even once she was vaccinated—and headed up I-95 for his meeting with the owner of the Curiosity Shop, who had agreed to sign a new lease, albeit not at the per-square-foot price Joe had proposed.

He didn't have to drive to Nottingham Ridge for a lease, of course, but he was happy for the distraction, happy to do anything that didn't involve staring into a computer. He was surprised by the volume of traffic at midafternoon. Where were people going? Schools were still virtual statewide, restaurants and bars largely take-out. What if Joe just kept going up I-95? Could he outrun his problems?

The irony of his situation did not escape him. Because Joe had procured his second mortgage from a short-term lender that was not federally regulated, he could not protect himself from the balloon payment coming due on May 1. But Dev-pronounced-Dave as a commercial tenant in Joe's shopping center had *rights*. Rights and the upper hand. Joe wasn't obligated to negotiate with the guy, of course; he could have refused his counter and evicted him, but then what would he have? An empty store in a shopping center he was still trying to unload, a shopping center that already had a vacant 12,000-square-foot space where Modell's had once been. In the end, the renegotiated rent on the bookstore hardly mattered. He was circling the drain. A bookstore that specialized in World War I and II history was not going to make or break him. If he had a nuclear bomb, he would drop it on himself.

Except he wouldn't. If he knew anything about himself, it was his desire to live, and to live on his own terms. There had to be a solution to his troubles; there just had to be.

The bookstore was empty, but it had a happy hum to it. Clean, well-kept, well-organized. He asked to use the bathroom although he didn't really need it, because the bathroom was always a tell to how well the tenant was taking care of the property. Paper towels, Clorox wipes, a sandalwood-scented liquid soap.

He was almost tempted to browse. World War I had always interested him. He and Meredith had spoken often of visiting France, seeing the battlefields. Yet they never had. She could never afford the time away and, to be fair, he hadn't thought he could, either. All that work, all that devotion to their jobs, and for what? Would they ever see Europe now, get on a plane again?

"Are you going to get a tenant for the Modell's?" Dev asked. "I'm nervous about committing to two years if it's going to continue empty—"

"Oh, we've got someone impressive lined up," Joe said. "I'm not allowed to say, but it rhymes with Einmart-stay."

"I thought they were going to come out of bankruptcy as on-line only."

Shit, had that been reported? If so, Joe had missed it. "Like I said, I'm not at liberty to provide details."

Joe was old enough, just, to remember when shopping malls and department stores were grand, aspirational, the center of a teenager's life. Look how much time he had logged in Towson Town, mainly at the food court, during high school. Malls were still going strong when he had settled into his job at his uncle's real estate firm in 2003. It could be argued that Joe had terrible timing.

Or it could be argued that he always found a way to succeed, no matter what was going on in the world. He was a survivor. No, he was much more than that. Joe had never settled for mere survival. He was a thriver and striver, eyes set on the goal, always moving up and forward.

It was not yet three when he left Dev's store. He almost envied the man, clearly happy and satisfied inside his self-made kingdom, tiny as it was. He checked his schedule—there was a Zoom call at four, with all the partners. Business was beginning to pick up, but mainly in the regions that had resisted strict lockdowns: Florida, Georgia, Texas. He could race and make it back to the office or he could do the meeting from his car. He'd look enterprising, calling in from his front seat, a man on the move. What to do with the next hour? The day was bright, the temperature a balmy 55 degrees. He decided to head up 272, see if Plumpton Park Zoo was open.

North East had seemed cluttered and grimy to him, and he had all but snarled at the large shopping center Cordish operated near the I-95 exchange—twenty-two stores, all leased, most solid national tenants, that goddamn Walmart cockblocking him. But within a mile, just past the community college, the landscape reverted to the countryside he remembered as a child, visiting his father's father. Gentle hills, a sky that seemed so much bigger than the sky over Baltimore. Authentic country.

He pulled into the zoo's parking lot. Lord, it was little. He had expected that much; places from one's childhood always seemed smaller. But he had also expected it to be seedier than it was in his imagination, and in that, he was pleasantly surprised. He had a dim memory that the zoo had run into hard times in the 1990s, but then a new family had bought it ten years ago or so and started emphasizing conservation.

He couldn't help himself: After checking the time, he bought a ticket, feeling a little weird—what kind of fortysomething man on his own dropped by a small zoo on a Friday afternoon?—and began walking the familiar paths. Had there been tigers here when he was a boy? He didn't think so. The cage seemed small for the pair, one Bengal and one Siberian, but they appeared content. According to the sign outside their cage, which identified their "conservation status" as near extinction, they had been at another zoo and would have been put to death if Plumpton hadn't been able to take them in. Maybe they were smart enough to know they had been saved.

He made his way up the path, skirting the male peacock, the one animal given the full run of the place. A black-backed jackal ran anxious laps in his enclosure, and Joe noted his conservation status: "Least concern." Ouch. If they could put Joe in a cage, they'd probably slap the same status on his sign: "*Homo erectus*, cis, white. Age span in the wild, 75–80 years. Conservation status: Least concern." Of least concern to whom? Joe laughed at his own observation, but the laugh turned into a wheeze, and he had to find a bench where he could sit, reclaim his breath. Was the jackal happy? Who could tell? Was Joe happy? Did he look happy? He probably did, and yet he was screaming inside 24–7. He felt like he was in the garbage compactor scene in *Star Wars*—walls closing in, his own gunshots ricocheting off the walls, and then a low growl, the feel of something moving past your leg, a single hairy eyeball—and then things got *really* bad.

Suddenly wobbly, he got up and began walking toward the zoo's exit, passing a lone giraffe, two bison, some goats, a macaw whose cage warned: "He bites." He stopped only once, to take in the eerie stumps of *Taxodium distichum*—bald cypress, the state tree of Louisiana. They looked like a field of petrified prairie dogs to Joe.

Back in his car, he set the alarm on his phone and allowed himself a catnap. At 3:58 p.m.—he made it a point to be early for meetings, always—he checked into the Zoom waiting room. The host, his uncle, started the meeting at 4:05 p.m.

"Where the hell are you?" he asked.

"In my car. Up in Cecil County, near where my dad grew up."

"Weren't you trying to convince me that we should take a flier on a Class C up there? Back in 2019, before things really went to shit?"

He shook his head. "No, Tony, that doesn't sound familiar. Hey, Meredith thinks she can help me get bumped up the vaccination list. Once I've had both shots, I'm happy to start traveling again, scouting for good investments."

HER SECOND RIDE finished, Meredith grabbed her towel and cell phone and quickly calculated where her leaderboard position put her—11 percent. *Eleven percent!* How could she not have made the top ten? She had exceeded the metrics in cadence and resistance by at least five points. She wondered how much higher her ranking would go if she filtered her results for riders forty and older. But Meredith wouldn't dream of filtering her results according to age. Maybe gender. The bottom line was that the easier classes, the ones rated between 7 and 8, attracted ringers such as herself, those who essentially dropped down a class and then overrode.

A year-plus into her relationship with Peloton, Meredith preferred to remain invisible. She never took live classes. She followed no one and was a little unnerved by the fact that she knew only three of the five people who followed her, all from book club. Who were the other two freaks who followed MDSimpson? (Her username was her initials, but also could be construed as "Dr. Simpson.") She neither asked for nor received high fives. This wasn't *Romper Room*; she didn't need to be seen in the Magic Mirror at the end.

But she did like to measure her progress and she was proud today to note that her output, while not good enough to put her in the top 10 percent, had earned her a PR for a thirty-minute ride. Within a week, she should have her 500-ride badge.

Dismounting, she examined herself in the mirrored wall. Unlike most of the women Meredith knew, she had changed almost nothing in her home over the past year. It really couldn't be improved, except for the kitchen, whose dark cherry wood seemed dated to her. But, heck, wait another ten years and they would probably be stylish again. Home decor seemed a bit of a scam to Meredith.

She looked good, she decided, in her leggings and sports bra. And not good-for-her-age—actually good. But she had been too focused on cardio, staying lean, over the past year. She should probably start doing some of the strength-training classes available through Peloton, or use Joe's weights. Her arms and legs, while slender, were not as muscular as they could be. That said, she didn't like an overtly athletic look—and neither did Joe, thank goodness.

*Where is Joe?* He had said he needed to drive up to North East to go over a lease with one of his tenants at the shopping center and seemed defensive when she asked why that had to be done in person. She understood that Joe was restless; who wasn't? But he was particularly thin-skinned these days, hurt by the mildest teasing, jumpy and irritable. He had even seemed resentful that she had already gotten her first shot and would receive her second one next week. Meredith had actually exaggerated her mild side effects from the Moderna vax, hoping it would make Joe less envious.

Although she usually showered and changed as quickly as possible after a workout, disliking the smell and feel of her damp clothes, she padded around the kitchen for a while, trying to figure out dinner. She had never bought into the idea of a pandemic silver lining, but there had been enjoyable novelties, even new good habits. For a while, she had planned meals carefully, and her cooking, competent but seldom inspired, had improved. But she was tired of cooking, tired of their weekly walks, which they had somehow maintained through the relatively mild winter. She was tired of her house, beautiful as it was. She was tired of the friends she had, but she didn't want any new ones.

She was tired of everything and everyone—except Joe.

She had defrosted chicken thighs, but she could no longer remember why. Sheet pan something? A *New York Times* recipe? She looked for her phone, realized she had left it in the basement after using the calculator to figure out her percentage finish on her Peloton ride. She perched on the edge of Joe's chair in the office alcove, mindful to keep the dampest parts of her away from the cushion. The computer wouldn't turn on—oh, of course, Joe used Touch ID. But she could bypass that with his password, which she knew, of course, always had. He hadn't changed it in years. Why would he?

Melissa Clark's "Sheet-Pan Chicken with Jammy Tomatoes and Pancetta." Meredith hit print—she hated following recipes from screens—and in the time it took for the two pages to scroll from the printer, she found herself down a Google News rabbit hole. How stupid of that senator to force a six-hundred-page bill to be read aloud; how irrational people were becoming. She entered the letter C, which on her computer or phone would have led straight to COVID coverage. She wanted to see how cases were trending in Maryland.

But Joe's Google search box, presented with the letter C, asked if she was looking for Chanel. *Oh, what is this silly man up to now?* Meredith was of two minds about surprises, but she could wait until Valentine's Day to discover what he had in store for her. Chanel. Where had he gotten the idea to buy her something from Chanel?

*March 10, 2021*

JOE LATHERED UP with the lavender bath gel in the master—
*owner's*—bath. Clearly chosen for its color, which complemented
accents in the tile, it had a sweet, cloying smell that was far more
damning than any scent sex might have left behind. He stayed under the spray for a long time, desperate to rinse away every trace.

"Why are you showering?" Jordan demanded from the bed, her
voice at once sultry and offended. Strange, to have a mistress who
was so skeptical of him, when his wife, who knew nothing, and
Amber, who knew everything, always gave him the benefit of the
doubt.

"I'm supposed to be playing tennis with Zach tonight," he
shouted over the water. "I always shower after tennis."

"But you told Meredith you were playing outside, in that park near Locust Point. How would you shower there?"

*Look, I don't want to smell like you.*

"Actually, there's a community center there, with public bathrooms." Were there shower facilities there? Were they open? "But I'll tell her that Zach and I stopped at his house to shower, then went out to grab a bite. And I'll put my tennis clothes in the wash."

The rainfall showerhead was anemic. He wondered if prospective buyers ever thought to test the water pressure. People shopping for new homes tended to assume they were perfect, without flaws. Meredith had researched showerheads when they bought their house on L'Hirondelle and learned that the pressure remained constant whatever fixture one used, so the more diffuse the delivery, the softer the spray. If you preferred more of a stinging car wash experience—and Joe did—you were better off with old-fashioned fixtures. She had not only swapped out the showerheads, she had paid a plumber to adjust their pressure so Joe got the kind of blasting he preferred. The shower at the model always made him feel as if he wasn't truly clean. But maybe that's just how he felt after sex with Jordan now.

"You and Zach," Jordan called back, her voice now light and teasing, "should start playing more, I think."

"Once a week," he said. "Once a week is all I can muster for now."

Even during the winter months, when there was no tennis at all, before Jordan had come along, he had found a way to be with Amber twice a week, but he couldn't tell Jordan that. He missed Amber, but she was probably right about the risks Jordan posed to them both. Joe had been shocked at how matter-of-fact she was about it. No tears, no recriminations. Her instinct for self-preservation was as strong as his, possibly stronger. *I'm sorry*, Joe had said. *Why?* Amber asked. *She predates our thing. You didn't owe me anything then. You don't really owe me anything now. Let's take our time and figure out a foolproof solution.*

Easy for Amber to say. Joe felt like a gigolo, forced to engage with a woman who no longer interested him. Jordan's blackmail, or maybe the mere fact that she wielded power over him, made her undesirable to him. It was more akin to a workout, whether or not she realized it, not that different from rallying with Zach. Yet she seemed to be enjoying herself and remained as intent as ever on his enjoyment. Was she really having orgasms? Was everything a lie? Had she set out to entrap him from the beginning, believing she could force him to leave Meredith, all the while pretending she was a free-spirited party girl without a care in the world?

When he came out of the bathroom, she was still naked in the king-sized bed, scrolling through her phone, probably on Instagram. The staged bed in the staged bedroom in the staged house.

"Aren't you worried?" he asked.

"About what?"

"People noticing the lights are on after dark? That's not typical in a model home, having people here in the early evening." Freeland Acres, which had seemed so unpromising to Joe, had sold out its lots in the first six months of the pandemic. The pandemic had made people claustrophobic, desperate for backyards and firepits and driveways big enough for basketball courts, room for swimming pools, although there was a wait list for pool builders now.

The pandemic had also made Jordan even more successful. She was still the number one saleswoman for Decca Builders, a fact she dropped a little too often for Joe's comfort. Jordan was not

privy to Joe's specific troubles, of course, but she knew that residential real estate was booming while commercial limped along.
It was really in bad taste, her casual humblebrags about how well
she was doing. She had a new car, a cherry-red Porsche, and she
seemed to be wearing a new pair of $400 shoes every time he saw
her. *What else do I have to spend money on?* she had said at one
point. *Nowhere to go, nothing to do. Might as well look good.*

It was, he realized, another way of saying, *I'm lonely.*

"The people who live around here are incurious by nature. The
whole point of having lots this big is you don't have to know your
neighbors. My real fear is that we'll end up selling the model.
You'd be shocked by how much people have offered."

Joe thought of his sad little shopping center—the empty
12,000 square feet where Modell's had once been, the barely
patronized Sizzler. He really had believed that food and sporting
goods, sub sandwiches and books were enough to create a little
village, that people wanted places to congregate. They would,
eventually. He just needed to survive these lean months.

"It's still a long way out here," he said.

"Not a problem," Jordan said, "when people are working from
home. Who knows? Maybe offices are over forever."

He put on his pants, tucked in his shirt. "Thanks for wishing
my industry dead."

She realized she had been insensitive and lifted her eyes from
her phone, smiling at him kindly. "Your field will be fine, Joe, when
the dust settles. Just—different. Transformed."

"Vaccinations are starting," he said. "Meredith has gotten hers.
We're finally going to turn this thing around." He didn't mention
that he was going to be getting his first jab soon as well. He was
sheepish about Meredith gaming the system for him.

"And when things are normal again," Jordan said, "we can think about our future."

God, he hated her. Hated himself for not seeing through her sooner. He thought longingly of Amber. No tricks, no surprises. No jealousy. Whereas Jordan was always asking him if he still slept with Meredith. Of course he did—he had never stopped. He has, however, assured Jordan they have changed their minds about having a baby.

In the car, he changed out his watches—risky as it was, he still kept Jordan's 2019 Christmas gift in the glove compartment and wore it when they were together. She needed those kinds of re-assurances. She had bought him a watch and now he was buying time. God, how much did time really cost and how much would he buy if he could? He would buy himself at least nine months, create almost a year between now and the date when his balloon payment was coming due.

It was just past eight. He rationalized that he had time to go out for a sandwich and a beer, which is what he would have done if he had actually played tennis. It was book club night tonight, made possible, as the pretext of tennis had been, by an unexpect-edly balmy string of March days. Meredith probably wouldn't even notice he was out late.

Could he swing by Amber's? Just to say hello? It's not like Jordan had him under constant surveillance.

MRS. DALLOWAY DECIDED *she would light the firepit her-self.*

Meredith surveyed her patio. After noting the long-range fore-cast a week ago, the book club had agreed, by a vote of 10–2 in an "emergency" Zoom meeting, that an outdoor gathering would be okay. Meredith was the only vaccinated member, but others had begun lining up their first shots, many through the help of a dedicated Facebook page. They had decided to have drinks, but no food would be served. It was strictly BYOS—bring your own snacks.

The weather, as predicted, was kind—almost 60 degrees today, although the temperatures began falling rapidly after the sun set. In just three days, it would be setting an hour later. Meredith had chairs arranged in a circle around the firepit, her Valentine's Day gift from Joe and exactly what she wanted. She had, in fact, requested it, but Joe had the good sense to give her something personal as well. Not Chanel, as it turned out, but an Elsa Peretti necklace, which impressed her. She was surprised Joe even knew the designer's work.

"Where's Joe?" Wendy asked.

"Playing tennis."

"After dark?"

"They usually grab food or a beer after."

"You're letting him eat indoors at restaurants now?"

"I don't *let* Joe do anything," Meredith said with a laugh. "Besides, we're outside—I'm sure they are, too, given the weather."

"I mean—you've been so careful because—"

Meredith cut her off. "I've had both my shots and Joe is getting his first one next week."

"How did you swing that?"

She smiled serenely but declined to answer.

"Where do they play? The club doesn't open until April."

"They've found a public court, in the city. I found it, actually, on one of our walks. Latrobe Park. We passed it when we walked the length of Fort Avenue, all the way from the railroad tracks to Fort McHenry and back again. Joe wanted to show me a penthouse apartment in Locust Point that's been languishing on the market. As if we'd ever give up this house."

By 7:35, all the women were there, even those who had voted against reconvening when they first floated the idea. The chosen book was *Circe*, picked because most of them had already read it, and Meredith was keen to discuss it; she had found it unexpectedly moving. In fact, she had wept openly at the book's end. It was the only depiction of a marriage she had ever read that felt similar to her own. Was she not a sorceress in a sense? Had she not made herself mortal for Joe, agreed to support and forgive his early mistakes so that he could know what it was like to live, forgiven and redeemed?

But, as usual, the women had trouble getting to the book, or staying on topic once there. And, as usual, some had not read it and were clearly faking their way through with Wikipedia and Google to guide them. Darla's drinking no longer seemed as shocking, however, because everyone was pounding their wine.

What was different was that all they could talk about was the pandemic. How it affected their kids, their lives. It was the only story. No one had gone anywhere or done anything. COVID had made their worlds small—and they hadn't been that big to begin with. Meredith was one of the few who was not working from home. Not an option for a surgeon. Her long-caged friends were tense with an almost feral energy. She noticed which ones had gained weight, then felt bad about noticing. It also was clear who had returned to salons for cut and color and who was relying on DIY techniques. Meredith had learned to do her own waxes (thank you, Flamingo strips) and she had a home dermabrasion kit, but she had scheduled her first haircut within seventy-two hours of her second shot.

"Did anyone read her first book?" Wendy Asher had. Dutiful Wendy, still clinging to the fantasy that this was a serious group of women, capable of extending their intelligence beyond their day-to-day lives and gossip.

"If you ask me," Ann said, topping off her glass, "it's a bit of a cheat, rewriting myths. Couldn't anyone do this?"

"People have always recycled stories," Wendy protested. "Think of *Romeo and Juliet*, or *Clueless*, which is based on a Jane Austen novel."

"Did you hear," Darla put in, "that Nancy and Todd broke up? They're telling everyone it's not a pandemic divorce, that they were planning to separate last February and it was just too impractical at the time."

Meredith did not like to encourage personal gossip at book club, but she couldn't let this go for some reason. "Why would anyone care whether it's a pandemic divorce or not? How does that matter?"

"I guess," Darla said, "it's a bit of a cliché and Nancy never wants to be seen as part of a cliché."

"Divorce is always a cliché, in the end." Meredith regretted her words the moment she said them. She didn't even believe them and now she would be asked to defend them.

Sure enough: "What do you mean?" Wendy asked.

"I always thought Tolstoy was wrong, actually. It's the unhappy families that are alike. Not in the particulars—there are all sorts of reasons to be unhappy, for marriages to end. But put aside the really big things, such as abuse or addiction, and the main reason marriages end is because people don't try hard enough."

"Maybe they shouldn't," Brynn put in, her voice hard with an emotion Meredith couldn't identify. "My first marriage ended because I made a mistake. He was a loser. I walked away, no regrets."

"Maybe they shouldn't," Meredith agreed. "And maybe I should rephrase what I said. Marriages end because people no longer wish to be married."

"Because at least *one* person no longer wishes to be married."

Meredith shrugged. She didn't want to have this conversation. She wanted to talk about Circe, her amazing gift to Telemachus. How had the book phrased it? *If you want it, I will do it.* That was sorcery. That was magic.

"What about adultery?" Ann asked.

"In the book?"

"Isn't that reason to end a marriage?"

"It depends," Meredith said.

She remembered then that Ann's husband had cheated on her and the marriage had ended, but that had been *his* choice. Ann had forgiven him and been willing to do whatever was necessary to stay together; he wasn't interested. That had been years ago and Ann had rebounded; she had met a perfectly nice orthodontist in the fall of 2019 and the pandemic had accelerated their relationship; they were living together and seemed happy. But it was a sore subject. Stan—Stan and Ann, how they had joked about the rhyme, as if it had created some magical bond, and yet it had not—had been excommunicated from their social circle. The husbands were allowed to see him, stag, but they didn't want to, and wasn't that all one needed to know about Stan? The men had dropped him of their own volition.

The temperature dipped and the wind began to rise. Meredith had stadium blankets at the ready, extra gloves and hats. The women wrapped themselves tightly and the silence lingered a bit too long, making it difficult to find safe footing back into the conversation.

"I think she overwrites," Brynn said. "I found it a bit of a slog."

"She writes beautifully," Meredith protested. "These are sentences where one should be happy to linger."

"I have a life. I'm reading at night. I need things to be a little more propulsive."

Meredith thought of *her* life, the hours-long surgeries, how she toiled over creating beauty, how tired she was at night, yet still eager for Joe or a book as moving as *Circe*. Maybe that was why she could appreciate Miller's lush sentences, the unhurried pacing. Beauty took time.

They said their goodbyes, crossing fingers that their next meeting might be in someone's house or, more amazing still, in a restaurant. The world was opening back up again. There was talk of summer plans. Trips, beach rentals.

She heard Joe come in and head straight upstairs, the telltale click and whoosh of the washing machine starting up. He was always conscientious about doing a wash after he worked out or played tennis. But Meredith would have to check to make sure the clothes weren't left in the washer overnight, where they would begin to smell. She would put them in the dryer before she went to bed.

AMBER WAS UPSTAIRS in her bedroom when she heard a car moving slowly down Puritan Lane. She told herself that all cars moved slowly down Puritan Lane, but then this one stopped. Door slam, feet on the pavement, and, sure enough, a knock. Soft at first, then building, until Joe added his voice: "Amber? Amber?"

Her car was in the drive; it was past eight o'clock on a Wednesday night. Where else would she be? Sighing, she went downstairs and let him in.

"I thought we agreed you wouldn't come to the house or the gallery for a while. Until we figure out what to do about—" She gestured, having no words for Jordan, a loose grenade rolling around in some amped-up action film, the new ones that played with physics and reality, showcasing impossible stunts, beyond human resilience. It was only a matter of time before Jordan went off. The question was where and who would bear the brunt of her explosion.

"I can't take it," Joe said. "I can't take this."

"Such a hardship, having to have sex with a gorgeous young woman who adores you. You used to do it voluntarily, not that long ago."

Joe, comfortable in her house by now, walked into the kitchen and pulled a bottle of red from the wall-mounted rack. "Brouilly," he said. It was his favorite. He uncorked it and poured them both healthy glugs in the stemless wineglasses Amber preferred.

"You said you would help me," he reminded her. "That you would do anything."

"I think," Amber said, taking a seat at the tiny bistro table she used in the kitchen, "that I have been helping you by accepting the fact that you have no alternatives. I don't think most—" Again, she was at a loss for words. What was she to Joe? "I don't think most women would accept this. I know we were both hoping that once she had what she thought she wanted, she'd get bored quickly. But it's barely been two months. It's too early to give up."

"I'm beginning to think it's like a competition to her," Joe said, slumping in the chair opposite Amber. "She's placated, for now, but she won't stay that way. She won't be satisfied until I leave Meredith. Which I can't afford to do even if I wanted to."

"You don't want to." Spoken flatly, a known truth, one she had never doubted. Still, there was the tiniest sting.

"Not for Jordan, no."

She wanted to shout: *This is not what I want.* But what Amber wanted she could never have. What she wanted was the highly compartmentalized world of the second half of 2020—her work, her twice-weekly meetings with Joe, their bubble world. Jordan had burst that.

And now spring was coming, and with it, apparently, vaccinations. Joe was about to get his first. Amber had found a slot for her first shot in early April. The world was going to open up, with them or without them. Joe would be able to start traveling again for work. This was ending.

This *had* ended.

"I need Jordan to go away," he said. "Voluntarily. She's clouding everything, making it impossible for me to focus, figure out what I really want. All I know is I don't want *her.* But I need a reason to stop seeing her that won't make her irrational or vengeful—I can't allow her to hurt you. I won't."

She was touched, but also wary. What was Joe trying to say? What was he asking of her?

"Amber, I'm in a hole, financially. It's the darndest luck, something I never could have foreseen. I bought this shopping center, thinking I could flip it—and I could have, if it weren't for the pandemic, then Modell's going bankrupt—"

*Joe Simpson is flunking French and needs a tutor. Are you interested, Amber? Do you think you can help him bring his grade up to passing so his college applications won't be affected?*

"I took out a second mortgage on our house and the note is coming due. I also sold a lot of our stocks—the only savings I have left are in retirement savings, and I'll pay stiff penalties if I touch those—"

*Don't be a tease, Amber. Kaitlyn was a tease.*

"I need an infusion of cash. And the fact is, Meredith needs to slow down. She's become manic. She works all the time. It's not healthy. Everyone else is gaining weight—well, not you—but I swear, Meredith has lost fifteen pounds in the past year, and she didn't have fifteen pounds to lose. She doesn't sleep, she barely eats. It's almost like she requires an intervention to stop working herself to the bone."

*I'm going to join the Peace Corps after college, I think, then see the world. Maybe climb the famous summits, or hike the Appalachian Trail. There's so much I want to see and do.*

*I'm going to go to Paris and never come back.*

"Have I ever told you," Joe said, "that Meredith's hands are insured? If she were hurt, if she couldn't work—we'd get a lot of money. Like, a lot. And, really, I would be saving her from herself. She works too hard, she's obsessive, she has no off switch. Plus, if I had to take care of Meredith in the wake of an accident, Jordan couldn't fault me for that. Not even Jordan is that heartless."

"Why are you telling me this, Joe? What can I do?"

"You know people. People who have been in prison."

"I know artists. Horace helps me find *artists*."

"Are those the only people he knows?"

"Joe—"

"I can't see clearly, Amber. I don't know what's right or wrong, anymore. I think you're the person I want to be with, but with all these things pressing on me, I can't figure anything out. I need time, Amber. Time and money, and a foolproof way to make Jordan give up on me. And you're so clever—look what you did with the Valentine's Day gifts. You're so much smarter than I am. You've always been. You've always been—*Amber.*"

He looked at her, his eyes heavy lidded. He had been in another woman's bed less than an hour ago. Within another hour or two, he would be in bed with his wife. Yet he belonged to her in a way he had never belonged to anyone else. They were yoked together after all these years by her decisions, decisions she had made without consulting or confiding in him. She could never get over the feeling that she owed him an enormous debt.

He wouldn't let her.

"When do you have to be home?" she asked.

"It's book club night," he said. "I don't think she'll even notice when I come in."

*March 22, 2021*

THE VACCINATION SLOT Meredith had secured for Joe was at a CVS all the way down in Federal Hill, near the shoe store he liked, the one where the pro athletes shopped. Ugh, why did people want to live in the city? He was glad now that he hadn't been able to interest Meredith in that creepy penthouse. He had to park two blocks away from the pharmacy, and it was one of those systems where you had to go to a machine, get a ticket, and return to the car. The only rationale Joe could see for the new machines was that no one would ever again know the serendipity of sliding into a meter with time left on it. He wondered if it would be possible to design an app that allowed people to bestow their unused minutes on another driver. Some sort of virtual bulletin board? But how would you get it to the dashboard of another car? He quickly abandoned his brainstorm. Not his kind of thing anyway. Joe liked concrete, tangible things—land, raw space, buildings.

Like Cross Street Market, for example, all spiffed up with new food stands and seating areas, a new restaurant going in where the old fish market had once stood. Bad timing—or maybe not. Vaccinations were here. By summer—god, maybe by summer they would be back to normal. He would sell Nottingham Ridge, pay off the refinanced second mortgage. Re-creating the stock portfolio would be trickier, but luckily Meredith had never paid attention to their investments. Once he had that $6 million in hand—

In hand.

*Was he really going to do this? Let someone attack his wife— well, only her right hand—in order to save them from financial ruin?* But it wasn't just the money. Jordan was an even bigger problem in some ways. If he couldn't avoid hurting Meredith, what should he choose, her heart or her hand? Her hand would heal.

He just missed stepping into a gelatinous mass—good god, was that vomit? Now he had to wonder if the excrement he saw along the sidewalks was human or canine. Jesus, look, three-quarters of a pizza, sitting on top of a manhole cover. Yet people paid more per square foot to live here than Joe and Meredith had paid for their house. Crazy.

He wondered if Amber understood that he was going to have to be fully committed to Meredith. She must. That was probably the real reason for her reluctance. He wasn't asking her to risk that much. By the time her friend found yet another "friend," there would be so many degrees of separation that no one could trace it.

The money was trickier. Joe couldn't afford to have a large sum leaving his account, and besides, he didn't have the cash flow.

Amber was going to pay up front because she was flush. Then Joe was going to pay her back by buying "artwork" at inflated prices. She had tried to get him to consider one of those ugly-ass scarecrows from that crazy guy on the Eastern Shore who had gotten so much attention. "You have the space for it," she said. "Meredith would kill me," he replied, and then they both heard what he had said and no one had anything left to say.

The last time he had talked to Amber, she said she still hadn't been able to put the deal together. But she would. Amber had said she would do anything for Joe, and unlike most women, she actually meant it.

He was five minutes early for his time slot, and the appointment ahead of him had already been jabbed and was sitting in the only available chair for the mandatory fifteen-minute waiting period. The pharmacist took her sweet time getting ready for Joe, but she was good at what she did. He barely felt anything as the needle slid in and out.

And then he felt a sensation so powerful that his knees buckled when he rose from the chair.

"You okay, sir?"

"I'm fine." He was more than fine. Once she had retracted the needle from his arm, he had allowed himself to articulate the fear he had refused to acknowledge all these months. *I'm not going to die. I'M NOT GOING TO DIE.* Life was precious. *His* life was precious. He promised himself to make the most of it.

"Do I have to sit here, for the fifteen minutes?" he asked. "Or can I walk around the store?"

"Feel free to browse," she said, handing him a sheaf of coupons. *The revolution will be televised and the pandemic will be monetized.*

You wouldn't think a CVS in the city would be that different from the one he normally used in Towson, but it felt like another world. He couldn't believe the things that were under lock and key here—deodorant, razors, bodywash. And it was dingier over-all, with stacks of boxes blocking aisles, waiting to be unpacked. It reeked of—poverty, even if it was in a zip code with a lot of high-end real estate. No trees, no yards—he could never live this way. He had been willing to change if that's what Meredith wanted, but—she didn't want it. She loved the house on L'Hiron-delle even more than he did. That's why he had to do whatever was necessary to save it. If any part of Joe's body were worth $6 mil-lion, he'd lop it off right now.

He found an aisle full of weird old-fashioned penny candy—circus peanuts, Bit-O-Honey, orange slices, spiced gum drops. The kinds of things sold at the original penny candy store in Notting-ham Ridge. Had his nostalgia for Plumpton Zoo and that musty old candy store set him up to make a mistake? No. His only fault was in not being able to see the future. Who could have predicted the past twelve months? Anyone who claimed to have done that was a liar or a witch.

His fifteen minutes up, he waved at the pharmacist.

"Just wanted you to know I'm heading out," he said.

She looked at him as if she had no memory of him at all. Maybe she didn't even see faces, only arms.

MEREDITH HAD AWAKENED stiff and strangely fatigued, tried to soldier through the day, only to give up by lunchtime. She had no appointments that afternoon, and while there was always something to do, she decided to listen to her body for once. No fever, no other symptoms, but something was definitely off.

She often wondered if that terrible cold on Super Bowl weekend had been COVID. She had even gone back to her calendar and reviewed her appointments from the end of January, reread her notes. There was one woman who had been in Europe, Paris to the best of her recollection, and although she hadn't mentioned Italy, who knew?

Yet Meredith was increasingly concerned that she not only had contracted COVID, but that she might be a long-hauler. Her energy had been at a low ebb for weeks. Her focus and concentration were not what they usually were. Of course, perimenopause could cause such symptoms as well. As could any kind of stress. But she refused to acknowledge she was under stress, especially since she had been vaccinated. As for the other possibility, perimenopause—uh-uh, no way. Still, once she was in the car, she did something she seldom did: She called her mother, just to talk.

She kept it chatty at first. Her parents were semiretired now, more consultants than full-time physicians, which meant, best Meredith could tell, they started drinking earlier in the day. Whatever their issues, they had never chanced being anything but stone-cold sober during their working hours. They believed this meant they didn't have a problem; Meredith saw it as proof that they did. Non-alcoholics didn't have to plan for sobriety. But, of course, they never spoke about it. If Meredith had expressed concern about their drinking, one of them might finally speak about why they drank as they did, and they couldn't possibly have *that* conversation.

It was hard enough, after desultory chat and gossip—*so strange to have a year without Mardi Gras, the Reynolds are breaking up, the Bonhams' grandson announced his pronouns are now they/them*—to introduce the subject of perimenopause. They were a family of doctors, yet shy when the topic was their own bodies. Meredith was already in front of her own gate on L'Hirondelle, but instead of engaging the opener, she idled before it.

"Mama," Meredith said, "may I ask when menopause started?"

"You mean historically? If we go back to Adam and Eve, I guess the question is, did the first woman go through menopause? While the Bible doesn't tell us how old Eve was when she died—"

"*Mama,*" Meredith said, a note of pleading in her voice. It had been hard enough to pose the question once; she couldn't bear to do it a second time.

"Oh, you want to know when I started? Late, very late. I was almost fifty before I had any symptoms and I wasn't truly in menopause until I was fifty-five. It wouldn't be surprising if you followed suit. That said—you might start earlier. Because—"

Meredith knew. Because of the chemo.

"I'd almost rather you'd already started," her mother said. "You got your period at thirteen—"

"Fourteen."

"Are you sure?" *Of course I'm sure,* Meredith thought. *Because I was there and you were not. You were at work. A friend had to talk me through it.* But she said only: "I'm sure. June 1994."

"Anyway, that's twenty-seven years of uninterrupted cycles, which can be associated with breast cancer risk. Obviously, I worry about that, too."

"Twenty-six. Only twenty-six years."

"Twenty-seven, Meredith, or almost. It's 2021, remember?"

"Oh, right." She had forgotten. She was going to turn forty-two in June. It didn't seem possible. The last year shouldn't even count, because it was barely a year in some ways, despite all the things that had happened, which were a kind of non-happening, an undoing—death upon death upon death. "Anyway, it's not like I was going to conceive just for the sake of improving my odds against breast cancer."

"You might still have time."

It took Meredith a beat to understand what her mother meant. "To conceive? No, never. Joe and I agreed from the start—"

"You were nineteen," her mother said. "And you both had known such significant traumas. You aren't wedded to decisions you made when you were nineteen."

"We married at twenty-three. Are we bound by *those* words, our wedding vows? It was only four years later."

"I'm not tryna to pick a fight with you, Meredith."

It was one p.m. in Baltimore, noon in New Orleans, and her mother's words were already a little mushy. Meredith imagined her on the back porch, gin and tonic in hand. The drinks would start out as mostly tonics, with a nice squirt of lime. By four p.m., they would be mostly gin.

"We're happy," Meredith said. "We've never regretted our choices."

"Half my friends who have kids are separating. It's the pandemic."

*A non sequitur*, Meredith told herself. Her mother was already in her cups, and that was a non sequitur.

"Honey," her mother said abruptly.

"Yes?"

"When menopause does start, take it seriously. Find a good doctor. Address the symptoms. It's not as cut-and-dried as they once thought, hormone therapy and cancer survivors, and it's important—"

"Mama, I'm a doctor, too, okay? I know the science." Besides, she would never neglect that part of her marriage. Most of the marriages that broke up, Meredith was pretty sure it was about sex, the drudgery that leached all the romance from the relationship. Use it or lose it? Use it or lose *him*. That was not Meredith and Joe's problem.

"Anyway, I don't think this is perimenopause. You know I had COVID last year."

"I know that you keep telling everyone that, yet you refused to be tested for antibodies. My two cents—you want to believe you had it. And now you'd rather see yourself as a long-hauler than as a former cancer patient going into early menopause. You hate being sick, but you hate being ordinary even more."

And this was why she seldom called her mother.

Despite feeling shitty, Meredith took a long, soaking bath when she got home and then applied a charcoal mask, a sight so comical that she almost uploaded it to Instagram, then realized it looked as if she was in blackface, and she would never dream of doing anything that could be inferred as offensive, no matter how lighthearted her intent. She used her Flamingo strips to tidy her bikini line and put a conditioning mask on her hair. Yet Joe, who had no appointments beyond his morning vaccination, still wasn't home by four. Where was Joe?

Then she realized: Joe didn't know she was home, so why would he feel any urgency about being there? He was driving a lot these days, covering endless miles in his car. Meredith had noticed the odometer when she used his Range Rover for a run to the dump last week, but decided not to mention it. Before the pandemic, Joe had flown at least twice a month, had always been on the go. Now he spent most of his time on Zoom calls. Of course he was restless.

When he hadn't shown up by five, she walked down their driveway, almost a tenth of a mile, and grabbed the mail from the box. Joe was obsessed with the mail. It was the first thing he tended to upon homecoming. Then, once the mail was open and divided into piles—bills, recycling—he always tore the recycling pile in half, which made no sense to Meredith, as it created much more of a mess if the can tipped over. Left to her own devices, she chucked the obvious junk mail straight into recycling, not even bothering to open it.

Like today, this piece of mail labeled "urgent" from some unknown loan company, addressed to Joe and Meredith. Really, it should be illegal to send such obvious hoaxes. She took it, the inevitable catalogs, and a solicitation from the Fraternal Order of Police and threw it all in the recycling bin. Time to start dinner. She was less rigorous in her planning than she had been before she was vaccinated, given that an unplanned trip to the grocery store no longer seemed an unacceptable risk. But she also was looser, better at improvisation. She found some shallots, checked the pantry for anchovies. Yes, they could have that lovely anchovy pasta for dinner with a simple green salad.

"YOU DON'T WANT to do this."

Amber shrugged. "I already have, right? As far as everyone's concerned, I've done something far worse."

She was sitting at a bar on Highway 1 with Horace, a place favored by bikers. And, apparently, Horace, although he didn't have a motorcycle and never had, not to Amber's knowledge. But the bar was set up so one could drink outside, which was why they had chosen it. God knows, Amber needed a drink for this conversation.

"It's going to cost a lot."

"I can afford it."

"And he's not going to pay you back."

"I know," Amber said. "But he thinks he is. Joe always thinks he's going to do what he says he's going to do."

It was five p.m., rush hour, the traffic on Highway 1 steady and fast. People were moving again. Amber herself was going on the road in less than two weeks, heading out on her first buying trip since January 2020.

"There are a dozen ways this could go wrong. Want me to list 'em?"

"No. I know what they are."

"You're an odd woman," Horace said. "Maybe the oddest I've ever met."

"Perhaps I am odd," Amber conceded. "I know what I want. But I also know what I can have."

"You sure you've thought everything through?"

"I'm sure I haven't. Because no one ever does. But I know where I'll be on April first, and I know where Joe will be. It's the rest of it I need your help for, Horace."

Horace shook his head. "No. I won't be party to this, Amber. You're on your own. I won't tell anyone about this conversation, if it comes to that. I'm no snitch. But I'm not going near this."

"You think I won't do it myself if it comes to that?"

"That's *exactly* what I think. You're a good person. You finally know that about yourself. Why risk everything you've built up? Just let it be. Walk away."

It was good advice, she knew. So why couldn't she take it?

*April 1, 2021*

THE HAMPTON INN in Opelika, Alabama, was bustling, and Amber would have been okay with that if people had followed the hotel's stated mask-wearing policy, but most guests were flouting it, their snotty-nosed kids running amok in the breakfast bar. No yogurt or Cheerios for her this morning. Why were there so many families? Then Amber remembered—it was spring break. Easter was only three days away.

She had left Baltimore March 30, and although she could have made it to Opelika in one hard day of driving, she had chosen to spend the first night on the road at the Ritz-Carlton in Charlotte. She had rationalized that a woman who was about to drop $100,000 on a cache of outsider art would be able to stay in the

Ritz-Carlton. But she really just wanted to know what it was like to slide into a perfectly made bed and order room service.

Joe, aware that he would eventually have to pay Amber a significant amount of money, had thought he could buy a single artwork from her, but while there was visionary art that went for extraordinary amounts, Amber didn't think that served their purposes. Instead, she proposed that she go for quantity, picking up dozens of pieces and bringing them back to Baltimore, where they could eventually be stored in the empty Modell's in Joe's shopping center in North East.

And the great thing is that Amber's purchases would be recorded as all-cash. Not even a check or Venmo trail, which was common among the artists she knew.

The thing is, it just wasn't terribly efficient, or even healthy, for Amber to spend days on the road driving a U-Haul, as she used to. She needed one artist with a wide variety of unsigned work, which was why she was in Opelika. Denny Cummings wasn't good, but he was prolific, and he worked in a wide array of media and styles. For a big enough sale, he would happily drive his "art" to Baltimore.

She disliked Cummings on sight and then felt bad for disliking him. A lean, craggy white man, probably years shy of the age he appeared to be, he was that saddest of specimens, a would-be creator who had no talent for creating. Instead, he imitated whoever was in vogue—Bill Traylor, R. A. Miller, Howard Finster. He'd even had a Henry Darger phase, although that was blessedly short-lived, as he managed to convey all the creepiness and none of the charm of the Chicago artist's work. She picked out forty of the least offensive pieces and offered him $20,000 in cash.

"Do you think I might have my own show?"

"One day," she lied. She didn't have the heart to tell him that she was going to itemize his work as the unsigned creations of the artists he imitated. No one knowledgeable would be fooled, but Amber wasn't going to show or sell this work, so she wouldn't be committing fraud. Joe believed he needed a legitimate-appearing way to give her $100,000, once he had it, and this was the solution she had proposed.

"You goin' to see Wetumpka while you're down here?" Cummings asked. God, he was so pitiable. Why do the pitiable arouse fury in us?—or was Amber unusual in her dislike for the obvious victims in the world? She knew only that she had seemed pitiable once and it enraged her to this day. It enraged her more than ever.

"I hadn't planned to."

"They made that television show there. The one where they redo the homes."

"I thought that was Waco, Texas?"

"Like that, but smaller. They have the *Big Fish* house."

She had no idea what he was talking about. "The one thing I do want," she said, "is some white sauce barbecue."

Cummings scratched his chin. "Chuck's in Opelika is good. But it's a mustard base."

*Why*, Amber wondered, *am I asking for food recommendations from a man who looks as if he smokes more than he eats?* She decided to use her phone and found that her best bet was probably Decatur, which was not in the direction she had planned to drive, but then—it didn't matter in which direction she drove, as long as she was on the road. She stopped at Big Bob Gibson's about two p.m., then continued on to Nashville, checking into the Hermitage.

*It's happening*, she told herself, sipping red wine, too full from her late barbecue lunch to do more than pick at the salad she had ordered from room service along with a bottle of Brouilly, although she managed to find room for a slice of coconut cake. *It's happening right now.*

MEREDITH'S THURSDAYS WERE always long, and while daylight saving—how she disliked people who got it wrong, said *daylight's saving* or, just as nonsensical, *daylight's savings*—was providing a little more light, it was near dusk when she left her office just past seven. Thank god Joe had tennis tonight. Cold as it was, he and Zach insisted on playing the first day the club opened for the season; it was a tradition for them. She could pick at something from the fridge, not worry about making him dinner.

She had run out at noon to mail a package and been forced to park on the far edge of the lot when she returned. She walked quickly, her boots loud on the pavement. This time of day, the only other sounds were the *zhush* of Beltway noise and the croaks of what she believed were grackles, although it seemed too early for grackles, too cold. But then, given the weather, everyone was so confused.

*Everyone was so confused.*

She thought she saw a man lurking nearby, and, while she knew she was being paranoid, she quickened her steps, got into her car. As she pulled out, she noticed a car right behind her. Her usual route would have been to go left on Joppa, but traffic was heavy and she grew impatient, turned right instead.

The car she had noticed in the parking lot, a dark, nondescript sedan, followed her onto Falls Road instead of 83. Most cars got on 83. She became truly concerned when she turned left on Ruxton Road and the sedan, a Nissan, did, too. What was going on?

*Nothing,* she reassured herself. *Don't be silly—you know nothing is going on.* Still, she couldn't help herself. She picked up speed, risky on these curvy roads at dusk. All she wanted was to be at home, safe behind her own gates.

She hit the button for the gate before she braked, knowing how slowly it opened. She glanced in the rearview mirror, thought she saw the car from Greenspring Station coming around the bend. The gate was not all the way open, but the gap was large enough and—her eye caught sight of a shape to the left, approaching her car quickly. She jammed her foot onto the accelerator, only to feel something thump against the car. She tried to correct, pulling the wheel so sharply to the right that she ended up smashing into the stone pillar next to the gate.

She got out of her car, shaky and confused. The other car, definitely a Nissan, stopped and the driver got out.

"Are you okay?" A man's voice, but she couldn't really see him. He wore a hoodie pulled up high and tight, his face lost in its depths.

"I'm fine," she called. "Really—I'm fine. Please don't worry about me."

He kept walking, something tightly clutched in his hand.

JOE LABORED OVER Jordan—there was no other word for it—but Amber had insisted he go through with this one last time. Thank god this would be the last time. It had to be, right? Even this needy, self-involved woman would understand that Meredith could be his only priority for the foreseeable future.

Did Amber understand? Did she get that? They would be over, too, of course. He would be good, he would be good, he would be good—

"Not so rough, please," Jordan said. "That's not what I'm in the mood for tonight."

Finished, he fought his instinct to flee and instead lingered in bed with her, running his hands through her hair, over her body, saying goodbye even if she didn't realize it. He forgave himself for being drawn to her, unpredictable and problematic as she had become. He hadn't been foolish. She was a desirable woman and she had not, in the beginning, given off that scent of crazy that warned a man not to get involved. She seemed to have been created for this kind of affair.

She would change, of course, when she married. Most women did. They married, they had children, they became . . . *different*. He had observed this in Meredith's friends. It wasn't always that they changed physically, although some did. Parenthood—to Joe, it was like getting on a boat for a day trip to another country somewhere in the Caribbean. The new destination looked the same; there was no real reason to go there except everyone was going there and you'd get a stamp in your passport, so why not. Then you got there and you couldn't leave, it turned out. Again, the country looked the same. It was the same, in many ways. But you had been repatriated, you were now a citizen of a different world. Jordan would take that trip, eventually. Almost all women did.

Meredith had not. Neither had Amber.

Had he loved Amber? He had loved the way he felt when he was with her, her adulation, her willingness to do anything for him. But things had gotten so crazy. How could he have ended up here? He never meant to hurt anyone, truly. He would have avoided it if he could. But in the end, it would all be for the best. He would take care of Meredith, provide for her. Their house would be saved. Amber would graciously fade into the background, understanding there could be nothing between them ever again. That had not been his intention when he asked for her help. But he saw now that it was the only possible outcome, and it was for the best. He couldn't save *everyone*. And, as they said on airplanes, you had to put your own oxygen mask on first.

He left Freeland Acres at four and went straight to tennis. It was Amber's idea to stack his alibi, as it were. ("If they push back, ask you to account for where you were earlier and you end up telling police you were with your girlfriend, who could doubt you? No one would lie about that.") His game was off, but who could blame him? He reached home by seven thirty. He poured himself a beer, then wondered if he should be drinking a beer. He was probably going to have to drive to the ER soon. It was impossible to act as if he didn't know what was about to happen. He assumed it would be in the parking lot at Greenspring Station—where else could Meredith be approached? Would she fight back? She was a sensible woman. She'd let a man with a knife take her car. God, what if the guy stole her car and didn't manage to—

The intercom, the one connected to their gates, pealed.

"Yes?"

"Joe?" Meredith. Voice shaky, on the edge of tears. "Could you come down here?"

"Are you okay?"

"Please, just—I can't get up the driveway, I—"

Jesus, it never occurred to him that the guy would attack her outside their home. Yet the slow-moving gate, the house's relative isolation, their lightly traveled road—it made sense. Thank god Amber had kept him in the dark about the details; his fear was staggeringly real. He ran out the front door and down their drive. The night had gotten so cold. The gate was open, but he couldn't see her. He sprinted to the street and saw—

A dead deer on the side of the road, Meredith's right fender badly damaged. But she was . . . okay. *Meredith was okay.* Her airbag had deployed, but there was not a mark on her. Some guy in a hoodie was standing nearby, talking on his cell phone.

And suddenly he was happy for whatever fate had intervened, maybe this deer, maybe the hired guy—the contractor, as Joe thought of him—had tried to approach her as she waited for the gate to roll open and then a deer had jumped and she had hit the accelerator by mistake, he didn't care, he didn't care, oh thank god, this was Providence, he had been prevented from his own terrible, stupid plan. It was a sign. As Meredith had told him so long ago, it was never too late to start being good.

He walked her up to the house, called AAA, then animal control. Meredith's car would be towed to their mechanic up on Joppa, and the deer could be taken away by whatever county agency took deer away. He examined Meredith's hair and clothes for glass—nonsensical as the windshield had been intact, he just wanted an excuse to touch her—put her in a hot shower, brought her dinner in bed.

At nine thirty, he was washing up when he heard the gate intercom again. "Mr. Simpson, it's Baltimore County police, can you let us in?" He opened the gate, surprised that a police report was required. But he'd probably need it for the insurance agency, so why not get it over with?

"Mr. Simpson, could you tell us where you were this afternoon?"

"Well, I—" Why was he being asked this question when nothing had happened? "I played tennis at L'Hirondelle Club."

"And before that?"

"I don't see how this is relevant—"

"Were you at the model for Freeland Acres? With Jordan Alt-man?"

Jesus, what had the crazy bitch done now?

"Could I come to your offices and speak about whatever this matter is tomorrow? My wife had a terrible scare this evening, she hit a deer down by our front gate and—"

"Just yes or no, Mr. Simpson. Were you there? We were told your car, a green Range Rover with a vanity plate, was parked there for at least an hour this afternoon."

*He had told Jordan that people watched, people saw.*

"Well, yes, but, officers—if we could speak of this tomorrow—" Giving them his best man-to-man smile.

"We would like you to come to Baltimore County Department of Public Safety headquarters tonight, sir."

He was still smiling because something was up, he just couldn't figure out what he was missing. Was he being accused of trespassing? Corporate espionage? Who cared where his car was parked? "Should I bring a lawyer?"

"That's your call, sir."

"As in my one phone call?"

"As in—that's your decision. We want to talk to you. But if you want to bring a lawyer in, well, sure, we can go ahead and charge you."

"*Charge* me?" The *thing* could not be traced to him, the *thing* had never happened, the *thing* was not a *thing*, it was as if these men had arrived from a parallel reality. How could Joe be held responsible for a crime that had been averted, possibly because of a deer bolting across his driveway at the perfect moment? He felt the panicky terror he had known all those years ago, the sheer unfairness of being confronted with something that was not his fault. The terror—and the rage.

"Jordan Altman is dead, Mr. Simpson. Her body was found by a security patrol who noticed her car was still at the model at eight."

*May 27, 2021*

RELOCATING, SAID THE sign on the Amber Glass Gallery. EVERYTHING MUST GO.

Much to Amber's amusement, some shoppers had inferred this meant sharp, desperate discounts. Yes, everything must go—to New Orleans, to storage. Amber was going to be exclusively online for the near future. She didn't need to sell anything. Oh, she entertained offers below the list price, but some were insultingly low. If a customer really annoyed her, she showed them photos of Denny Cummings's hideously derivative work, quoted an absurdly high amount, then accepted what the customers believed to be cagey lowball offers. Everybody won. The buyers left believing they had scored a bargain and Amber had one less piece of Denny Cummings's crap in her back room.

A woman in dark glasses and a green sundress hesitated outside the door, then pressed the bell. Amber buzzed her in, although she knew at a glance this was not a serious customer.

"Are you really leaving?" the woman asked, pushing her sunglasses into her hair.

"Yes, Meredith, I am."

Her eyes looked bloodshot, and there was the faintest hint of gray at her temples. By Meredith Simpson's standards, she was really letting herself go.

"Without telling me?"

"Why would I tell you?"

"Because we have unfinished business."

"On the contrary," Amber said. "We never had any *business* at all, you and I."

*March 15, the house on Puritan Lane, a car, a knock. Amber assumed it was Joe and she was pleased in spite of herself that he would risk so much to see her.*

*But the person who came to her door that night was Meredith.*

*"I know about you and Joe," she had said without preamble. "But do you know about Joe and Jordan Altman?"*

*"Yes," Amber had said. "I know everything."*

*She could tell Meredith was surprised, that she had expected Amber to be hurt or shocked or angry, that she believed she was equipped with information that gave her the upper hand. But Meredith regrouped quickly, her eyes taking on a sly cast.*

*"You don't know 'everything,'" she said. "You never have. I know something about Joe that would shock you to your core."*

*"I could say the same."*

*"You've left me at a severe disadvantage," Meredith said. "It's*

almost as if you wanted to hurt *me*. Why? I never did anything to you."

"I guess the money stuff is catching up to you," Amber said, continuing to pack items from her desk. "The loan that was coming due on the house, the savings he used to buy the shopping center up in Cecil County. But those things have nothing to do with me. Joe made those decisions on his own."

"They can't foreclose on the house, because Joe forged my name on the loan application. It's voided and the lender has to reach terms with me. And his uncle is going to buy the shopping center, although at a rock-bottom price. But I can't afford that house on my own. I'm going to have to downsize. Joe's legal bills alone—"

Joe had pleaded not guilty, although DNA evidence put him at the scene and no one else had been seen coming or going that evening from the model home in Freeland Acres, a place that noticed big, shiny Range Rovers with vanity plates . . . but people? People, not so much. A person could hike into Freeland Acres from the main road, do what they had to do, and hike back out. The gun had yet to be found. The gun, Amber knew, would never be found.

"Whereas if *Joe* had been murdered, you would have gotten life insurance and the house would have been paid off automatically? Was that what you expected from me? Or did you just hope I would kill Jordan without implicating Joe?"

"I never asked—"

"No, you merely assumed. Why were you so sure I would turn on him, Meredith, once I knew everything? Because that's what you would have done? Because that's what you did?"

*"There's something you have to hear. The night of the prom—Joe did go back to the room. He found you passed out in the bathroom, heard the baby crying. He killed the baby, Amber, not you. He killed the baby and ran away, leaving you to deal with the consequences."*

*"That's not possible,"* Amber said. *"The door was locked, there was only one key. He told police he knocked—"*

*"Why would he lie about what happened, Amber? To me? What would be the point? He killed the baby. He took so much from you in that moment. Now he's going to do it again. Pursue what he wants and leave you in the lurch."*

*"What are you talking about?"*

*Meredith didn't have an answer to that. Good. So she didn't know what Joe had been planning to do to her, what he had expected Amber to arrange for him. But she knew about Joe's affairs, affairs to which she had been willing to turn a blind eye until now. In that moment, Amber realized just how intertwined Joe and Meredith were, how dangerous they were to anyone who came between them.*

She said now: "I guess I can't blame you for thinking everyone's a killer at heart, Meredith. And if you expected me to be enraged when I found out what Joe had done, you were right. I've never been so angry in my life. But unlike you, my first instinct isn't to kill someone who disappoints me."

"I don't know what you're talking about."

"Have you forgotten how small New Orleans is? How insular? One call to my friend there and I had the whole story. Heck, she tried to tell me last Christmas, but we were talking past each other, thinking the other understood what we were referencing— *that thing with their daughter,* she said to me. I thought she meant your illness, but it turns out she was referring to how you killed your boyfriend."

"An accident," Meredith said. "It was ruled an accident."

"Sure, fine. You were fifteen, and you shouldn't have been driving at all, but you had the advantage of being sober. Your boyfriend—ex-boyfriend by then, the gossip is he had just broken up with you—was the one with the blood alcohol limit of .20, which made it seem as if you were doing the conscientious thing when you agreed to drive him home—then drove straight into a live oak on Exposition Boulevard. You turned just before impact, so he took the brunt of it. Even if he had survived, he wasn't going to be able to take advantage of his golf scholarship to UNC. But he didn't survive."

"An accident," Meredith repeated.

"You sure do know a lot of unlucky people, Meredith. A boyfriend fatally injured. A husband who killed a baby, according to you, and is now accused of killing his lover. Remind me not to get too close to you."

"I know he didn't do it," Meredith said. "I just don't know why he's not telling the detectives everything. Joe's never been able to hide anything from me. *You* did this. Why won't Joe tell the truth? Why won't he admit you were involved?"

"Ask him, Meredith," Amber said, serene in the knowledge that while someone might be able to prove she slept with Joe, there was nothing to link them financially. She had paid for Denny Cummings's art, she had taken delivery of it. "You two always liked to share your darkest secrets, right? Well, the good news is, you're not done yet—you both have lots more to tell each other."

Meredith, used to getting her way, was not easily dismissed. "That poor woman didn't deserve what happened to her. I don't know how you live with yourself."

"How do you live with yourself? How does anyone live with

themselves, in the end? The way I see it, you either admit to your-self exactly who you are—or you lie to yourself the way you lie to the rest of the world. Now, if you'll excuse me, I need to lock up and head for the shore before traffic gets bad."

She could not bring herself to hate the woman who walked out of the no-longer-gallery, her head held high. But Meredith had made the mistake of forgetting that someone willing to do your dirty work could do their own as well. Jordan, who had threatened to expose Amber, was dead. Joe would rather go to prison than ever tell Meredith what he had planned for her. Meredith faced an uncertain future, one in which she would be the one thing she feared most: pitiable. This arrangement had, as Amber had told a dubious Horace when he refused to help her set it up, fixed *everything*.

And, who knew, maybe Joe would convince a jury that he had no reason to shoot the woman who was lousy with his semen, a woman he had been seeing secretly since before the pandemic, something Meredith had known for weeks, ever since she checked the messenger app on his desktop computer after Valentine's Day, when she didn't receive something from Chanel. That was the revelation that had sent her running to Amber, certain that she would explode, if not over Joe's infidelity, then at the knowledge of how he had framed her years ago.

It was odd, police conceded, that Joe had killed his lover ex-ecution style—one shot, from behind. But maybe that simply showed how cold and calculated he could be. Occam's razor was good enough for homicide investigators, it turned out.

Amber had to swing by her house to grab a suitcase for her overnight stay in Snow Hill, and by the time she was on the road, the Waze app warned her there was an accident on the Bay Bridge that had created a miles-long backup. She was better off going up and around the Chesapeake, a longer drive, but one that would allow her to move swiftly and constantly, which was always Amber's preference. Forward, swiftly and constantly.

She reached the outskirts of Belleville well after dark. She gave Everett a check for more money than he had ever earned on his artwork, although its memo line described it as a "commission." He gave her a glass of iced tea. They sat outside in the dark, a country dark, thick and flat, the first fireflies of the season sparking. As her eyes adjusted, Amber could see what appeared to be a subtle glow on the limbs of the scarecrows that rose above them, Everett's makeshift family, terrifying yet ultimately benign. There was a new piece, womanly, in very high, pink heels.

"Was she really a bad lady?" Everett asked. "Was she really going to hurt you?"

"Yes," Amber said. *Who knows*, she thought. Amber had tried, she really had. She had told Jordan everything, hopeful to persuade her that they could be a formidable team, that together they could destroy the man who had wronged them. Jordan hadn't believed Amber, and she refused to see herself as anyone's victim. She doubled down, said she would sell the salacious story of the reunited teen lovers with the added bonus that each one now claimed the other was the killer. Amber believed Jordan would have done just that. For Joe. All for the sake of Joe.

Who, in the end, was this ordinary man, why had he been allowed to rampage through life, careless and reckless? Why had Amber romanticized him, catered to him, done whatever he asked? She imagined the world through Joe's eyes, a chorus of women—mother, Meredith, Jordan, and yes, Amber, she was one of them, no use pretending she hadn't been—rising up, singing of his glories and accomplishments, assuring him that he was entitled to love and riches and success, that nothing and no one should block his path.

The spell had been broken and she was free. He was just a man. Maybe not even that. Joe's tragedy was that the excuses to which he had availed himself again and again—*I was only a boy, I was a kid, I didn't know*—became a destiny he could never outrun.

*May 1997*

# THE BOY

JOE GOT OUT of his car, not exactly refreshed by his catnap, but no longer nauseous at least. It was past five, probably too late to drive out to the reservoir, but he could change, maybe even grab a quick shower, then meet Zach and Susannah at the diner. If Amber didn't answer the door, he could probably go to the front desk and get a second key card. Or he'd just go in his tux if it came to that.

The door wasn't quite closed. Had it been like that when he had gone to check on Amber before leaving for the after-party? He honestly didn't know. He had tiptoed up to the door mostly for show—a soft knock or two, barely whispering her name because, truth be told, he was hoping Amber wouldn't rally. Kaitlyn had given him a note, Kaitlyn said she still thought about him all the time.

Now he saw that Amber's wrist corsage had somehow gotten caught—it must have fallen as she dashed to the bathroom, pulling at her dress, ready to vomit—and kept the latch from engaging. A white flower on a ribbon, pressed between the door and the frame. His mother had told him the name of that flower, but he couldn't remember it.

God, he hoped she would be asleep, or too sick to come out with them. Now that he had slept a little, his stomach had settled, and he was hungry. He couldn't wait to tell Zach about Kaitlyn, what had happened in the limo. Obviously, he wouldn't do that in front of Susannah. And he wouldn't tell Zach unless he asked. But Zach always asked.

There was a weird noise coming from the bathroom. Who made sounds like that while puking? "Amber? Amber?" When she didn't answer, he figured he better poke his head inside. If she was throwing up, she wouldn't want to come to breakfast at the diner anyway. He wasn't risking that much.

He found Amber passed out, her face scary white. But her chest was rising and falling, she was breathing. Should he call the front desk, ask for paramedics?

Then he realized the source of the sound was—shit.

*No*, he thought. *No. You can't. You mustn't. Be quiet. I'm a good guy. This isn't my fault. I'm a good guy. This isn't my fault. This is so unfair. I didn't know about you, she never told me. What am I supposed to do? You're going to ruin my life. Please stop, you've got to stop, you've got to stop, you've got to stop—*

# ACKNOWLEDGMENTS

**WHERE TO START?** I have to begin with Sarah Marshall, from whose podcast, *You're Wrong About,* I stole the title of this book. But the true spark was Sarah's observation that a young woman's body *is* a mystery to her more often than not. As I delved into the real stories of untimely births/tragic deaths (not always at proms), I discovered that one couple involved in such an incident had reconnected on Facebook, albeit as platonic friends. That was the second spark. To be clear, this is a work of fiction that is not inspired by any single event. As it happens, Sarah became a friend during the past two years after she suggested that she "accompany" me on a walk one day, via our phones. We still talk regularly as I amble around Baltimore.

Bailey Wight of Jeanine Taylor Folk Art, a place where I have bought several pieces of outsider art, talked me through a day, week, month in her work life. Long before this conversation, she had gone above and beyond to help me procure a Mary L. Proctor piece, whose shipping cost would have been prohibitively expensive were it not for Bailey's ingenuity. However, the piece described in this book is a product of my own imagination, an amalgam of multiple Proctor pieces. Carol Ott brainstormed Joe Simpson's mortgage dilemma; Melody Simmons gave me a crash course in commercial real estate. Ronnie Mund provided me with a wonderful overview of what it was like to chauffeur prom-goers in the 1990s. Katelyn Burns shared a hilarious detail from her own high school prom and was generous when I asked: "May I steal that?" She also gave me helpful feedback on the character of Miss Margaret. I didn't need to interview a reporter who wrote about a dress-shopping expedition because I was that reporter, although my subject never became notorious. Spencer Short told me where well-dressed mid-Atlantic men get their shirts and other wardrobe items, although it was my idea to give South Baltimore's Dan Brothers a shout-out; he also advised me to move my Cecil County Class C shopping center from Rising Sun to the more densely populated North East.

It should be noted that Towson High School is a real place that has never known a tragedy such as the one imagined for this book. But while the shopping center on York Road may appear to be real, it is very much a figment of my imagination. (How I wish there were a French bistro in that location.) L'Hirondelle Club also is a real place; I have never had the privilege to play tennis there, but I'm sure it's lovely and that all its members are very nice people.

My recent work has been a process of rethinking and reexamining my relationship to novels that had a profound impact on me. This novel is like a very long prequel to *Double Indemnity*; I love James M. Cain, but, boy, his characters do jump right in when it comes to brazen criminal acts. This book also owes something to John Updike's Rabbit series, especially as they are interpreted in Mary Gordon's essay "Good Boys and Dead Girls." (Although, unlike Gordon, I love the Rabbit books and reread them frequently.)

I began this novel in January 2021, eleven months after the end of my marriage. It's not that I *recommend* having a small personal crisis during a global pandemic, but it does have the advantage of keeping one on an even keel: Whenever I tired of feeling overwhelmed and sad about the one, I just switched to feeling overwhelmed and sad about the other. That said, my separation and divorce were about as amicable as such things can ever be and I managed to write this book, in part, because I enjoy enormous support from my co-parent, David Simon. Our amazing daughter, Georgia Rae, also was supportive, accompanying me to Plumpton Park Zoo and discussing what animals and plants were best for the purposes of this book. Molli Simonsen makes everything work; my household would be lost without her.

My friends to whom this book is dedicated—I couldn't begin to name them all. Because I've been working from home for twenty-plus years now, I long ago constructed a world in which I relied on "virtual" communication, checking in daily with a wide variety of people across multiple platforms and devices. Every single "How are you?" text, email, DM mattered to me. But there is a team, assembled early in 2020, when I was at my lowest, who deserve special recognition. So thank you, Todd Bauer, Taffy

Brodesser-Akner, Alafair Burke, Nancy Greenberg, Greg Herren, Ann Hood, and Joyce Jones. We say a bride needs something old, something new, something borrowed, something blue. What I needed was somebodies old and somebodies new, friendships ranging from two to almost fifty years.

Laura Lippman
*Baltimore, Maryland*
*May 2022*